A TREASURE
FOR MY DAUGHTER

A Treasure
For My Daughter

Edited by BESSIE W. BATIST

Recipe section compiled by
SARAH EIN, ANNE WARSHAW, MARY DAVIDS

HAWTHORN BOOKS, INC./PUBLISHERS/NEW YORK

FIRST EDITION
First Printing, 1950
Second Printing, 1952
Third Printing, 1953
Fourth Printing, 1955
Fifth Printing, 1958
Sixth Printing, 1961
Seventh Printing, 1964

SECOND EDITION
First Printing, 1965
Second Printing, 1968
Third Printing, 1968
Fourth Printing, 1969

A TREASURE FOR MY DAUGHTER is a voluntary project and all royalties due the Ethel Epstein Ein Chapter of Hadassah–WIZO in Montreal will go to Hadassah in Israel. Assistance in preparing the book was provided by Lenora Weinrauch, Sarah Policoff, Ida Gefter, Gertrude Steinberg, Anne Taviss.

CONTENTS

Introduction	Lenora Weinrauch	9
Preface	Bessie Batist	11
Betrothal and Marriage	Anita Schwartz	14
Mezuzah	Rita Kert	19
Kashrut	Millie Wittenberg	21
This is Hadassah	Bessie Batist	25
Sabbath	Frances Schwartz	32
Rosh Hashanah	Shirley Epstein	45
Yom Kippur	Rose Miller	60
Succot	Lillian Freeman	68
Chanukah	Lenora Weinrauch	78
Chamishah Asar Bishvat	Shirley Epstein	90
Purim	Gertrude Steinberg	95
Passover	Shirley Epstein	104
Lag b'Omer	Lenora Weinrauch	145
Shavuot	Riva Lack	
	Sybil Steinberg	150
Three Weeks and Tisha b'Av	Shirley Epstein	160
Miscellaneous Recipes		163

CONTENTS

Circumcision, Pidyon Ha-Ben,
Bar Mitzvah   Edith Epstein   228

Laws Concerning Mourning   Ada Efros   234

Benedictions and Grace   Bessie Batist   237

Twenty-five-Year Calendar   Gertrude Steinberg   247

Yahrzeiten   260

Family Anniversaries   261

Essential Books for the
Jewish Home   263

General Index   265

Index to Recipes   267

A Woman of Virtue

*Who can find a virtuous woman? for her
price is far above rubies. . . .
She looketh well to the ways of her
household, and eateth not the bread
of idleness.
Her children arise up, and call her blessed;
her husband also, and he praiseth her.
Many daughters have done virtuously, but
thou excellest them all.
Favour is deceitful, and beauty is vain:
but a woman that feareth the Lord, she
shall be praised.*

Proverbs 31:10, 27–30

INTRODUCTION

The Ethel Epstein Ein Chapter of Hadassah was formed December 17, 1947, as a tribute to the memory of the late Mrs. Hyman Ein.

It is fitting indeed that the united effort of the Chapter's members should have resulted in a book of this nature.

Almost immediately after the first meeting, the Program Chairman, Bessie Wittenberg Batist, suggested the publication of a book on Jewish festivals, traditions and customs with menus and recipes, as a service to Hadassah and the community. Various papers were assigned to the members for preparation.

From the writing of the first assignment on the *Sabbath*, which set the style for the entire book, to the title, which was suggested by Miss Shirley Epstein and Mrs. H. L. Schwartz, there has been splendid co-operation, harmony and perseverance on the part of each and every one.

We have attempted to show that to live by the principles of Judaism enhances the beauty and significance of the Jewish religion. This book, however, is not doctrinal.

How closely related our religion is to other elements of Jewish culture, ethics, history, literature, as well as to law and customs, is evident throughout this book.

We are pleased that in publishing this evidence that Jewish home life is a beautiful way of life, we are directly aiding those thousands of Jews who have been deprived of their homes and have lost their near and dear ones. Proceeds from the sale of A TREASURE FOR MY DAUGHTER go toward the rehabilitation of war victims and the building of new homes to enable them to start life anew in Israel.

When this project was begun, reference was made to Palestine. Then, by the grace of God, we were fortunate to be able to refer to Israel, the Jewish homeland today.

Mention has been made elsewhere of the many who have encouraged and helped us in this work. Mrs. Batist has the deep gratitude of every member of the ETHEL EP-STEIN EIN CHAPTER, for without her aid and constant stimulus this book would never have been finished. The Recipe Section Committee, headed by Miss Sarah Ein and assisted by Mrs. Anne Warshaw and Mrs. Mary Davids, are to be commended for the excellent results of a very difficult piece of work. It has been an honor and great privilege to be associated with the group of women that constitutes the membership of the ETHEL EPSTEIN EIN CHAPTER. Like all Hadassah women, we realize that "service to others, in reality, is service to oneself."

Lenora B. (Mrs. Ralph) Weinrauch
Founder-President
ETHEL EPSTEIN EIN CHAPTER OF HADASSAH-WIZO

PREFACE

This volume has been written for the purpose of answering the questions of our young Jewish homemakers who, in their desire to observe the Jewish traditions, often find themselves uncertain of the details in carrying out these practices.

We have endeavored to answer these questions in the form of a conversation between a mother and her daughter, Hadassah, who is about to be married. This volume does not pretend to carry authority in doctrine; rather it is a compendium of current practice in the modern Jewish home.

It has been our object to give the reader a fairly detailed outline of the Jewish holidays, the preparation for them and their observance in the home, as well as the services performed in the synagogue.

The appropriate benedictions for the various rituals and ceremonies for each occasion are also included.

The members of the ETHEL EPSTEIN EIN CHAPTER OF HADASSAH compiled this book in the hope that it may bring a clearer understanding of our heritage, our faith, our ideal of duty and our pride in the principles of our religion.

As a further help to the homemaker we have compiled traditional menus appropriate for each festival and the recipes for each dish.

The compilation of this volume required much research. I am deeply indebted to all the members of the

ETHEL EPSTEIN EIN CHAPTER OF HADASSAH, who have contributed so much of their time and energy in carrying out their assignments preparing the articles to make this book possible.

Grateful acknowledgment is hereby made to Rabbi Wilfred Shuchat of the Shaar Hashomayim Congregation, who read the entire manuscript. For his most helpful criticism I wish to express my deep appreciation. We are also indebted to Rabbi Maurice Cohen of the Shaare Zion Congregation for the use of his library and his kindly interest.

We are grateful to the distinguished scholar, Rabbi Pinchas Hirshprung, for his trouble in reading the text and for his approbation.

To Mr. David Rome for his advice in the preparation of this volume for publication and for his tireless effort in our behalf in the editing, and to Mr. Abraham Goldberg for his technical assistance—our sincere thanks.

Sincere thanks are extended to the judges of the book-title contest, Mrs. H. Singer, president, Hadassah Organization of Canada; Mrs. A. Raginsky, Sr., honorary president, Dominion Hadassah; Mrs. Henry Nathanson, president, Montreal Hadassah; Mrs. M. B. Weinstein, honorary president, Montreal Hadassah, and to Mrs. Jesse J. Schwartz, one of the most active members of the women's Zionist movement.

To the ladies who served on the book committee with me, Mrs. R. Weinrauch, Miss Sarah Ein, Mrs. S. Warshaw, Mrs. H. L. Schwartz, Mrs. S. Itel, Mrs. E. Davids, Miss Shirley Epstein and Mrs. Sidney Schwartz, I extend my grateful thanks. We are also grateful to Mr. Harry M. Epstein, of Montreal, and Dr. William B. Ein, of Newark, New Jersey, for their co-operation.

We owe special thanks to my husband Joseph Batist, who helped in the research and editing, for ever so many helpful suggestions and encouragement.

BESSIE W. (Mrs. Joseph) BATIST
Editor

BETROTHAL AND MARRIAGE

"Hadassah, I am delighted that you and David have decided on a formal betrothal, before your marriage. Most couples today become engaged without any ceremony."

"We thought it would please you and Father and David's folks. Mother, what are the traditional customs in these things?"

"Well, dear, a contract or *tnaim* is often drawn up wherein the parties promise to be married at a certain time. This is followed by the sacred ceremony, when the marriage is formalized by the groom handing his bride a ring, or in the olden days a Palestinian coin, pronouncing the words, 'Thou art consecrated to me,' or any phrase conveying the same idea."

"We will need your help in setting our wedding date, Mother. I understand there are certain times of the year when weddings are prohibited."

"The favorite time for weddings is immediately after Shavuot, or in the month of June. Weddings are prohibited between Pesach and Shavuot—the *Sephirah* season—which is a period of half mourning because of repeated calamities that befell the Jewish people in ancient days during this time of the year. However, weddings are permitted on Lag B'Omer, for, according to tradition, these calamities stopped on that day, and it was set aside as a day on which weddings and other festivities were permissible. Weddings are also permitted on Rosh Chodesh (the New Moon), and on the fifth of Iyar, the anniversary of the establishment of the State of Israel, Yom Haatzmaut.

"Weddings are not permitted during the three weeks before Tisha B'Av, since the greatest misfortunes in our history have occurred during the three weeks from the 17th of Tamuz to the 9th day of Av. Nor is it permissible to solemnize weddings on the Sabbath or on holidays."

"We were fortunate in procuring the synagogue for our ceremony."

"Yes, the synagogue is the favorite place because of its sacredness."

"Mother, I would like to know your ideas about the Jewish laws on marriage."

"Marriage, Hadassah, is a divine institution, a holy estate in which man lives his true and complete life. The Jewish husband loves his wife as himself and honors her more than himself. 'I will work for thee—I will honor thee —I will support thee' is to this day the husband's vow in the Jewish marriage contract. The affectionate consideration shown to the Jewish wife, as well as the domestic purity and the devotion that are the glory of Jewish womanhood, are largely the fruit of our Torah. The holiness of the home is basic in all human relations. It is an ideal that has distinguished the Jewish people throughout the ages.

"Marriage is a primary religious duty. Important as it may be that love precede marriage, it is even more important that it continue after marriage. The modern attitude stresses the romance before marriage. The old Jewish view emphasizes lifelong devotion and affection after marriage. The purpose of marriage is twofold. Firstly, there is the duty of building a home and rearing a family. 'Be fruitful and multiply' figures in the Torah. Secondly, companionship—woman is to be the helpmate of man, socially, spiritually and physically. Hadassah, there is a purity law concerning the physical relationship—the cessation of marital relations in every form each month. It is called the *Nidah* period. Through guidance in these vital matters, which our laws provide, Jewish men have been taught respect for womanhood, moral discipline and ethical culture.

"There are important laws about personal and marital purity that go far back in our history. Our ancestors traditionally placed great importance upon the *Mikveh*. I do hope that you will be in touch with a rabbi to discuss these matters with him from the point of view of Jewish law. For our Jewish women these laws have given protection from uncurbed passion and taught them to view marital life in a sane and practical manner.

"It is this idea that is expressed by the word *kiddushin* (sanctification) that is applied to Jewish marriage. *Kiddushin* is the dedication of two human beings to life's holiest purposes."

"Mother, what is this custom of the bridegroom, or *chosson*, being called up to the Torah on the Sabbath before the wedding ceremony?"

"The custom is explained in the Talmud in this manner: King Solomon had a special gate for bridegrooms built in the Temple where the people of Jerusalem would gather on the Sabbath to congratulate the fortunate young men. After the destruction of the Temple it was ordained by the sages that the bridegrooms go to the synagogue so that they may be congratulated there.

"After the services, the congregants are invited to a *Kiddush* to celebrate the occasion with the families of the bride and groom."

16

"Is it customary for the groom to be called only on the Sabbath preceding the marriage?"

"No, Hadassah, he may be called on a Monday or a Thursday, as the Torah is read on those days as well as on the Sabbath.

"It is also customary for the bride and groom to fast on their wedding day until after the ceremony. For the bride and groom it is as solemn as Yom Kippur, because on that day they are forgiven all their sins. If the wedding takes place on Lag B'Omer, Chanukah, Rosh Chodesh, or some other festive occasion, the bride and groom do not have to fast."

"Why is the marriage ceremony performed under a canopy?"

"In ancient times the *tallis* (prayer shawl) was used as a canopy at the nuptial ceremonies. Later the canopy was in the form of a bower of flowers. In the course of time the details of the wedding ceremony changed. The *chuppah* (bridal canopy) was transformed into a portable canopy resting on four poles.

"The bridal procession is a festive affair in which the groom is first led under the *chuppah* by his parents, usually to the accompaniment of music; then the bride is escorted by her parents. This signifies the surrender of the daughter to the man who is to be her husband. The bride is usually dressed in white, which exemplifies purity, and wears a veil that is used to cover her face during the ceremony.

"The rabbi welcomes the couple by saying, 'Blessed be he who comes in the name of the Lord. We bless you from the house of the Lord.'

"The marriage service consists of the blessing of the betrothal followed by a benediction made over a cup of

17

wine, of which the bride and groom partake. Wine is a symbol of joy; joyousness at a wedding is a religious duty. The marriage contract, the *ketubah*, is read. This tells the obligations of a man to a woman in married life. Then the groom places the wedding ring on the forefinger of the bride's right hand, saying, '*Harai at mekudeshet li betabaat zu kedat Mosheh V'Israel*.' ('You are hereby betrothed to me by this ring in accordance with the laws of Moses and Israel.') The couple then again drink from the cup of wine —an indication of their resolve to share whatever Providence may allot them. Finally, the breaking of the glass by the groom recalls the destruction of Jerusalem at the hands of the Romans."

"Mother, why do we have to have a reminder of this tragedy at this festive occasion?"

"This is in fulfillment of the pledge that is recorded in the Psalms, 'Let my tongue cleave to the roof of my mouth, if I remember thee not; if I set not Jerusalem above my chiefest joy.' It is also a promise by the couple to do their share for the firm restoration of Israel, which has lain so long in ruins.

"The reception follows, at which the *Hamotzi* (benediction over bread) is made over a *chalah* (large loaf of bread) which each guest partakes of. After the meal, grace is said, followed by the chanting of the seven blessings of sanctification *(Sheva Brachot)*."

MEZUZAH

"You promised to tell me of the significance of the Mezuzah."

"Yes, Hadassah, the Mezuzah is a piece of parchment bearing a text from the Bible and enclosed in a case, which we Jews attach to the doorposts of our homes. It is usually placed in a slanting position on the right doorpost as one enters. In many homes it is also fastened to the doorpost of each room.

"The case is made of various types of materials such as metal, glass, or olive wood imported from Israel, and has an opening through which may be seen a single Hebrew word, *Shadai* (Almighty), written on the back of the parchment scroll. The parchment is made from the skin of sheep or calves. The writing on the scroll is governed by the same strict rules that pertain to the writing of the Sefer Torah."

"Is there any particular ceremony in connection with the hanging of the Mezuzah?"

"Yes, a benediction is usually pronounced."

"Mother, you mentioned that the Mezuzah contained a text from the Bible. Which part of the Bible is written on the parchment?"

"The Mezuzah contains the first two portions of the *Shema*."

"What is the *Shema*, Mother?"

"The opening words of the *Shema* are '*Shema Israel, Adonoy Eloheinu, Adonoy Ehad*' ('Hear, O Israel, the Lord our God, the Lord is One'). This prayer is the fundamental basic reading of the Jewish religion, and these words enshrine Judaism's greatest contribution to the religious thought of mankind, that there is but one God. The Mezuzah on the doorpost of a home is a solemn declaration that the people who live within subscribe to the principles enunciated in the *Shema* and are devoted to its ideals. The second portion stresses the moral obligation. The *Shema* is also a symbol of God's watchful care over the house and its dwellers.

"According to the old custom, we place the index and middle fingers of the right hand on the Mezuzah and then touch the lips with them whenever we enter or leave the house as a token of our homage to the words of the Almighty.

"The story is told of a very rich person who sent a pearl of great value to Rabbi Judah as a token of his personal regard. In return, the Rabbi sent him a Mezuzah, explaining that the pearl, having a great material value, would require a mortal guardian to watch it, whereas the Mezuzah had a spiritual significance and would bring upon the owner and his household the benign guardianship and protection of Almighty God."

KASHRUT

"Mother, I received a gift of a new Jewish cookbook. The recipes are very good but there is no information there on *kashrut*."

"The dietary laws, Hadassah, are the foundation on which the Jewish home is built and have been an important factor in the preservation of the Jewish race. The Torah takes the whole of human life as its province. In the eyes of the Torah all human beings are sacred. A healthy soul in a healthy body is its ideal. Among the laws of purity first place is given to the subject of food, because the daily diet intimately affects man's whole being. The Jew who keeps *kashrut* is reminded of his religious identity at every meal.

"The basis of *kashrut* in Jewish life is essentially and fundamentally religious but it has an historical and sanitary aspect as well.

"Modern research has proven that the Jewish dietary laws are based on sound hygienic principles. Certain animals are breeders and carriers of disease germs; consequently the flesh of such animals is harmful to people. Those animals are excluded from the Jewish diet. Furthermore, the flesh of all animals used by us for food must be thoroughly drained of blood. This is most effectively done by the Jewish traditional kashering of the meat before it is eaten.

"According to the laws in the Bible we are permitted to eat the flesh of only those animals that have a cleft hoof and chew their cud. It is forbidden to eat the hindquarters, unless the sinews and fat from these parts are removed, a process requiring great skill with which modern butchers often do not concern themselves. Therefore this meat is not used by Jewish people.

"Only such cattle and fowl as are slaughtered according to the Jewish ritual are permitted to Jews. A *shoichet*, a religious man who has studied the Jewish laws of slaughter, kills the animal or fowl by cutting the jugular vein with one stroke of the *chalef* (a very sharp knife), giving the animal the least pain, and thus being a most humane method of slaughtering animals. If a *shoichet's* hand is unsteady, he may not kill.

"After the animal is killed, the lungs and other vital organs are inspected *(bdikah)*, and if they are found free of all symptoms of disease, the meat is declared kosher. All meat and poultry to be considered kosher must be under the supervision of Jewish authorities.

"When meat is brought home, the traditional kashering is done. First it must be thoroughly washed and placed in a vessel with enough water to cover the meat and left to soak for half an hour. This is done to remove the blood and dirt which may have clung to it in the handling. Then it is removed from the water and placed on a board in a slanting position or on a grid to allow the water to drain off. It is immediately liberally sprinkled with salt on all sides and left to stand for one hour. The salt is used to draw out any blood that may be left in the meat. At the end of an hour the meat is thoroughly washed three times to make certain that all the salt and blood are removed.

"The utensils used for soaking the meat must not be used in the preparation of any other food.

"The hearts of animals must be slit before soaking to free them of any blood. The lung must be cut to open the large veins that it contains before soaking. The liver, which contains a large quantity of blood, cannot be made ready for cooking by the usual process of soaking and salting. It must be seared over a fire in order to draw out the blood and slightly salted while it is being seared. No meat may be kept after seventy-two hours unless it is kashered in the interval. Steaks and chops do not have to be kashered if they are to be broiled. No bird or beast of prey is permitted, such as eagles, vultures, owls or lions.

"If on opening fowl for kashering, a foreign substance such as a needle or nail is found, a rabbi should be consulted as to whether such a fowl is kosher. The veins of the neck are removed, and the tip of the wings and the claws from the feet must be cut off. Eggs found inside poultry require kashering but are kept separate from the meat. Such eggs must not be eaten with dairy foods."

"Mother, I noticed that sometimes you did not use certain eggs."

"The reason for that, Hadassah, is that an egg with a blood clot on the yolk is considered fertile and must not be used.

"Only such fish are permitted as have scales and fins. No shellfish are considered kosher for they are called the scavengers of the sea and are therefore unclean.

"Separate dishes and cutlery are used for meat and dairy meals, both for the preparation and the serving. Cracked or chipped dishes are considered unclean and should not be used.

"The separation of meat and milk foods is based on a law which is repeated three times in the Torah: 'Thou shalt not seethe the kid in its mother's milk.'

"Food known as *pareve* is that made without either dairy or meat ingredients and is prepared in separate utensils. Glass dishes are considered *pareve* and may be used for serving either meat or dairy foods.

"An interval of six hours must elapse before one may eat dairy food after a meat meal.

"Through the dietary laws the Torah has exerted a profound influence on the domestic life of every Jewish home. These laws are primarily religious and have their foundation in the Bible, Mishnah, Gemara and the studies of the sages. *Kashrut* has played an important part in maintaining the Jewish people. It is also believed that persons who have conformed to these principles are less susceptible to certain diseases. In the Middle Ages, when epidemics occurred often, the Jewish population was less affected. This gave rise to the malicious accusations that the Jews were responsible for the plagues by poisoning the wells. Authorities attribute the healthy characteristics of the Jews to their observance of the dietary laws."

THIS IS HADASSAH

"It is a good thing, Hadassah, that my interest in Hadassah led you to join the Junior organization. There are advantages in becoming familiar with Zionism early in life."

"You are so right, Mother. We in our group have found it most interesting to take an active part in Hadassah work.

"The Junior Chapters of Canadian Hadassah are comprised of Jewish girls between the ages of eighteen and twenty-six. They constitute a most important, integral part of Canadian Hadassah. It is a transient stage and the membership is renewed every three or four years. As the girls become a little older, they enter the very fine business and professional groups, and the intermediates, and the married girls enter Senior Hadassah. As the Juniors become Seniors, they give new vitality to the work and strengthen the movement and thus help to maintain the continuity of the organization.

"Junior Hadassah have their own educational program and their own practical projects for Israel. Among these is an annual subsidy, raised for the Acco Baby Home in Acre and for the Canadian Hadassah's Children's Village—Hadassim. The Junior membership is specially active for the National Fund, clearing boxes, etc. We take an active role in the Youth Aliyah Drives, the United Israel Appeal, and so on.

"For the younger group there is Young Judaea. Through Canadian Hadassah-WIZO, Young Judaea extends practical assistance to boys and girls between the ages of eight and sixteen, coupling advisory and financial aid. Scholarships are provided for leadership training, summer schools and visits to Israel.

"The members of Junior Chapters of Hadassah participate in all national conventions and conferences and hold special sessions and seminars.

"The young Jewish women are proud of their role and are keenly alert to the needs of Israel today. Among our activities are discussion groups, study groups, reading circles, festival programs, drama groups, choral groups, art and literary groups, practical workshops, courses on Jewish customs and ceremonies, a film library, Hebrew classes, public speaking and debating."

"I think, Hadassah, your development and the development of the family, when you become a homemaker, stand a better chance if you realize early in life your responsibility to your people as well as to your home. There is nothing so stimulating as that sense of belonging."

"Isn't it a strange coincidence that both my name and that of our organization should be Hadassah?"

"We named you Hadassah because you were born on Purim and as a tribute to Queen Esther, who was also known as Hadassah. The Hadassah organization took this name to identify itself as a group dedicated to the re-establishment of Palestine as a national home for the Jews. Their very first meeting took place on a Purim night.

"Canadian Hadassah was organized in 1916 with the formation of two chapters, one in Toronto and one in Montreal. Several other chapters also sprang up in isolated cities. In 1917 it was decided to form these chapters into a national organization; in that year the Hadassah organization of Canada came into being, with the late Lillian Freiman, of Ottawa, as president. It is interesting to know that Canadian Hadassah was organized before the Women's International Zionist Organization, popularly known as WIZO; but when WIZO was founded in 1920, Canadian Hadassah became one of its first federations and has remained one of the strongest links in the international chain.

"From small beginnings in 1920, WIZO spread out across the world and today there are 250,000 Jewish women in all walks of life, the world over, united in this great movement. Our work has a twofold purpose—education and the securing of funds."

"Just how and by whom are these monies distributed?"

"The first in importance is the Jewish National Fund, the Keren Kayemeth, which buys land for settlements. This land remains the property of the JNF. While it may be rented to individuals for a period of not longer than 99 years, it may never be sold."

"Does the Keren Kayemeth only buy land?"

"No, Hadassah, the funds are also used for the conservation of soil by drainage, supplying water and planting trees, which is very important in order to bring back the fertility of the soil."

"Are the $2.00 tree certificates that we buy at our meetings helping the reforestation of Palestine?"

"Yes. Today one of the major projects in this soil conservation is in the Negev, in the southern half of Israel. The JNF is the main agency developing this area since 1943."

"What has been done there?"

"Settlements were set up on the basis of experimentation. Data was gathered on temperature, moisture and char-

27

acteristics of the climate. Deep wells were sunk and experiments for conserving local rainfall as well as water coming down from the mountains were carried out. On the basis of these experiments it was found that, with proper methods, the desert wasteland could be made fertile. In fact, it has proven so successful that crops now obtained are four to five times greater than had been previously obtained. This has encouraged us to continue this work for complete rehabilitation of this desert area.

"One popular method of raising funds is the National Fund Blue Box. For decades, thousands of Jewish homes in all lands have had this box for their regular contributions. This has always reminded housewives, children and visitors in the home of their duty to Israel. These boxes are cleared periodically.

"Then there is the eternal Golden Book, where for payment of $100.00 are inscribed the names and occasions the Jewish people will always remember. The *Sefer Hayeled*, where inscriptions are $10.00, is for children and there is the *Sefer Bar Mitzva*—in which the inscription may be made for $25.00. Land may also be purchased for the JNF at $25.00 per *dunam* (equivalent to a quarter of an acre in Canadian measure). In addition, the JNF depends upon legacies and bequests."

"What is the Keren Hayesod, Mother?"

"It is the Construction Fund, and provides for industrial and agricultural development, such as public utilities, harbors, wharves and educational facilities. In fact, we may say that the Keren Hayesod looks after the cultural, industrial and educational needs.

"The annual United Israel Appeal campaign is for both the Keren Kayemeth and Keren Hayesod.

"There is also the Youth Aliyah, or Child Rescue fund,

a humanitarian movement that has spread throughout the world. In this country, Canadian Hadassah has been the official agency of Youth Aliyah since 1936. Since the inception of Youth Aliyah, more than 125,000 children have been rescued from the war-torn countries of Europe, and now from North Africa and other Eastern countries, and given a new lease on life in Israel. Through a carefully planned program of training and education, the children have been transformed from broken youngsters into wholesome, healthy children once again. Through the years they have proven themselves to be the finest citizens of the country and many from the early groups are now in the front line of the pioneering effort. They have helped to build the Jewish State. They have been integrated into every phase of life in Israel and will help to make it flourish as a nation. Through the efforts of the members of Hadassah in Canada, many additional thousands of children have been saved.

"As a further project, Canadian Hadassah has established a Children's Village in Israel called Hadassim, where more than 500 children—most of them from Youth Aliyah —have found a home and are receiving the finest education in ideal surroundings.

"A section of 500 *dunams* of land was bought in the Sharon. This village has facilities for 400 children, but the plan provides for an ultimate capacity of 650. The ages of the children are from six to seventeen. They are given the opportunity of developing their natural talents in the arts and crafts as well as a general education. The girls are trained in domestic science, home economics and sewing. The children help in the housework and the kitchen. The cleanliness of the village is the responsibility of all. The graduates are trained to take their place in the youth movements."

"Mother, what is Nahalal?"

"It is another of the major projects of Canadian Hadassah in Israel—the Agricultural Training School for girls and boys at Nahalal. This was established in 1921 and has played an important role in the agricultural development of the country. There is nothing so vital to the economy of Israel as the training of its youth for farming. This school is training about 400 boys and girls for life in Israel and Canadian Hadassah is thus helping to build up a generation of builders and growers."

"Mother, as you tell me of these funds, I understand the value of helping others and being proud of our heritage. It helps us to understand our past and to look forward with courage to the future."

"Hadassah, dear, fund-raising is not our chief aim. You must realize that Zionism strives for a national regeneration —a return to our true Jewish cultural heritage which has become thinned out by assimilation and by the idea that philanthropy alone is important. In order to combat this and to rebuild ourselves, education is necessary, to gain dignity and self-respect by emphasizing our Jewish values. It is not charity that has kept us alive throughout the generations, but the Jewish spirit, which survived all obstacles to preserve itself."

"Mother, I believe that Zionism is one of the guiding spirits helping Judaism to be reborn everywhere. Zionism can be compared to the little *shames* on Chanukah, ever ready to rekindle all the unlit candles of the menorah—Judaism."

"The work of our organization enriches our lives, Hadassah, as well as those in Israel by giving our lives significance.

"The establishment of the Jewish State has given us a

new pride and dignity. Israel will be the center of Jewish life. It has given a new birth of freedom to our people. Through Hadassah's vital program, each member achieves a new dignity as a Canadian citizen and new understanding as a Jew, as well as a new sense of solidarity with all who honor liberty and fight for justice. We are proud of the role that Canadian statesmen have taken in assisting in the birth of Israel.

"Our great cultural traditions are finding rebirth in Israel. There has been revived, first of all, the Hebrew language. Rejuvenated and modernized, it has evoked a vigorous modern Hebrew literature (both in poetry and in prose), which reflects the ambitions and ideals of our people. An authentic folk music has sprung up spontaneously throughout Israel; native arts and handicrafts have appeared; a school system crowned by the Hebrew University in Jerusalem conveys the heritage of the past and the problems of the present. In brief, Zionism has made possible, at least in one land, a full Jewish life—a revival of a complete and ancient civilization.

"The work of Hadassah enlarges our vision, revives the source from which we sprang, and of which we have every reason to be proud.

"To know our history is to add to our self-respect, and so the work of rebuilding Israel is tied up with our own salvation."

SABBATH

"Mother, what are you doing? Oh, preparing gefilte fish for tomorrow."

"Yes, Hadassah, tomorrow is Friday, when every Jewish homemaker prepares for the Sabbath. Soon you will be a homemaker yourself, and you will be busy preparing for the Sabbath and other holidays."

"You know, Mother, I have some qualms about my ability to manage my own home in the traditional Jewish way. I have always taken the routine of this home for granted."

"That is something that will come naturally to you because you were brought up with it. For instance, you know that no cooking is done on the Sabbath, and that it begins at sundown on Friday, as we count our days from sunset to sunset."

"Yes, I remember the undercurrent of excitement every Friday night even as a child when we all took part in the preparations."

"Our Jewish religion provides very well in this respect for the children. I always allotted some special duty to each of you in the preparation for the Sabbath meal. One of you spread the tablecloth, another placed the two covered *chalahs* which, by the way, represent the double portion of manna gathered on Fridays when the Jews were wandering in the desert on their way to Palestine from Egypt. You always brought the wine and the *Kiddush* cup, and of course, I prepared the candlesticks with the candles."

"Is there a set rule as to the number of candles to be kindled?"

"No, Hadassah, but the minimum of two is required, though some people add a candle for each child in the family. The Sabbath candles are lit twenty minutes before sunset. The benediction is recited in silence with covered head and the eyes shielded with the palms of the hands."

"May one add a personal prayer, Mother?"

"Yes, most Jewish women do after the benediction."

"You know, Mother, after you have lit the candles and said the prayer, when we gather around you to say 'Good Sabbath,' peace and joy seem to settle over our home; sometimes I think I can see that peacefulness and joy, not only feel it."

"I, too, feel very much as you do, Hadassah. In fact, you will experience it even more in your own home, because you will be the one who ushers in the Sabbath by lighting the candles, and you will bring that joy and peace into your household.

"When Father comes home from the synagogue, there is also a deep feeling when he blesses each of the children by placing his hands on your bowed heads and says 'God make thee as Sarah, Rebeccah, Rachel and Leah' to the girls and 'God make thee as Ephraim and Menasseh' to the boys. After this solemn moment we all join him in singing *Shalom Aleichem,* our joyous Sabbath hymn. Do you know that when the father is away the mother may recite the blessing over the children, as well as chant the *Kiddush? Kiddush* is chanted over a goblet of wine. It is a symbol of joy and cheer. Then the ritual of the washing of the hands is performed, after which the *Hamotzi* is recited over a *chalah*, of which we each partake and repeat the benediction. Then the meal is served. After the meal, grace is chanted and then we all enjoy *zmirot*, the traditional thanksgiving songs."

"We often go to the late Friday night services and the *Oneg Shabbat*. Mother, what does *Oneg Shabbat* mean?"

"*Oneg Shabbat* means the Pleasure of the Sabbath and assumed its present form in Tel Aviv, in 1923, when Chaim Nachman Bialik modernized the old custom of group study during *Shalosh S'udot* and *Havdalah*. After lectures and discussions, they sang *zmirot*, Hassadic tunes and new Hebrew songs. In Israel, *Oneg Shabbat* is usually held Saturday afternoon about two hours before sunset. The custom has been followed in other countries. In some synagogues it is held after late Friday-night services."

"I like going to the synagogue with you and Father on Saturday morning. We are proud of the way the Junior Congregation conducts the services, the way everything is explained so that all can understand what is being read and are able to follow the service."

"It is a fine preparation for the participation in the adult congregation and its various functions. As soon as you have your own home I would suggest that you join the synagogue sisterhood."

"That is a good idea. I would like to be like you and to follow your example in all customs. I will continue inviting a guest as you have always done to our Sabbath dinner."

"That custom of sharing Sabbath and holiday meals is traditional. The Sabbath is our day of complete rest and when we come home from the synagogue and *Kiddush* is chanted and the *Hamotzi* is made there is more time to enjoy our meal and relax with our guest and family."

34

"We abstain from work and usually visit our friends and relatives on the Sabbath. Mother, I usually read a Jewish book on Saturday."

"There is a beautiful prayer which every mother recites at twilight on the Sabbath, seeking the well-being of the Jewish people, which begins with the words, 'O God of Abraham, Isaac and Jacob, guard Thy people Israel for Thy Praise.'

"After the stars appear, the Sabbath ends with the *Havdalah* ceremony. This prayer emphasizes the distinction that God made between holy days and days of work, between light and darkness. The prayer is said over a twisted multicolored candle, over the *besamin* or spice box and over a glass of wine.

"You know, Hadassah, that all care, grief and sorrow are forbidden on the Sabbath. All fasting (except on the day of Atonement) is forbidden, and all mourning is suspended on the Sabbath."

"I suppose that is because it is considered the holiest day."

"The Sabbath is one of the first institutions observed by our ancestors dating back to the days of the Exodus. There are two foundations for the Sabbath: one, the religious, that God created the world in six days and rested on the seventh day; therefore the Sabbath is the anniversary of the Creation. The other approach is historical. When the Israelites were freed from slavery they received the Ten Commandments on Mount Sinai, the fourth of which is *Remember the Sabbath to keep it Holy*. The Jews were the first people in the world to observe a Sabbath that means rest."

"Mother, then the Fourth Commandment can be considered the first labor law of mankind?"

"Yes, because no other nation conceived this idea of man dedicating one day in the week to rest."

"I think that it is one of the greatest contributions Israel has made to the world."

"The Sabbath, Hadassah, has become a boon to mankind, one of the glories of all our humanity. As Claude G. Montefiore said, 'For if to labor is noble, of our own free will to pause in that labor is nobler still'."

"What a beautiful statement! Mother, you have always explained all the festivals—not only the Sabbath—and made an interesting Jewish home for all of us. We always looked forward to the Jewish holidays. You would be surprised at how many of my friends feel about the observances. To them the Jewish holidays are sad and difficult. How did you manage to convey the spirit of the Jewish ceremonies and customs to us without making us think them burdensome?"

"I wanted our home to be a gay place where our friends could come and enjoy themselves in a Jewish way. I worked hard to develop our home, as you will too, I am sure. I always had a Jewish calendar so that I would know well in advance when each holiday would come and I always had ample time to plan and prepare. As for being sad, Hadassah, our holidays are sad to a certain extent, because we always remember the hardships of our ancestors and their struggle for happiness. But at the same time, we celebrate their success in overcoming these hardships and pray that the future will bring complete fulfillment of our age-old struggle for restoration. I know that in carrying on the Jewish beliefs in your home, you will find it no more burdensome than I did. You may make minor changes here and there, but basically you will do as has been done for centuries, and what Jews will continue to do as long as this world exists.

MEDITATION BEFORE KINDLING THE SABBATH CANDLES

May the Sabbath-light which illumines our dwelling cause peace and happiness to shine in our home.

Bless us, O God, on this holy Sabbath, and cause Thy divine glory to shine upon us.

Enlighten our darkness and guide us and all mankind, Thy children, towards truth and eternal light.

Amen.

—Abraham Millgram,
Sabbath, Day of Delight,
Jewish Publication Society, 1944

DINNER MENU FOR FRIDAY EVENING
Erev Sabbath

Wine   Chalah

Gefilte Fish on Fresh Vegetable Salad

Horse-radish   Nahit   Celery and Olives

Chicken Soup with Rice

Roast Capon   Noodle Kugel   Kishke

Compote of Rhubarb and Strawberries

Eier Kichel   Tea and Lemon

CHALAH

1½ teaspoons salt	or 2 envelopes active
1 tablespoon sugar	dry yeast
2 tablespoons oil	¼ cup lukewarm water
2 cups hot water	4 eggs
2 cakes compressed yeast	8 cups sifted all-purpose
	flour

Add salt, sugar and oil to hot water, stir to dissolve. Dissolve yeast in lukewarm water, then add to slightly cooled first mixture. Add 3 of the eggs, well beaten, and stir in the flour, ½ at a time. Blend well, then turn dough out on lightly floured board or counter top and knead steadily for at least 10 minutes, pressing dough away with palms of your hands, then fold over, press down, roll and work with fingers until dough is smooth and elastic and no longer sticks to your hands or the board. Place dough in greased bowl, brush oil over top, cover with waxed paper or cloth towel and set bowl in warm place (about 80°F) until trebled in bulk. Knead down again, allow dough to rise once more, then divide dough in half; cut each half into three equal parts. Roll these lengthwise to about 1½ inches thick. Make braids of the three rolls, pinching together at ends to seal. Place both braids on an oiled baking sheet and again allow to rise until more than doubled in bulk. Beat the fourth egg, brush over top of braided dough, then sprinkle with poppy or caraway seeds and bake in an oven pre-heated to 400° for 20 minutes. Reduce heat to 375° and continue baking an additional 40 minutes until crust is golden and crusty. Makes 2 loaves. Before forming loaves take off small piece of dough, pronounce the appropriate benediction (see p. 237). Burn this portion.

Note: If preferred, one of the loaves may be frozen. After baking, cool thoroughly, then wrap in plastic wrap or aluminum foil, sealing securely. To defrost, allow about 3 hours at room temperature.

GEFILTE FISH

Fish Balls

6 pounds whole fish (fresh-water variety such as whitefish, carp, yellow pike) or 3½ pounds fil-leted mixed fish
1 large onion, minced
1 medium carrot, grated
1 tablespoon oil
2 teaspoons sugar
Salt, pepper to taste
3 eggs
1 cup ice-cold water

Fillet the fish, saving bones, skin and head for the stock. (If using filleted mixed fish, ask butcher or fish man for 1 small whole fish or several fish heads for the stock.) Chop fillets very fine or put through food grinder. Add the onion, grated carrot, oil, sugar, salt and pepper to fish, blending well. Beat in eggs and cold water. Chill this mixture in re-frigerator while preparing the stock, then form into balls, enclosing a small piece of carrot in each. Makes 18 to 24 balls, depending on size.

Fish Stock

Place in a large kettle the reserved bones, skin and head of fish along with 1 large onion, sliced, a diced carrot, 2 stalks celery and 1 tablespoon salt. Add 4 cups water, bring to a boil and continue boiling for 5 to 10 minutes, simmer while preparing the fish balls. Remove skin, bones and head from stock, and discard. Carefully drop fish balls into boiling stock, cook uncovered over low heat for 2 hours, adding 1 cup cold water after the first hour. Cool slightly before removing fish balls to a bowl or platter. Stock may be strained over the balls and chilled. Serve either as appetizer or entree.

PREPARED HORSE-RADISH

Wash and peel ½ pound fresh horse-radish roots. Grate, or put through medium blade of food grinder, or cut in small pieces and add to electric blender at medium speed. Add to the grated horse-radish 1 tablespoon sugar and white vinegar to cover, about ½ cup. If desired, a little canned borsht, 3 or 4 tablespoons, may be added for color. Place in sterilized jars, seal.

NAHIT (Chick Peas)

Soak 1 pound dried chick peas overnight. Drain, add fresh cold water to cover and 1 tablespoon salt. Bring to a boil, covered, cook over very low heat until tender, about 1 hour. Drain, season with salt and pepper to taste, toss with 1 or 2 tablespoons oil and, if desired, 1 tablespoon minced parsley. Good hot or cold. Makes 6 to 8 servings.

CHICKEN SOUP

1 stewing chicken, about 4 pounds, cut up
1 veal knuckle or beef marrow bone (optional)
2 carrots, scraped, diced
3 celery stalks (including leaves), diced
1 large onion, quartered
8 cups water
2 teaspoons salt, or to taste

Place chicken and veal or beef bones in large pot with vegetables. Cover with water, add salt. Bring to a boil, lower heat, cook covered until chicken is very tender, about 2 hours. Skim occasionally, discarding scum that rises to top. Remove chicken pieces when tender, set aside. Remove and discard vegetables and beef bone. Chill clear broth. When cold, scrape off fat. Meantime, cut chicken meat from bones for use in chicken casserole, salad or sandwiches; discard skin. Makes 6 to 8 servings. Leftover soup may be refrigerated to serve again. Serve with cooked rice, noodles or mandlach (see p. 49), though for Passover, none of these may be used.

SAVORY ROAST CAPON EN PAPILLOTE

1 capon, about 6 pounds oven-dressed
2 tablespoons grated onion
1 teaspoon paprika
½ teaspoon mixed poultry spices (thyme, basil, sage)
½ teaspoon salt
Large brown paper bag

41

Remove giblets from cavity of oven-dressed capon. Rub or brush outside of capon with the grated onion. Sprinkle all over with mixture of paprika, poultry spices and salt. Let stand at least ½ hour, then place inside paper bag. Twist opening of bag to seal. Place bag in pan in oven preheated to 350°, bake 2 to 2½ hours. When done (leg should move very easily), remove capon from bag to platter. Chicken should be brown and crisp on outside, the flesh moist and tender. Serves 6.

NOODLE KUGEL

3 cups flat noodles, ½-inch wide
8 cups boiling salted water

½ cup clarified chicken fat or oil
4 eggs, beaten
Salt, pepper

Cook noodles in boiling salted water until tender, about 10 minutes. Drain. Place in bowl with the chicken fat, the beaten eggs, salt and pepper to taste. Beat quickly to distribute fat and eggs. Spoon into preheated greased 1½-quart baking dish and bake in oven preheated to 400° until top is browned and fat bubbly. Makes 6 servings.

For Fruited Kugel: Add to drained cooked noodles ¼ cup sugar, 1 teaspoon cinnamon, 1 cup grated apple or 1 cup drained pineapple chunks and ½ cup seedless raisins. Beat together the eggs, salt, pepper and chicken fat or oil as in basic recipe, adding 1 teaspoon cinnamon and ¼ cup sugar. Spoon into greased baking dish and bake as above.

KISHKE

Beef casing (trimmed)
1 cup all-purpose flour
1 large onion, diced

¾ cup chopped uncooked chicken fat
½ teasoon salt, or to taste
Dash freshly ground pepper

Scald casing thoroughly, drain well. Mix flour, onion, chicken fat, salt and pepper. Stuff casing with this mixture; cut to fit and seal both ends by twisting. Heat water in a pot until boiling rapidly; add the stuffed kishke, cook 2 minutes, remove with slotted spoon. When cool enough to handle, scrape scum from outside with knife. Replace in boiling water; cook, covered, 2 hours. Remove from water, drain. Serve this way, or if preferred, sauté in additional chicken fat in a skillet until browned on all sides, or roast in pan with chicken. Makes 8 to 10.

COMPOTE OF RHUBARB AND STRAWBERRIES

3 pounds fresh rhubarb, diced
1/4 cup water
Pinch of salt (1/16 teaspoon)

1 quart (2 pints) fresh strawberries, rinsed, hulled
2 cups granulated sugar

Dice unpeeled rhubarb stalks, place in heavy saucepan with water and pinch of salt. Cook slowly, tightly covered, for 10 minutes. Add salt, berries and sugar. Replace cover, continue cooking over low heat another 10 minutes. Cool. Serve warm or chilled, with or without whipped topping. Makes 10 to 12 servings. Leftovers can be kept in refrigerator for serving again.

EIER KICHEL

3 eggs
1 tablespoon oil
2 tablespoons sugar
1/4 teaspoon salt

1/2 teaspoon baking powder
1 2/3 cups sifted all-purpose flour

Beat eggs until foamy, add remaining ingredients all at once, beat with wooden spoon until smooth. Form into dough, knead slightly with fingers, roll out on lightly floured board or counter top to ⅛-inch thick. Cut in circles with cooky cutter, or in diamond shapes with sharp knife. Place on well-greased baking sheet, brush with oil. Sprinkle with a little sifted granulated sugar, if desired. Bake in oven preheated to 375° about 20 minutes until light brown. Remove at once from baking sheet with spatula.

Fried Kichel: Instead of baking, fry squares or circles of dough in deep fat heated to 375°, until golden brown, about 7 minutes. (Kichel will rise to top of fat.) Drain on absorbent paper, then sprinkle with confectioners' sugar.

ROSH HASHANAH

"Hadassah, with the approach of the New Year, you may be interested to know the difference between the high holy days and the other holidays in the Jewish calendar. Rosh Hashanah and Yom Kippur are the high holy days given over to prayer and earnest self-judgment by each person; these holy religious days are the most solemn of the Jewish religious observances, whereas other holidays either celebrate great historical events in the history of the Jewish people or celebrate the various harvest seasons."

"That is when the shofar is blown, is it not, Mother?"

"Yes, Hadassah, the solemn period is announced by the blowing of the shofar each day in the synagogue during the morning service after the beginning of Elul. Every day during this time, with the exception of the Sabbath, the shofar is sounded, reminding the people that the high holy days are drawing near and urging them to begin thinking seriously of their spiritual state."

"The ceremony of the blowing of the shofar is a very important one, for it impresses me with a feeling of intense solemnity. There is always a hush in the synagogue when it is blown, and the congregation is listening with awe."

"That is so because the shofar has deep significance. The blowing of the shofar is preceded by the chanting of Psalm 37, recognizing God's supreme power over all the people. This beautiful prayer, *Lamnatzeach*, is repeated seven times in succession. After this, the shofar, which is a ram's horn, is sounded. It produces sounds called *tekyah*, *shevarim* and *teruah*, which are sounded in different sequences. *Tekyah* is sounded as one long note. *Shevarim* consists of three broken short notes. *Teruah* is sounded as nine quick sharp notes.

"Tradition explains that these ancient notes honor the patriarchs Abraham, Isaac and Jacob. They call to mind many events of our history; for example, the *Akedah*, which was the offering of Isaac to God by Abraham, and God's rejection of a human sacrifice. The primary purpose of this command was to demonstrate that God abhorred human sacrifice. Unlike the cruel heathen deities, it was spiritual surrender alone that God required. We recall God's revelation at Mount Sinai when the commandments were given to Moses. It reminds us of the desecration of the Temple. The shofar is a holy symbol associated with important events, high ideals, and new hopes—above all, it inspires us with the hope of everlasting peace and good will in the world.

"First of all there are the *Selichot* services, which are held nightly before Rosh Hashanah and end on Yom Kippur. There is need for such a period of solemn thought, prayer, repentance, and self-examination.

"A special *Selichot* service takes place after midnight on Saturday before Rosh Hashanah, at which time special prayers of repentance and forgiveness are said. Some of these prayers recall the hardships of exile and persecution that Jews have suffered during the past."

"Are any other prayers recited before Rosh Hashanah?"

"Yes, Hadassah, a benediction is said when the candles are lit at sundown of Erev Rosh Hashanah and also at sundown on the next day. We observe Rosh Hashanah for two days. These days fall on the first and second day of Tishrei."

"Mother, this is a very solemn holiday, for we remember past failings and pray to God for forgiveness of sins committed."

"Yes, Rosh Hashanah is known as the Day of Judgment, the Day of Memorial and the Day of Shofar Sounding. Jewish tradition visualizes a court of justice, over which God sits enthroned to pronounce judgment on all people. Before Him lie the books in which all the deeds of all men are inscribed. These are opened on Rosh Hashanah and judgment is passed on all creatures of the world. During the ten penitential days, which commence with the first day of Rosh Hashanah, we can pray for remission of punishment. Prayer, fasting and charity are invoked to soften the judgment. On Yom Kippur, the Day of Atonement, the judgment is sealed. In this way, Jewish religion emphasizes that all we say or do or think is a matter of permanent record, written both in our own memories and in the lives and thoughts of those who come under our influence.

"Rosh Hashanah is the Day of Memorial or remembrance for, as you mentioned, this is the time when the Jew examines his thoughts and deeds of the past, and prays that God will remember him kindly."

"I recall the beautiful prayer *Untaneh Tokef*, which is like a poem."

"That prayer, Hadassah, was written by Rabbi Amnon to express the greatness of God and the humility of man. It tells how man is judged on Rosh Hashanah. It says that on these days God determines who may live and who shall die, who will prosper and who will not, who shall have rest and peace, and who is destined to wander and suffer. However, through prayer, charity and repentance, one's sins will be forgiven. Do you know the *Taschlich* service?"

47

"I know that on the afternoon of the first day of Rosh Hashanah, Jews attend the *Taschlich* service, but I do not think I really understand the full meaning of this ceremony."

"This takes place on the bank of a river or some other body of fresh water, and we symbolically throw our sins into the water where they are carried away. The ceremony signifies that it is within man's power to rid himself of sin and correct his ways."

"I would like to feel that I realize the deep significance of Rosh Hashanah. I would certainly like to live up to its ideals the year round."

"That is a fine thought, Hadassah, for the result of our actions is shown in the habits we develop and the character we achieve. An ancient rabbi said, 'Punishment of an evil deed consists of the increased tendency toward evil; the reward for goodness lies in its increased tendency toward righteousness.'

"We have been discussing the ceremony and meaning of Rosh Hashanah. One custom that we Jews observe at this time is the visiting of the graves of parents and relatives during the month before Yom Kippur. There is also the gracious custom of sending New Year greeting cards to relatives and friends, and of greeting people by saying '*L'Shanah Tovah Tikatevu*,' which means 'May you be inscribed for a good year.'

"On this holiday, after earnest self-judgment and honest regret for sins committed, we pray that God in His judgment will consider us worthy to be inscribed favorably in His books. Our highest wish is expressed during the service that the time will come when all individuals and nations will live in brotherhood, justice and peace in conformity with His will."

DINNER MENU FOR ROSH HASHANAH I

Wine   Honey and Apple

Gefilte Fish (see p. 39)   Lettuce and Cucumber Salad

Chicken Soup (see p. 41)   Mandlach

Roast Chicken with Potato and Liver Stuffing

Carrot Tsimes with Knadel   Green Beans

Apricot Whip

Honey Cake   Tea   Stuffed Prunes and Dates

MANDLACH (Soup Nuts)

3 medium eggs   2 tablespoons oil
2 cups sifted all-purpose   1 teaspoon salt
flour

Combine all ingredients, beat to blend, then knead slightly to make a dough just firm enough to roll with the hands (it will be a soft dough). Divide into 2 or 3 parts and roll into ropes ⅜ inch thick, using the palms of your hands to push over lightly floured board or counter top. Cut into ½-inch pieces, place in shallow well-greased roasting pan. Bake in oven preheated to 375° until golden brown. Shake pan occasionally so that nuts brown evenly on all sides. Use as many as desired in soup; store remaining mandlach, after they have cooled completely, in a covered jar.

ROAST CHICKEN WITH POTATO AND LIVER STUFFING

6-pound roasting chicken or capon

49

Stuffing

4 medium potatoes, boiled, mashed
1 sliced onion, sautéed in fat until lightly browned
½ pound liver, baked, minced
2 tablespoons chicken fat
1 green pepper, minced (optional)
Salt, pepper to taste
2 tablespoons grated onion
Paprika, salt

Remove giblets from cavity of dressed chicken. Combine stuffing ingredients, blend well, seasoning to taste. Fill both breast and neck cavities with stuffing, lace up cavities, then rub chicken all over with grated onion, sprinkle all over with paprika and salt from shaker. Roast at 350° for 2 hours until leg moves easily. If it browns too quickly, cover loosely with tent of aluminum foil. Serves 6 to 8.

CARROT TSIMES WITH KNADEL

Tsimes

½ pound brisket of beef
1 small whole onion
1 teaspoon salt
2 cups water
2 pounds carrots (about 12 medium carrots), diced
½ cup sugar

Place brisket, onion and salt in water, bring to a boil, lower heat, simmer covered for 1 hour. Add carrots and sugar, continue cooking until carrots are very tender, 20 to 30 minutes.

Knadel

2 medium potatoes, grated
1 tablespoon matzo meal
1½ tablespoons chicken fat
1 tablespoon grated onion
½ teaspoon salt
¼ teaspoon black pepper

Drain the grated potatoes well to remove excess moisture. Add remaining ingredients, and spread over the top of the tsimes, place in baking dish and bake in 350° oven until lightly browned, about 20 minutes. Serves 6.

Note: For knadel dumplings, add 1 egg to above mixture, form into balls, place over tsimes. Bake as above.

APRICOT WHIP

¼ cup cooked dried apricots

2 tablespoons sugar
1 egg white, beaten stiff

Force cooked apricots through a sieve. Add sugar and beaten egg white, fold and blend lightly. Serve chilled. Makes 3 or 4 servings; double ingredients to serve 6 to 8 persons.

HONEY CAKE

½ cup oil
1 cup sugar
4 eggs, well beaten
1 cup honey
2½ cups sifted all-purpose flour
½ teaspoon baking soda
1 teaspoon allspice
3 teaspoons baking powder

½ teaspoon salt
½ teaspoon cinnamon
1 cup orange juice
Grated rind of 1 orange
1 cup chopped walnuts or almonds
½ cup chopped raisins (optional)

Cream together the oil and sugar, at medium speed in electric mixer, beat in eggs one at a time until mixture is light and fluffy. Add honey gradually with mixer in motion. Sift together flour and other dry ingredients, holding out ¼ cup. Add flour mixture to mixing bowl alternately with orange juice, continuing to beat at medium speed until very smooth and creamy. Toss nuts and chopped raisins with reserved flour, add to cake batter, stirring to distribute evenly. Pour into 9 x 4 x 3-inch greased loaf pan or 9-inch-square cake pan; bake in oven preheated to 350° for 1 hour or until top springs back when pressed lightly. Honey chiffon cake may be substituted.

HONEY CHIFFON CAKE

4 eggs	Grated rind of 1 orange
1 cup sugar	1 cup orange juice
3 cups sifted all-purpose flour	½ cup oil
	1 cup honey
½ teaspoon baking soda	1 cup chopped walnuts
1 teaspoon allspice	or almonds
3 teaspoons baking powder	½ cup chopped raisins
½ teaspoon salt	(optional)
½ teaspoon cinnamon	

All ingredients should be at room temperature. Separate the eggs. Beat egg whites to a froth, add sugar gradually and continue beating until egg whites stand up in peaks and become glossy. Sift flour, soda, allspice, baking powder, salt and cinnamon into large bowl. Make a well in flour mixture, add rind, half the orange juice, add oil and honey. Blend well. Add egg yolks and balance of juice. Beat well for 1 minute. Fold in egg whites, nuts and raisins. Place into 2 ungreased, paper lined, 9-inch tube pans; bake in oven preheated to 350° for 40 minutes or until top springs back when pressed lightly. To cool cake, suspend pans for 45 minutes before removing.

DINNER MENU FOR ROSH HASHANAH II

Wine   Honey and Apple

Sweet and Sour Meat Balls in Tomato Sauce

Chicken Soup (see p. 41)   Noodles (see p. 66)

Roast Duck with Orange Sauce

Potato Varenikes   String Beans   Tossed Salad

Fruited Gelatin Mold   Honey Teiglach   Tea

MEAT BALLS IN TOMATO SAUCE

Meat Balls

1 pound ground beef	1 small onion, grated
1 small potato, grated	2 tablespoons catsup
¼ cup water	¾ teaspoon salt
	Dash of pepper

Mix all ingredients, blending lightly. Form into 1-inch meat balls.

Sauce

1 small onion, chopped	½ teaspoon salt
2 tablespoons oil or fat	Freshly ground black
1 can (1 pound) tomatoes,	pepper
strained	4 tablespoons sugar

Sauté onion in oil or fat until soft. Force tomatoes through sieve into skillet; simmer, uncovered, over very low heat 15 minutes. Add salt and pepper. Drop meat balls into sauce; simmer, covered, 1 hour longer. Add sugar, remove cover, cook additional 15 minutes. Serves 4.

ROAST DUCK WITH ORANGE SAUCE

4- to 5-pound duck,	¼ teaspoon black pepper
dressed, oven-ready	1 cup sliced onion
1 teaspoon salt	1 navel orange, thinly
2 tablespoons grated onion	sliced
1 clove garlic, crushed	1 cup orange juice

The previous night, remove giblets from cavity of duck, sprinkle inside with ½ teaspoon salt. Rub mixture of grated onion, remaining salt, crushed garlic and pepper over outside of duck. Refrigerate. Next day, place duck over slices of onion in shallow roasting pan. Prick skin of duck all over with sharp-pronged fork to allow fat to run out. Cook duck in oven preheated to 350°, uncovered, for 1 hour. Pour off or spoon off all fat from pan. Place orange slices over top of duck, return to oven. Bake ½ to ¾ hour longer, basting occasionally with orange juice. When leg of duck moves easily, remove duck to platter, keep in warm place. Skim off all fat from drippings remaining in pan, bring skimmed liquid to a boil. Season sauce to taste with salt and pepper. Serve unthickened over sliced duck. Serves 3 or 4.

POTATO VARENIKES

Dough

2 eggs, beaten	2 cups (about) all-purpose
⅛ teaspoon salt	flour
	¼ cup water

To make dough, combine eggs, salt, water and flour, beat to blend, then with fingers knead into soft dough. Divide dough in half; roll out each on lightly floured board to ¼-inch thick. Cut in 2-inch squares.

Filling

6 medium potatoes, peeled, cooked	2 large onions, chopped
	3 tablespoons chicken fat
	Salt, pepper

Place 1 to 2 tablespoons filling in each square, fold over dough to make triangles, pinching edges to seal.

Place 1 quart water and ½ teaspoon salt in kettle or pot, bring to rolling boil, then drop in varenikes one at a time. When they rise to the surface, remove with slotted spoon and place in greased baking dish. Keep hot in oven until time to serve. Makes 24 to 30, depending on thickness of dough, enough for 6 servings.

FRUITED GELATIN MOLD

Prepare kosher gelatin as directed on package. Pour into slightly oiled mold. When beginning to set (consistency of unbeaten egg white), add 1 to 1½ cups well-drained cut-up fresh or canned fruit, such as peaches, bananas, seedless or seeded grapes, berries, melon balls, or canned pineapple (do not use fresh pineapple). Chill until very firm. Turn out of mold by dipping mold quickly in bowl of hot water, then pulling away molded gelatin from edge with fingers. Makes 4 to 6 servings.

HONEY TEIGLACH

3 eggs	½ cup honey
3 tablespoons oil	¼ cup sugar
⅛ teaspoon salt	1 tablespoon powdered
1 tablespoon sugar	ginger
2 cups sifted all-purpose flour (about)	1 cup chopped walnuts

Make soft dough of eggs, oil, salt, 1 tablespoon sugar, and the flour, kneading with fingers until smooth enough to handle easily. Pinch off small pieces of dough and roll out each on lightly floured board or counter top to ½-inch thick. Cut in ½-inch pieces. Place on well-greased baking sheet. Bake in oven preheated to 375° until light brown, about 20 minutes, shaking the pan once or twice. Remove from baking sheet with spatula. Meantime, combine honey, ¼ cup sugar and ginger, bring to a boil. When rapidly boiling, drop pieces of dough into syrup one at a time, then add nuts. Remove from fire, stir to distribute evenly, spoon into greased shallow baking pan, place again in oven with heat reduced to 350° until honey has been absorbed, about 20 minutes. Remove from oven, turn out on moistened board and pat down with knife or fingers. (If using fingers, dip hands in cold water.) Cut into pieces 2 inches high. Sprinkle coconut over top. Makes 36.

ROSH HASHANAH NOON MEAL

Wine   Honey and Apples

Brain Latkes   Tomato and Lettuce Salad

Breaded Veal Steaks   Cottage Potatoes

Peas and Carrots   Celery   Olives   Pickles

Apple Strudel   Tea

BRAIN LATKES

1 pair calf's brains	Salt, pepper to taste
1 egg	Matzo meal, about ¼ cup
1 teaspoon grated onion	2 tablespoons chicken fat

56

If brains are frozen, defrost first. Blanch by dropping into boiling salted acidulated water (containing 1 tablespoon vinegar for each 2 cups water). Cook 3 minutes; remove, pull off outer skin with sharp knife. Mash brains with wooden spoon. Add egg, onion, seasonings and matzo meal; blend well, forming paste. Heat chicken fat in skillet, add mixture by spoonfuls, fry until crisp and golden on each side. Makes about 12 latkes.

BREADED VEAL STEAKS

1 large onion, chopped
2 celery stalks, chopped
1 green pepper, seeded, chopped
1 tablespoon chicken fat
Salt, pepper
1 small can (3 ounces) mushrooms, drained

1 can (10 ounces) pareve tomato soup; or 2 medium tomatoes peeled and chopped
4 individual veal cutlets
1 egg, beaten
4 to 6 tablespoons oil or vegetable shortening
½ cup fine dry crumbs

To make sauce, sauté the onion, celery and green pepper in the chicken fat until tender, about 10 minutes. Sprinkle with ½ teaspoon salt and a dash of pepper. Add mushrooms and tomato soup (or the chopped tomatoes), simmer about 20 minutes.

Meantime rub salt into cutlets, using ½ teaspoon altogether. Dip each in egg, then in crumbs, then fry in sizzling hot oil or fat until well-browned and crisp on both sides. Place in large shallow baking dish, cover with sauce, bake in 350° oven until meat is fork-tender, about 30 minutes. If sauce cooks down too much, add ¼ to ½ cup hot water. Makes 4 servings.

COTTAGE POTATOES

Peel potatoes, allowing 1 or 2 potatoes per serving, and cut in very thin slices. In heavy skillet, heat 2 tablespoons fat; when sizzling, add potatoes, cover tightly, turn heat very low. Remove cover frequently to turn over potatoes. When potatoes are fork-tender, sprinkle with salt from shaker.

APPLE STRUDEL

Pastry

2 ½ to 3 cups sifted all-
    purpose flour
¼ teaspoon salt

1 cup vegetable shortening
⅓ cup water
1 tablespoon vinegar

To make pastry, blend flour and salt in large bowl. Add shortening, chop with knife or pastry blender until the size of peas. Add water and vinegar, knead to form smooth dough. Divide dough in half. Roll out each half very thin, forming rectangle.

Apple Filling

3 or 4 medium apples,
    peeled, grated
½ cup sugar

¼ teaspoon cinnamon
4 tablespoons seedless
    raisins

Cover each rectangle of dough with the apple filling, roll up, place on baking sheet with overlapping side down. Preheat oven to 350°; bake 45 minutes until pastry is crisp and golden. Cut strudel in portions while still warm. Serve warm or cold topped with hot lemon or orange sauce.

Lemon Sauce

2 tablespoons cornstarch
1 cup sugar
½ cup water

Grated rind and juice of 1
    lemon

Combine cornstarch and sugar, blending well. Add water, bring to a boil, cook over moderate heat about 5 minutes until thick and transparent. Add grated rind and juice after sauce has started to thicken. Makes 1 cup.

Orange Sauce

Use only ½ cup sugar and ¼ cup water, and instead of lemon, use grated rind and juice of 1 orange.

YOM KIPPUR

"Hadassah, we have been discussing Rosh Hashanah and, as Rosh Hashanah and Yom Kippur are related high holy days, it is now opportune for us to consider the meaning and observances of Yom Kippur.

"Yom Kippur is the tenth day of Tishrei and is the last of the ten penitential days that began with Rosh Hashanah.

"After the Temple was destroyed, the Jewish people had no altar on which to offer their sacrifices, so they developed prayer as a substitute for these sacrifices in the Temple. From this time prayer became the accepted form of atonement to God, instead of sacrifices, and Yom Kippur was set as the holiest and most important day for atonement. It is the Sabbath of Sabbaths, and is observed by total abstinence from work and by fasting and prayer all day.

"Just as on Rosh Hashanah we worship God as the King and Ruler of the universe, who shapes our lives and determines our future, so on Yom Kippur we reaffirm our belief and trust in the greatness of God through fasting, prayer and confession. We seek this forgiveness because the Jewish religion teaches us that if we sincerely repent the misdeeds we committed, we may be forgiven. The whole day of Yom Kippur, the Day of Atonement, is spent at the synagogue in meditation and prayer."

"Mother, the *Kaparot* ceremony is usually performed the evening before Yom Kippur, is it not?"

"Yes, Hadassah, it is an ancient ritual recalling the animal sacrifices in the days of the Temple. This ceremony consists of swinging a fowl over a person's head and saying, 'May this be a substitute for me. If it has been ordained that I die, may this fowl die in my place.' A rooster is generally offered for a man, a hen for a woman. After the ceremony, the fowl or its value in money may be donated to charity. You see, Hadassah, what an important emphasis is placed on charity in our religion?"

"Mother, I notice that two different kinds of candles are lit at home every year on Yom Kippur eve."

"Yes, the first kind of candle to be lit is the *yahrzeit* candle in memory of the dead, dedicated by those who have lost a parent or child. In addition, the two usual holiday candles are lit and the Yom Kippur blessing is recited over them."

"Mother, is there a law about when the fast actually begins and finishes?"

"Fasting begins after the evening meal, which is served well before sunset, and ends after sundown the following day. The meal is usually festive, but no highly seasoned food is served to avoid undue thirst, for water as well as food is forbidden during the fast. Everyone is expected to fast except children, boys under thirteen, girls under twelve and the sick persons."

"Mother, why do we fast?"

"My theory is that it is a self-inflicted abstinence from all pleasures of the body for the purpose of reflecting on the past, and leaving the spirit free to seek harmony with God. For this purpose, after the last meal on the eve of Yom Kippur is served, we go to the synagogue for the *Kol Nidrei* service.

"This service has always had a great appeal to me.

From the moment I come into the synagogue, the bright lights signify that this is no ordinary service. The appearance of the men wearing their *tallis* and some also wearing the long white robes, or *kittel*, gives me a feeling of joy and confidence. The *kittel* is reminiscent of the white color of purity, like the white dress of the bride.

"The congregation rises as the ark is opened and the scrolls are taken out. There is an intense interest and solemnity as the cantor sings the *Kol Nidrei*. I enjoy the congregation's joining in this service, repeating the beautiful prayer after the cantor three times. This reaffirms our profound trust in God and in His mercy.

"Let us stop to consider the meaning of *Kol Nidrei*. It is an all-inspiring holy night. It is really a statement rather than a prayer—a statement that for unfulfilled obligations between man and God, repentance on Yom Kippur brings atonement; for vows and obligations made between man and man, Yom Kippur brings no atonement until amends are made to the person wronged. That is why we should seek forgiveness from each other, and make amends to our enemies—the younger usually making the first gesture of friendship."

"Mother, do the prayers on Yom Kippur day have the same significance as the *Kol Nidrei* service?"

"Well, dear, on Yom Kippur the mood of *Kol Nidrei* night is continued, and the spirit of confession and repentance repeated and deepened. One of the most important prayers is repeated a number of times during the day. It is the *Al Chet* or Confessions. It enumerates many kinds of sin, since no one can be certain what sins he has committed and of what is a sin and what is not. Dishonesty, cruelty, stubbornness, haughtiness—these and many others are included in the *Al Chet* prayer. Confession is the main theme of the Yom Kippur service, for the Jewish religion teaches that if a man sincerely repents or regrets his misdeeds he will be forgiven. The confessions are all in the plural form for all Jews are responsible for each other.

"The service on Yom Kippur day is divided into four parts, *Shacharit, Musaf, Mincha,* and *Neilah.* These prayers are found in the *Machzor,* which is the prayer book used on this day. The *Shacharit* service includes the reading of portions from the Bible—the Torah and the Haphtorah. A most solemn moment of the day takes place after *Shacharit,* when the memorial service, or *Yiskor,* is conducted. In addition to prayers for his own relatives, the Jew prays on behalf of his fellow men, recalling the passing of all Jews who lost their lives in persecution or in defense of their country.

"*Musaf,* or the additional service, includes a description of the service of the high priest in the Temple in Jerusalem in ancient times, and the martyrology. A very touching prayer is dedicated to the great martyrs of Israel.

"*Mincha,* the afternoon service, includes the reading of further portions of the Torah and the Haphtorah.

"The concluding service is *Neilah.* It is a final appeal and the mood is of splendid solemnity and hope that our prayers and the regrets of our sins have been accepted. Yom Kippur services are concluded with the confidence that the day has helped us to renew and strengthen ourselves, and that the coming year will be one of peace and happiness.

"After *Kaddish* and the last benediction are recited, comes the sounding of the shofar, which takes the form of one long blast, denoting the final hope that our prayers have been answered. Yom Kippur is over. Ending the solemn season as it began, the sounding of the shofar recalls to us the achievements and struggles of the past and the hopes and promise for happiness in the future."

EREV YOM KIPPUR DINNER

Chicken Soup (see p. 41)   Kreplach

Boiled Chicken (see p. 41)   Vegetable Salad

Applesauce

Honey Cake (see p. 51)   Tea   Fresh Fruit

KREPLACH

Dough

2 eggs, beaten	2 cups sifted all-purpose
¼ teaspoon salt	flour (about)
¼ cup water	Boiling salted water

To make dough, combine eggs, salt, flour and water, knead until smooth and elastic (add 1 cup flour first, then the second cup of flour a little at a time, working after each addition; dough should be stiff). Roll out on lightly floured board to ⅛ inch thick. Cut into 2-inch squares.

Filling

1 pound stewing beef, cooked	1 small onion, chopped
	2 tablespoons fat
	Salt, pepper to taste

Put meat through food grinder. Sauté onion in fat until lightly browned, add to ground meat with salt and pepper. In each square, place a tablespoonful of the meat mixture, then fold over dough into triangle, pressing edges firmly together. Work quickly or dough may become too dry to handle easily. Drop meat-filled triangles into rapidly boiling salted water for 10 minutes or until they rise to top. Remove from water with slotted spoon. Add to clear soup. Makes about 24.

APPLESAUCE

2 pounds tart apples	¼ teaspoon salt
1 cup water	1 cup sugar
	¼ teaspoon cinnamon (optional)

Wash and quarter apples without peeling. Add water and salt, bring just to a boil, lower heat, simmer uncovered just until apples are soft. Force through strainer, immediately add sugar and, if desired, cinnamon. Makes 2 to 2½ cups applesauce.

YOM KIPPUR NIGHT DINNER

Fish Appetizers of Gefilte Fish Balls (see p. 39)

Pickled Herring   Chopped Herring

Chicken Soup (see p. 41)   Noodles

Mandlach (see p. 49)

Chicken Casserole with Vegetables

Radish Flowers   Celery   Olives

Mixed Stewed Fruit   Tea   Cookies

PICKLED HERRING FILLETS

2 salted herrings	¾ cup vinegar
2 medium onions, sliced	¼ cup water
1 pimiento, cut in small squares	1 tablespoon sugar
	¼ cup pickling spices

Soak herring overnight in cold water to cover. Drain. Remove head and tail, split down back, remove center bone. Cut each half in 3 parts. Place a square of pimiento in each, roll up, secure with toothpick. Place layers of rolled herring and onions in 1-quart jar. Combine vinegar, water, sugar and spices, bring to a boil, then allow to cool. When lukewarm, pour over herring in jar. Seal. Allow to stand at least 3 days in cold place before serving. Makes 12 pickled herring appetizers.

CHOPPED HERRING

2 salted herrings
1 tart apple, cored, chopped
1 small onion, chopped
1 thin slice pumpernickel bread, soaked in vinegar, squeezed dry

3 hard-boiled eggs, chopped
⅛ teaspoon cinnamon
¼ teaspoon pepper
Sugar to taste
3 tablespoons vinegar
2 tablespoons oil

Soak herring in cold water to cover for 12 hours; drain, skin and bone, then chop with sharp knife. Combine with remaining ingredients, blending well. Makes 8 to 10 servings.

NOODLES FOR SOUP

2 eggs
2 cups sifted all-purpose flour (about)

Beat eggs until light. Add flour gradually to make a stiff dough. Knead until smooth. Roll out on lightly floured board as thin as possible. Place between 2 towels until dough is partially dry, then roll up as for Jelly Roll (see p. 134) and with thin sharp knife cut into thin strips. Allow strips to dry completely before using. Makes about 6 cups noodles.

CHICKEN CASSEROLE

1 3- or 4-pound stewing chicken
1 medium onion, chopped
1 or 2 carrots, grated
1 stalk celery, chopped
2 tomatoes, peeled and chopped
1 package frozen cut beans
¼ pound chopped fresh mushrooms; or 1 3-ounce can mushrooms, drained (optional)
Salt, paprika
½ cup water

Remove and discard skin from uncooked chicken; then cut meat from bones. In a large casserole (2½-quart), place a layer of about ⅓ the mixed vegetables (defrost frozen beans just enough to separate), sprinkle with salt from shaker and a little paprika. Add a layer of chicken meat, then more vegetables, sprinkling additional salt and paprika over each layer until all ingredients have been used. Add water. Cover casserole (or use foil if casserole has no cover), bake at 400° for 2 hours. Makes 6 to 8 servings.

MIXED STEWED FRUIT

1 pound dried prunes
½ pound dried apricots
½ pound dried pears*
6 cups cold water
1 lemon, thinly sliced
½ cup sugar
¼ teaspoon salt

Soak fruit in water overnight. Place in large saucepan, add lemon slices, cover, cook slowly 45 minutes to 1 hour until fruit is tender. Add sugar and salt, stir to dissolve. Cool. Makes 10 to 12 servings, but will keep in refrigerator for several weeks.

* If dried pears are not locally available, use 1 pound dried apricots.

SUCCOT

"Mother, I asked David to have dinner with us tomorrow night. What will you serve?"

"How does turkey with all the trimmings appeal to you?"

"Fine, Mother, though it seems like a Thanksgiving menu and tomorrow is the first day of Succot."

"Why, Hadassah, Succot is the Jewish Thanksgiving. As a matter of fact the Pilgrim fathers in America based their Thanksgiving on our festival because they were steeped in the knowledge of the Bible.

"Succot, the Feast of Tabernacles, is observed on the 15th of Tishrei. This holiday has a twofold significance. In the first place, our ancestors in Palestine celebrated it as the festival of ingathering of the harvest, giving thanks to God for bountiful crops. Secondly, it is the Feast of the Tabernacles or Booths to commemorate the temporary shelters used by the Israelites during their forty years of wandering from Egypt to Canaan."

"Mother, I remember vividly our happy visits to Uncle Aaron's house at Succot. He always had a *succah* in his garden at the back of their home. Do you remember how beautiful it looked with the table set under candlelight and the moon and stars shining through the leaves and branches, which were the roof of the *succah*?"

"Yes, and I can still recall the expression on your face when Uncle Aaron raised you on his shoulders and allowed you to pick some of the fruit hanging from the roof. Remember how the walls, too, were decorated with all kinds of fruits and vegetables?"

"Mother, I still remember the excitement of waiting for my turn to shake the *lulav* and *esrog*."

"Succot is also called *Chag-Ha'asif*, or the Feast of Harvest. The *esrog* (citron) is held in one hand and the *lulav* (palms), the *hadassim* (myrtle sprigs) and the *araboth* (willow sprigs) bound together are in the other hand and a blessing is pronounced.

"Each morning during the first seven days of the holiday, except on the Sabbath, the *lulav* and *esrog* are brought into the *succah*, where each member of the family pronounces a blessing over them, holding the *lulav* in the right hand and the *esrog* in the left. The palm leaf is shaken lightly, after the benediction, so that it rustles. When one has no *lulav* or *esrog*, the ceremony is performed in the synagogue. The *esrog* must be without blemish, shapely and of good color. The *lulav* should be tall and straight, but flexible.

"The kindling of the holiday lights is performed in the *succah*. Evening services are brief in the synagogue, after which the family is ready for the festival meal in the *succah*. This begins with *Kiddush*. The *chalahs* are in the shape of ladders: the *hamotzi* is dipped in honey. Fish, soup, chicken, or turkey are on the menu.

"The third, fourth, fifth and sixth days are known as Hal Hamoed, being the ordinary days of the festival, the time for community celebrations and entertainments. In Israel it is the favorite time for hiking and overnight camping.

"The seventh day is called Hoshana Rabbah, which means Great Help.

69

"The eighth day is called Shemini Atzeret and is a distinct festival. A more serious mood prevails and the important prayer for rain (*Geshem*) is recited.

"The last day, Simchat Torah, is the jolliest. It is the day when the completion of the annual reading of the Torah in the synagogue occurs, and the reading is immediately resumed anew. The festival in a synagogue on Simchat Torah eve and the following morning is very enjoyable as the young folks and the old folks chant and make merry together. Children carry small flags with apples or other fruit stuck on the top of their small flagpoles. Then comes the *Hakafot*, the processional with the Torah scrolls. The rabbi, the learned men, the *gabbai*, the president and other notables are honored first, each one being given a scroll to carry. The *hazan* leads, followed by the rest of the congregation, all rejoicing, singing and kissing the Torah.

"The observance of this Thanksgiving or Feast of Tabernacles is an expression of our gratitude to the Almighty for His kindness in guiding our ancestors during their wandering and also for bestowing upon us His blessings."

SUCCOT DINNER I

Chopped Eggplant Relish on Lettuce and Tomato Salad

Clear Chicken Soup (see p. 41)   Egg Drops

Roast Turkey   Noodle Stuffing

Mashed Sweet Potatoes in Orange Halves

Cranberry Grape Relish   Asparagus

Orange and Pineapple Upside-down Cake

Tea and Lemon

CHOPPED EGGPLANT RELISH

1 medium eggplant
1 small onion, minced
½ green pepper, minced
1 small tomato, peeled, chopped

1 tablespoon oil
1 tablespoon vinegar or lemon juice
1½ teaspoons salt
¼ teaspoon pepper

Place whole eggplant in baking pan in 350° oven, bake until skin is wrinkled and soft. Remove from oven, peel off skin. Add onion, green pepper and tomato, chopping until well blended. Beat in oil, vinegar, salt and pepper. Chill. Serves 4 to 6.

EGG DROPS

2 eggs, beaten
⅛ teaspoon salt
1 tablespoon chicken fat

½ cup flour (about)
1 quart salted water, brought to boil

Beat together eggs, salt, chicken fat and flour enough to make a thin batter. Drop a tablespoon of batter at a time into rapidly boiling salted water, cook 5 minutes. As egg drops rise to top, remove with slotted spoon. Serve in clear chicken soup. Makes enough for 6 servings of soup.

ROAST TURKEY WITH NOODLE STUFFING

1 10-pound turkey, oven-ready

Wash turkey inside and out. Fill both neck and breast cavities with stuffing.

Stuffing

¾ pound medium egg noodles
1 medium onion, chopped
3 tablespoons chicken or turkey fat

4 eggs
1 tablespoon chopped parsley
Salt, pepper to taste
2 tablespoons grated onion
Salt, pepper, paprika

71

Boil noodles in salted water until tender, about 10 minutes. Drain thoroughly. Fry onion in chicken or turkey fat until lightly browned, toss with noodles. Beat in eggs, 1 at a time, then add parsley, salt and pepper. Spoon this mixture into turkey, fasten breast cavity with poultry skewers, close with thread or butcher's cord. Fold neck skin over stuffed neck cavity, fasten shut with skewer.

Rub grated onion over outside of turkey, sprinkle all over with salt, pepper and paprika. Roast uncovered at 350° for 2½ to 3 hours or until leg moves easily. If turkey browns too quickly, cover loosely with tent of aluminum foil. Serves 12 to 14.

SWEET POTATOES IN ORANGE HALVES

6 medium sweet potatoes, cooked in jackets
2 tablespoons chicken fat

Salt to taste
4 tablespoons brown sugar
6 oranges

Peel cooked potatoes, mash with chicken fat, salt and brown sugar. Cut oranges in half, scoop out fruit (save fruit sections for Upside-down Cake). Fill each orange half with mashed sweet potato, top with a little brown sugar and dot with fat. Place orange shells in muffin tins. Bake 30 minutes in 350° oven. Makes 12 servings.

CRANBERRY GRAPE RELISH

With fork, break up contents of 1-pound can or jar whole cranberry sauce. Add 2 teaspoons grated orange rind and ½ cup seedless white grapes, each cut in half. Stir to blend.

ORANGE AND PINEAPPLE UPSIDE-DOWN CAKE

Fruit Glaze

1 can (8 ounces) crushed
pineapple, drained
Orange sections from 4
oranges

10 maraschino cherries
½ cup granulated sugar
2 tablespoons cornstarch

Combine drained pineapple with diced orange sections, cherries, sugar and cornstarch; blend well. Place mixture in greased 9-inch-square or round cake pan.

Cake

¼ cup shortening
1 teaspoon grated orange
rind
½ cup granulated sugar
1 egg, beaten

1 cup sifted cake flour
¼ teaspoon salt
1½ teaspoons baking
powder
¼ cup orange juice

Cream shortening for cake, add rind and sugar, beat until fluffy. Beat in egg. Sift together flour, salt and baking powder, add to egg mixture alternately with orange juice, beating 2 minutes at medium speed until batter is very smooth. Spoon over fruit in pan. Bake in oven preheated to 350° until top springs back when touched. Remove from oven, cool in pan 10 minutes, then turn out on platter with fruit on top. Serve with or without sauce, as preferred. Makes 12 servings.

Hot Fruit Sauce

1 teaspoon cornstarch
¼ cup juice from drained
canned pineapple

½ cup cold water
Juice and grated rind of 1
lemon
½ cup sugar

73

Combine cornstarch with pineapple juice, add remaining ingredients, bring to a boil, cook 3 or 4 minutes until shiny and thickened. Serve hot. Makes ¾ cup sauce.

SUCCOT DINNER II

Cantaloupe Basket	Yellow Split Pea Soup
Southern Fried Chicken	Honey
French Fried Potatoes	Cabbage Salad
Peach Tarts	Date and Nut Loaf Tea

CANTALOUPE BASKET

Locate the center between the ends of a cantaloupe. One inch on each side of this point, make a cut downward ⅓ of the distance through the melon. Make another cut 1 inch on the other side of the center point, thus making a 2-inch strip through the center, down ⅓ of the way through melon. Cut from each end in toward center to this strip on each side and remove portions of melon, forming a basket. Remove edible portions of melon with French vegetable cutter or spoon. Fill basket with cut mixed fruit. Chill and serve.

YELLOW SPLIT PEA SOUP

1 pound beef plate or flank	¼ teaspoon pepper
Beef soup bones	1 onion, quartered
2 quarts water	2 carrots, diced
1 cup yellow split peas	3 stalks celery, diced
¼ cup dried lima beans	1 sweet potato, peeled,
2 teaspoons salt	quartered
	½ cup fine noodles

Place meat and bones in large soup kettle, cover with water, bring to a boil. Remove scum that rises to top. Add split peas, limas, salt and pepper, cover, cook over low heat 1 hour. Add vegetables and noodles, cook 1 hour longer or until meat is tender, adding more water if needed. Remove meat and bones; cut up meat and return to the soup. Makes 8 to 10 servings.

SOUTHERN FRIED CHICKEN

To serve 8, buy two broilers, cut up. Scald, pat dry. In large brown paper bag, place 1 cup flour, 1 teaspoon salt, ¼ teaspoon pepper and 1 teaspoon paprika. Shake a few pieces of chicken in the flour at a time to coat well. Heat vegetable shortening in a heavy skillet to a depth of ½ inch, fry the chicken until crisply brown on all sides. Drain on absorbent paper, then remove to casserole or roasting pan. Shortly before serving, bake in oven preheated to 350° for 15 minutes. Serve with honey.

FRENCH FRIED POTATOES

Peel large potatoes, cut each into long strips about ¼ inch thick. Let stand in ice-cold water 1 hour, then dry well on absorbent paper. Heat 1 pint oil in electric skillet or deep fat fryer to 375° (or, if using regular skillet, test until cube of bread browns in 60 seconds). Add potatoes to hot oil, avoid crowding. Fry until crisply golden, 7 to 10 minutes. Remove with slotted spoon (or fryer basket), drain on absorbent paper. Sprinkle with salt while hot.

CABBAGE SALAD

1 small firm head of cabbage
1 teaspoon salt
2 carrots, grated
1 green pepper, seeded, minced

3 green onions, minced
¼ cup vinegar
2 to 3 tablespoons sugar or to taste

Shred cabbage on large blade of hand grater, or cut with long-bladed knife on wooden board until minced fine. Toss cabbage with salt in bowl. Add remaining vegetables, vinegar and sugar. Makes about 12 servings; leftovers will keep in refrigerator several days.

PEACH TARTS

Pastry

1 cup vegetable shortening
2 cups sifted all-purpose flour

3 tablespoons water
1 teaspoon salt
1 tablespoon vinegar

Cream shortening by beating with electric mixer until fluffy. Add remaining ingredients, knead with fingers about 5 minutes until very smooth. Chill about 5 minutes, then roll out on lightly floured board or counter top to ⅛-inch thick. Cut in rounds 4 inches in diameter, fit over tops of inverted muffin tins, prick each in several places with a fork and bake in oven preheated to 400° for 15 minutes.

Filling

Drain large can peach halves or sliced peaches, saving juice. Place a peach half or overlapping peach slices in each baked tart shell. Cover peaches with syrup.

Syrup

Blend together ¼ cup sugar and 2 tablespoons cornstarch, add saved peach juice, bring to a boil, cook until smooth and thickened, about 5 minutes. Pour at once over peaches. Serve tarts hot or cold. Makes 6 tarts.

DATE AND NUT LOAF

1 cup dates, pitted, chopped
1 cup boiling hot water
1 egg, beaten
½ cup granulated white or brown sugar

1½ cups sifted all-purpose flour
1 teaspoon baking soda
½ teaspoon salt
½ cup shelled pecans, chopped
1 teaspoon baking powder

Cover dates with hot water, let stand until cool. To the beaten egg, add the sugar, beat to blend well, then add dates and water. Sift together the flour, baking powder, soda and salt; add the nuts, toss to cover with flour. Combine with egg mixture, beat briskly for about 50 strokes. Grease a loaf pan, 9 x 5 x 3 inches, pour in batter, bake in oven preheated to 350° for 1 hour. Allow to cool in pan, then remove, slice thick when completely cold.

CHANUKAH

"It was a treat, Hadassah, to sit in on the rehearsal of the Chanukah play that your Sunday school pupils are to present. I'm sorry I was not able to stay for the closing scene that was to show Chanukah in Israel."

"Thank you, Mother, I do hope you can see the play right through when we present it next week.

"That closing scene will depict the public service in Tel Aviv, which is unique and picturesque, and will bring all the children on the stage. In the background will be a charcoal sketch of the synagogue because in Tel Aviv this assembly of all high school pupils, as well as of the older children from elementary schools, takes place in front of the synagogue. Arranged in a semicircle, they face a decorated platform on which stand the most prominent citizens of Israel. On the platform there is a large menorah. Thousands of spectators witness this unforgettable scene. The ceremony begins at the first indication of dusk. The cantor walks up to the giant menorah and, chanting the benediction, he lights the candles for that evening. In our play we'll do the entire eight benedictions, of course. A loud chorus rings out: 'Amen.' Now the children light the little menorot they have brought with them. A band strikes up the *Maoz Tzur*, and everybody joins in lustily. The band plays and the audience sings again. When the signal is given, twinkling lights and flaring torches begin to move. The children, who have looked forward eagerly to this annual Chanukah parade, form a line of spectators, their little flags and menorot clutched firmly in their hands.

"Of course, we shall not be able to do quite all that, Mother, but the idea will certainly be conveyed, judging from the rehearsal this afternoon. My pupils are quite excited and look forward to this event. After the play, the Ladies' Auxiliary is serving a dairy supper, with *latkes* and cheese dishes."

"The custom of eating cheese delicacies is an old one. It seems that Judith, a daughter of the Hasmoneans, fed cheese to the leader of the enemy, making him very thirsty. The wine to quench his thirst made him so drunk that Judith was able to have him taken prisoner and subsequently beheaded."

"Chanukah is of special significance to us, Mother. It testifies that the Jew can be a soldier when the need arises. This festival, however, commemorates the victory of a great moral cause rather than the victory of the battlefield."

"Yes, Hadassah. Our rejoicing is not at the defeat of our enemies, but at the rededication of the Temple. In the Haphtorah reading for the Sabbath of Chanukah, the keynote is: 'Not by might nor by power but by My Spirit, said the Lord of Hosts.' Chanukah exemplifies the rebellion in defense of the inalienable rights of man. It is a protest against the denial of the freedom of worship. The victory of the Maccabees is that of godliness over paganism, Judaism over Hellenism, right over might, democracy over dictatorship. From this point of view, this victory assumes world-wide significance even today. Now we hope that our rededication to the ideals of our people will maintain the Jews as a contributing factor in the advancement of civilization."

"Shall I get the menorah, Mother? I'll give it an extra

polishing, so that it will shine as brightly as the Chanukah light that Dad will kindle this evening when he returns from the synagogue. It is beautiful, Mother. Just think of it. It is your mother's and my own grandmother's! Was she a wonderful mother like you? Was she a mother to guide and advise, was she a comrade to discuss all the aspects of living? I am so glad to be your daughter!"

"Thank you, Hadassah, dear. I am happy indeed, that you are not reticent about these matters with me. We are too apt to criticize our own immediate family, often leaving the nice things unsaid until it is too late to say them. On the threshold of your married life, Hadassah, you must think and plan to make your home a sanctuary where husband and children eagerly look forward to being together each day, weekday and holiday, in good times and in days of adversity. Only the sense of belonging brings happiness and understanding. Chanukah, you will recall, commemorates such families. Hannah's must have been a closely knit family. She was able to imbue her seven sons with such a sense of right and devotion that they were ready to give their lives for their people and for the privilege of belonging to an ancient nation of great tradition, a nation so great that even today the way of life of righteous men throughout the world is based on the Ten Commandments. It originated with our people during one of our periods of finding ourselves, our forty years' wandering in the desert. There was Mattathias and his five sons. Theirs is the story of Chanukah.

"During the reign of Antiochus Epiphanes of Syria (175–163 B.C.), Palestine was a part of his realm. Jews were greatly persecuted. Antiochus tried to force them to worship Greek idols and to become assimilated. Those who refused were put to death, martyrs for our faith. Mattathias, the high priest, raised the flag of rebellion, a banner with the cry, '*Mi L'Adonoy Elay*' ('Whoever is on the side of God, follow me'). Judas, who guided the people after the death of his father, Mattathias, led them under his banner, '*Mi Kamokha, Baelim, Adonoy*' ('Who is like unto Thee among the mighty, O Lord'). Considered phonetically, the initial letters of the words in this Hebrew sentence make up the name Maccabee.

"Our ancient Talmud records the event which inspired the kindling of lights during Chanukah. During the re-dedication of the holy Temple by Judas Maccabeus and his warriors, when the perpetual lamp was about to be lighted, there was found only one cruse containing sufficient pure oil for one day. As a result of a miracle it lasted for the eight days required to prepare fresh oil. The following year, an eight-day festival called Chanukah was declared and has been celebrated with songs of praise and thanksgiving ever since. The 25th of Kislev is the beginning of the eight-day festival of the Kindling of the Lights."

"Mother, Chanukah is a minor festival, yet candles are lit."

"Yes, Hadassah, Chanukah is also the Festival of Lights. It differs from other festivals in one important respect. Its origin is not hidden, but remains clear in the light of our old history. It is a festival which commemorates great events in the history of the Jewish people. Although it is a minor festival and is not mentioned in the Pentateuch or the Bible, a special prayer, *Al Hanissim*, is recited during Chanukah. This prayer contains thanks for deliverance from the enemy of the Maccabees.

"Chanukah is a tribute to the five sons of Mattathias, who lived nobly and died nobly, leaving their great names to be remembered: Eleazer, whose high courage was an example to every soldier in Judea; John or Yohanan, who cared little for glory but was content to serve his brothers; Jonathan, the good high priest; Simon, the wise gentle ruler, and Judas, the fearless, fiery general who overcame the vast armies of the Syrian king and led the people back to their holy Temple."

"Mother, Chanukah, like all other Jewish festivals and holidays, means so much to children."

"Yes, Hadassah, all these holidays begin at sundown, almost invariably with the lighting of candles. A ritual such as that of the candles inspires even little children, and when we explain their meaning the educational and religious goals are attained. We cannot all be scholars in the Talmud, but we can all enjoy the practice of our religion in our homes and synagogues. Our heritage is so rich that it is our obligation to the children to impart as much of the meaning of our observances as we possibly can.

"This evening, Hadassah, when the menorah is placed on the table, and Father recites the benedictions as he lights the candle with the little *shames*, we shall all be gathered around to answer, 'Amen.' Then we shall chant in chorus the hymns, *Hanerot Hallalu* and the *Maoz Tzur* (Rock of Ages)—our hymn of thanksgiving, and play *dreidel* games. The four-winged spinning top, which we use in these games, bears the Hebrew letters, *nun, gimel, hei* and *shin* which stand for. . ."

"I know, Mother! *Ness gadol hayah sham*, which means, 'A great miracle happened there.' There are also other games and, most important of all to the children, there is the Chanukah *gelt* and other gifts that are given. We always give part of this money to charity."

"Father will be home soon, Hadassah, and with all our nephews and nieces coming for *latkes* and Chanukah *gelt*. . .

I had better get things started in the kitchen! Why, before we know it, Father will be kindling the first Chanukah candle."

CHANUKAH DINNER I

Meat Halishkes

Pea Soup with Hominy

Roast Capon   Corn Flakes Stuffing

Potato Pancakes   Peas and Carrots

Cranberry Aspic

Blueberry Roll   Tea

MEAT HALISHKES (Stuffed Cabbage)

1 large cabbage

Remove core from head of cabbage, place cabbage in pot. Cover with boiling water, cover tightly, allow to cool. This makes cabbage leaves easy to separate. Drain well. Lay out leaves to be filled.

Filling

1 pound ground meat   ½ cup uncooked rice
1 medium onion, grated   ½ cup water
1 small potato, grated   1 teaspoon salt
                             Dash of pepper

To make the filling, combine all ingredients, blending well, then place 1 tablespoon of the mixture on each cabbage leaf. Tuck over ends and roll up like a cigar, but loosely, allowing room for rice to swell with cooking.

83

Sauce

1 large onion, chopped
2 tablespoons fat
½ teaspoon salt

1-pound can peeled whole
tomatoes
½ cup sugar

To make the sauce, fry onion in fat until soft, add tomatoes and salt, boil 5 minutes, then lower heat. Carefully place halishkes in the sauce, overlapped side down. Cook covered over very low heat for 1¼ hours. Add sugar, continue cooking ½ hour longer. Makes 36.

PEA SOUP WITH HOMINY

1 pound beef flanken
Marrow bone
2 quarts water
1 tablespoon salt, or to taste
1 cup split green peas

¼ cup barley
¼ cup fine noodles
1 medium onion, minced or grated
2 carrots, grated
2 stalks celery, minced
1 cup canned hominy

Cover meat and bone with the water, add salt; bring to a rolling boil, remove scum that rises to top. Add all remaining ingredients but hominy, simmer covered over very low heat 2 hours. Remove bone and meat, discard bone, cut up meat and return to pot along with the canned hominy. Cook 15 minutes longer. Makes 5 to 6 servings.

ROAST CAPON WITH CORN FLAKES STUFFING

6- to 7-pound capon, oven-ready
2 tablespoons grated onion

Paprika
Poultry seasoning
Salt, pepper

Stuffing

1 medium onion, thinly
   sliced
3 tablespoons chicken fat
4 medium potatoes, grated
1 cup corn flakes
½ cup Rice Krispies
½ cup fine dry bread
   crumbs

2 eggs
3 tablespoons flour
3 large mushrooms, sliced
   or chopped
½ teaspoon salt
¼ teaspoon pepper
¼ teaspoon cinnamon,
   optional
1 teaspoon sugar, optional

To make stuffing, sauté onion in chicken fat until golden, add remaining ingredients, blending well. Remove giblets from capon, fill breast and neck cavities with the stuffing, truss with poultry skewers and lace up. Rub outside of capon with onion, sprinkle with seasonings. Place capon in large brown paper bag, tie up bag and place in ungreased roasting pan. Bake in 350° oven for 2 to 2½ hours. Remove from bag; capon will be brown, crisp and tender. Serves 6 to 8.

POTATO PANCAKES

6 medium potatoes, grated
1 small onion, grated
2 eggs, beaten
2 tablespoons flour

2 teaspoons baking powder
1 teaspoon salt
Dash each of cinnamon and
   black pepper, if desired
½ cup fat

Combine all ingredients but fat, mixing well. Heat half the fat in skillet, add mixture by tablespoons, fry until well browned on both sides, adding additional fat to skillet as needed. Serves 8.

CRANBERRY ASPIC

1 package lemon-flavored kosher gelatin
1½ cups boiling water
2 cups whole cranberries
½ navel orange
1 cup sugar
½ cup chopped walnuts
½ cup minced celery

Dissolve gelatin in boiling water. Chill in 1-quart mold until it starts to set (consistency of unbeaten egg white). Put whole cranberries and the orange (including rind and pulp) through medium blade of food grinder. Combine with sugar, nuts and celery, add to gelatin, stirring to distribute evenly. Chill until very firm, 3 to 4 hours. Unmold by dipping quickly in hot water, pulling gelatin away from edges with fingers, then invert on platter or plate. Makes 8 servings.

BLUEBERRY ROLL

Pastry

½ cup sugar
½ cup oil
2 eggs, beaten
1 teaspoon vanilla
Juice and grated rind of ½ orange
2½ cups sifted all-purpose flour
2 teaspoons baking powder
¼ teaspoon salt

To make dough, beat together the sugar and oil, add eggs, vanilla, orange juice and rind. Sift together flour, baking powder and salt, add to egg mixture, blending well and kneading with fingers. Divide dough in half, roll out each half on lightly floured board to ¼-inch thickness, forming a rectangle.

Filling

1 quart blueberries   ½ cup sugar
                      2 tablespoons cornstarch

Wash and drain berries, combine with sugar and cornstarch. Spread half the berry mixture on each rectangle of dough, roll up as for Jelly Roll (see p. 134), place with overlapped side down in shallow baking pan. Bake in oven preheated to 350° until crust is golden, about 40 minutes. Serve hot or cold, cut into thick slices. May be served with Fruit Sauce or Lemon Sauce (see pp. 73, 58) if desired. Makes 8 to 10 servings.

CHANUKAH DINNER II

Mock Liver Appetizer   Vegetable Salad

Cream of Celery Soup   Crackers

Fillets of Sole with Kasha Stuffing

Buttered Beets   Cole Slaw

Sour Cream and Cheese Pancakes

Cake and Cookies   Coffee

MOCK LIVER APPETIZER

1 large onion, sliced   1 pound wax beans,
3 tablespoons butter   cooked, chopped
3 hard-boiled eggs,   ½ teaspoon salt
  chopped fine   ¼ teaspoon pepper

Cook onion in butter until well browned; chop fine. Combine with remaining ingredients, beat vigorously by hand or in electric blender to form a pâté. Serve on lettuce as an appetizer or as a spread with rye bread. Serves 4 as an appetizer, 8 as a canapé spread.

CREAM OF CELERY SOUP

5 stalks celery, chopped fine	2½ tablespoons butter
1 small whole onion	2½ tablespoons flour
1 quart milk	2 teaspoons salt
	1 cup cream

Cook celery and the onion in 2 cups of the milk for 20 minutes. Remove and discard onion. Make a cream sauce of remaining ingredients: melt butter, stir in flour, cook until bubbly, then add remaining 2 cups milk, simmer until smooth and thickened. Add salt and cream, stir into celery-milk mixture. Makes 8 servings.

FILLETS OF SOLE WITH KASHA STUFFING

3 pounds fillet of sole	2 cups boiling salted water
½ teaspoon salt	1 medium onion, sliced
¼ teaspoon pepper	6 tablespoons butter
½ pound kasha	1 cup milk

Wash fish and pat dry with paper towel. Sprinkle with salt and pepper. Cook kasha in boiling salted water until all water is absorbed. Meanwhile, fry the onion in 4 table-spoons of the butter until soft and yellow. Add ½ the fried onion to kasha, mixing well. Spoon some of this mixture on each fillet, roll up fillets and secure with toothpicks. Place remaining fried onion in bottom of shallow baking dish. Place rolled-up fillets over the onion. Cover fish with the milk, dot with remaining 2 tablespoons butter. Bake in oven preheated to 350° for 30 minutes. Makes 6 to 8 servings.

COLE SLAW

5 cups grated or shredded
  cabbage
2 carrots, grated
1 small onion, grated

4 stalks celery, minced
1 tablespoon sugar
1 tablespoon celery seed
2 tablespoons vinegar
¾ cup mayonnaise

Combine vegetables in salad bowl. Make sauce of remaining ingredients and pour over cabbage mixture. Chill thoroughly. Makes 8 servings.

SOUR CREAM AND CHEESE PANCAKES

½ pound (8-ounce pack-
  age) cottage cheese
½ cup sour cream
3 eggs, beaten
½ teaspoon salt

1 tablespoon sugar, or to
  taste
¾ cup sifted all-purpose
  flour
⅛ teaspoon baking powder
2 tablespoons butter

Beat cottage cheese and cream until well blended; add beaten eggs, salt and sugar, then the flour blended with the baking powder. Beat until smooth; if batter seems too stiff, add a tablespoon or two of milk. Melt butter in skillet or griddle (if using an electric skillet or griddle, set at 375°), drop in batter by tablespoons, cooking until golden on each side. Serve immediately with additional sour cream and jelly. Serves 4.

CHAMISHAH ASAR BISHVAT
(The Festival of the Trees)

A people who no longer have the vineyard
but still celebrate the vintage
will one day again have the vineyards.
—Benjamin Disraeli

"Studying the calendar, Hadassah?"

"Yes, I am very much interested in this new 25-year calendar. Today is the 15th of Shvat, a day of special significance for Jewish people the world over. Chamishah Asar Bishvat is a nature festival without religious associations and might have been forgotten after the Jews were expelled from Palestine, where this observance first originated. That it has lived on to this day shows how deeply rooted was the longing of the Jews for the soil of Palestine, and this feeling has been kept alive through the many centuries. Even when they lived in countries where severe frost and snow reign during Shvat, Jews have continued to celebrate Chamishah Asar Bishvat each year to this very day, though observing it slightly differently in some countries.

"In ancient Palestine, a beautiful and practical custom was observed on Chamishah Asar Bishvat. A tree was planted upon the birth of a child, a cedar sapling (strong and tall) for each boy born that year, and cypress or pine (fragrant and small) for a girl. When the children married, branches of these trees were cut down and used as posts for the *chuppah*."

"Mother, how did you celebrate Chamishah Asar Bish-vat when you were a young girl?"

"The observance of Chamishah Asar Bishvat spread from Palestine to Europe, and the New Year of the Trees became an occasion for rejoicing with nature. It was a day of happiness in what was often an otherwise bleak existence. We ate fruits, and an effort was made to include some fruit from Palestine. Due to the difficulty of getting such fruits until recently, however, European Jews had to content themselves with carobs or 'boxer' which, being dried, could be imported from the Holy Land. Nowadays fruits such as olives, dates, pomegranates, citrons, grapes, figs, quinces, nuts and boxer, are imported from Israel."

"Mother, I have often wondered why it is important to plant trees."

"Well, Hadassah, trees play an important role in the upbuilding of Israel. They are necessary for the beauty of the country and for the fruits they bear; for shade and shelter to man, beast and bird; for lumber to build homes and to make furniture; for protection from winds and storm; for prevention of soil erosion and—most important—for draining the malaria-breeding swamps.

"In Israel, therefore, Chamishah Asar Bishvat is de-voted to planting trees and, since it has always been a chil-dren's festival, the privilege is often accorded them. Then, too, as the farmers and workers of tomorrow, the children must be imbued with a strong attachment to their country. A child who plants a tree with his own hands unites himself lastingly with the soil upon which it grows. Only with the revival of life in Israel has the New Year of the Trees come into its own in recent decades. Under the influence of the Zionist rebuilding of the land, the day has resumed its ancient meaning and again has become the time of the planting of trees."

"Now I can see how important it is for all Jews, young and old alike, to support the Keren Kayemeth, the Jewish National Fund, by buying trees. When I marry wouldn't it be a wonderful idea to donate money to that fund to commemorate our marriage?"

"Yes, Hadassah, I had thought of that, but I am glad that you suggested it yourself."

On barren hills we plant the slip
　　Who shall not taste the tree.
The lengthening root, the ripening fruit
　　We may not hope to see.

But, oh, the joy of planting trees
　　And, oh, the keen delight
When unafraid beneath their shade
　　We rest in dreams at night.
　　　　　　　　—Jesse E. Sempter

TEA MENU FOR CHAMISHAH ASAR BISHVAT

Harlequin Pears   Cheese Balls

Date and Nut Bread Sandwiches

Assorted Cakes   Cookies

Tea or Coffee

Candies   Nuts   Israeli Fruits

HARLEQUIN PEARS

8 small Bartlett pears*   1 cup seedless raisins
½ cup sugar   1 cup salted peanuts
2 cups water   Mint sprigs
1 teaspoon peppermint   Lemon wedges
  extract   Cheese Balls
Few drops green vegetable   Whipped cream
  coloring

Peel pears; halve and core. Boil together sugar and water
5 minutes, add pears, cover, simmer 10 to 15 minutes or
until tender. Remove pears, measure syrup. To ½ the syrup,
add peppermint extract and food coloring. Place 8 of the
pear halves in this, chill until pears are tinted green. Chill
remaining pear halves in clear syrup.

Meanwhile, put raisins and nuts through medium
blade of food chopper, moisten with 3 tablespoons of the
clear pear syrup. Combine each green pear half with an
untinted pear half, with the fruit-nut mixture as a filling.
Place on lettuce, top each with small Cheese Balls and garnish with whipped cream. Makes 8 servings.

  * Or, use a large can of Bartlett pear halves with the canned
syrup, omit sugar and water.

CHEESE BALLS

Combine 1 pint creamed pot cheese or farmer cheese with a tablespoon or two of pear syrup and 6 to 8 chopped maraschino cherries. Beat to blend well, form with fingers into balls ½ inch in diameter. Roll each in shredded coconut or crushed nuts.

DATE AND NUT BREAD

1 cup dates, pitted, chopped	flour
1 cup boiling water	1 teaspoon baking powder
¼ cup butter	½ cup chopped nuts
1 cup sugar	1 teaspoon baking soda
1 egg, beaten	dissolved in 1 teaspoon
1 teaspoon vanilla	warm water
1½ cups sifted all-purpose	Softened cream cheese

Pour boiling water over dates, let stand while mixing cake. Cream butter until fluffy, add sugar, beat until very light, then beat in egg, vanilla and the dates softened with water. Sift together flour and baking powder, add nuts, so that nuts are well coated with flour. Combine with dates and butter-egg mixture, beat to blend, add soda dissolved in water, beat until batter is smooth. Pour into well-greased 9 x 5 x 3-inch loaf pan. Let stand in pan 15 minutes while preheating oven to 350°. Bake 35 to 40 minutes until top springs back and is crusty brown.

PURIM

"Hadassah, I have invited the children for a Purim party or *S'udah*, and have asked them to dress up in costumes from the story of Purim. When they are here, we will tell them the story around the table, for this is customary on this holiday. I have written the story so as to be certain of all the details."

"Mother, why not read it to me first."

"That is a good idea. I begin like this:

"Purim is an important holiday in the history of our people. It commemorates an event which took place during the reign of King Ahasuerus about 485 B.C. When Vashti, wife of Ahasuerus, refused to obey his commands and to display her beauty before his nobles, she was banished. The beautiful niece of a pious Jew named Mordecai was chosen to replace Vashti as queen. Her name was Esther. Mordecai happened to overhear a plot to kill King Ahasuerus and told Esther about it, who in turn informed the king. In this way Mordecai saved the king's life and the fact was written down in the king's chronicles.

"Some time later, Haman, who was prime minister to Ahasuerus, became so impressed with his own importance that he expected everyone to bow to him. Mordecai, the Jew, refused to do this for he would bow to no man—he bowed only to God. In his rage, Haman vowed that he would avenge the insult, not only upon Mordecai, but upon all the Jews in the empire. Haman spoke to Ahasuerus and deceived him into believing that the Jews were not faithful citizens of the empire but a people who refused to obey the laws of the land. Believing these tales, the king authorized Haman to issue a decree ordering all the Jews to be put to death on a certain day. To select the tragic date to carry out the scheme, Haman cast lots (*purim*) which fell on the 13th of Adar. The name of the festival is Purim. It is often called The Feast of Lots.

"When Mordecai heard of this decree to put all the Jews to death, he hastened to Esther, and asked her to speak to the king on behalf of her people. Esther hesitated, for she feared that to appear before the king without permission could mean her death. But Mordecai convinced her that because of her position it was her sacred duty to plead for her people. She spent the day before appearing before the king in fasting and prayer seeking divine guidance. She then came before the king and invited him and Haman to a banquet."

"It seems unfair that Ahasuerus should so soon have forgotten that Mordecai had saved his life."

"It seems so, Hadassah. However, he was reminded of this fact during one of his sleepless nights when he had the records in his chronicles read to him. Then he recalled that Mordecai was a Jew. To continue with the story . . .

"When Ahasuerus and Haman came to Esther's banquet, she implored the king to spare her life and the lives of the other Jews. On hearing this, Ahasuerus turned in rage against Haman for having led him to believe that all Jews were unfaithful. He ordered that Haman should be hanged from the same scaffold which had been erected to put Mordecai to death. The Jews, having been freed from this danger, and allowed to carry on their peaceful way of life, proclaimed a holiday of feasting and gaiety. This holiday has been carried down through the ages and is called Purim. The day before Purim is observed as a fast day called *Ta'anit Esther* or The Fast of Esther, to commemorate Esther's fast on the day prior to appearing before Ahasuerus."

"The story is very clear and the children will enjoy it. Would it not be a good idea to tell some of the customs observed on this holiday?"

"I will write them down now, Hadassah.

"Although no candles are lit for this holiday, we go to the synagogue the evening before Purim and on Purim morning. As we enter, it is customary to drop a coin, usually half a dollar, into the plate provided for that purpose in remembrance of the half shekel Jews contributed in Adar toward the Temple repair and sacrifices. Today this money is turned over to the Jewish National Fund. The *Megilat Esther*, which is a scroll containing this story of Esther, is read by the *hazan* or by a learned person whom the congregation wishes to honor. The reading of Haman's name is usually greeted by the children with rattling of the graggers (noisemakers) and the stamping of their feet.

Shalach manot (gifts) are exchanged with relatives and friends. The most popular *shalach manot* items are cakes, candies and fruits, but books, wearing apparel and other useful gifts are also given. At this time we remember those less fortunate than ourselves and distribute money to charitable causes and give Purim baskets to the poor."

"Purim is such a jolly holiday that it is celebrated not only in the home and synagogue, but also in community centers."

"Yes, Hadassah, it is a happy festival for we invite relatives and friends to our home to enjoy our holiday fare. The main traditional food served is *Hamantashen*, which is triangular in shape to represent Haman's hat. We tell Purim stories and sing songs. At community centers Purim is celebrated by banquets, dances, Purim plays and masquerades. Purim carnivals also have become popular."

"The children will be delighted to know that they may wear their costumes in the streets and that they may go from house to house collecting *shalach manot*, gaily singing and dancing."

"Purim each year bids the Jew have courage and hope. On this holiday we remember that every Haman in the present and future must and can be overcome. Anti-Semitism may be overcome by good will and by courageously living up to our ideals as Jews and citizens."

PURIM MENU

Sweetbreads and Mushrooms

Tomato and Rice Soup

Rib Roast   Browned Potatoes

Glazed Carrots   Tossed Salad

Strawberry Mousse

Hamantashen   Teiglach (see p. 55)   Mohnelach

Tea

SWEETBREADS AND MUSHROOMS

1 pound sweetbreads
½ to ¾ cup fine dry
   crumbs
1 cup diced onions

½ pound (1½ cups) fresh
   mushrooms, sliced
2 tablespoons chicken fat
½ teaspoon paprika
Salt, pepper

Defrost sweetbreads if frozen. Blanch by cooking in acidulated salted water (2 tablespoons vinegar and ½ teaspoon salt in 1 quart water) for 15 minutes. Drain, cool and cut in cubes. Roll in the crumbs. Sauté the mushrooms and onion in the chicken fat until lightly browned, sprinkling with paprika, salt and pepper. Add the sweetbreads, cook 30 minutes longer over low heat, turning occasionally. Makes 6 to 8 servings.

TOMATO AND RICE SOUP

Brisket soup bones	1 medium onion, grated
2 cups water	1 teaspoon salt
1 large can (1 pound, 14	¼ cup rice
ounces) tomatoes, forced	1 teaspoon sugar
through strainer	

Place bones in kettle or large saucepan, add water, bring to a boil, remove scum which rises to top. Add remaining ingredients. Simmer 2 hours. Makes 4 to 6 servings.

RIB ROAST AND BROWNED POTATOES

2- to 3-rib standing roast of	¼ teaspoon celery salt
beef	½ teaspoon dry mustard
1 tablespoon flour	1 or 2 onions, sliced
1 teaspoon salt	6 potatoes, peeled,
½ teaspoon pepper	quartered

Weigh meat after it has been trimmed. Allow 18 to 20 minutes' roasting time per pound for rare (for accurate results insert meat thermometer in solid part of meat without touching bone, cook until thermometer registers 140°). Combine flour and seasonings, rub over outside of meat. Place meat in shallow roasting pan with fat side up. Fasten onion slices to fat of meat with toothpicks. Place meat in oven set at 500° for ½ hour, reduce heat to 350°. Onions may be removed after ½ hour if desired. Do not cover meat; do not add water. After fat has accumulated in bottom of pan add peeled potatoes, allowing 1½ hours for them to cook. Turn potatoes at least once to brown evenly. Serves 6.

GLAZED CARROTS

6 medium carrots, scraped, cut in lengthwise strips

Cook the carrots in salted water until tender; drain. Place in casserole.

Syrup

½ cup water   ½ cup brown sugar   2 tablespoons fat

Cover carrots with syrup, bake uncovered in 350° oven until liquid is absorbed, about 20 minutes. (During Passover, only granulated sugar may be used.) Serves 6.

STRAWBERRY MOUSSE

2 cups (1 pint) strawberries   1 cup sifted confectioners'
2 egg whites, beaten stiff   sugar
                                                ½ cup walnuts, ground

Wash, trim and slice berries. Add sugar, then stir into stiffly beaten egg whites, distributing evenly. Spoon into sherbet dishes, leave in refrigerator until time to serve. Sprinkle walnuts over top just before serving. Makes 4 to 6 servings.

HAMANTASHEN I

Pastry

2½ cups sifted all-purpose   3 eggs, beaten
    flour   ½ cup sugar
  2 teaspoons baking   ½ cup oil
    powder   Juice and grated rind of ½
  ¼ teaspoon salt   orange
                                            1 teaspoon vanilla

Sift together flour, baking powder and salt. Combine 2 of the eggs with the sugar, oil and vanilla, add flour mixture, knead until smooth. Roll out on floured board to ¼ inch thick. Cut into circles with round cooky cutter or glass tumbler. Place a spoonful of filling in center of each. Draw up 3 sides to form a triangle, pinching edges together. Brush the third egg, well beaten, over the top of the pastries. Bake in oven preheated to 350° for ½ hour.

Filling

½ cup raisins
½ pound prunes, pitted, chopped

½ cup chopped nuts
Juice and grated rind of 1 lemon
½ cup granulated sugar

Soak raisins in warm water overnight; drain. Combine with remaining ingredients.

Hamantashen II may be substituted.

HAMANTASHEN II

Dough

4 cups sifted all-purpose flour
1 teaspoon salt
1 teaspoon baking powder

1 teaspoon baking soda
1 cup sugar
3 eggs
¾ cup oil
½ cup water

To make dough, combine flour, salt, baking powder, soda and sugar. Place in bowl, make hole in center, add eggs (unbeaten), oil and water. Beat vigorously to blend well, then knead with fingers until smooth. Place on floured board, roll out as for pie crust, cut into circles with cookie cutters or glass tumbler about 2½ inches in diameter.

Filling

1 pound dates
½ pound crushed nuts
1 pound prunes

1 pound raisins
Juice and rind of 1 lemon
1 6-ounce jar jam or marmalade

Combine filling ingredients. Place a spoonful of filling in each. Proceed as in Hamantashen I.

MOHNELACH (Mohn Candy)

1 cup poppy seeds   1 cup honey   ½ cup chopped nuts

Place seeds in cheesecloth bag, rinse through several waters. Let drain suspended in the cheesecloth overnight. Add drained seeds to the honey, boil together, stirring constantly, until mixture forms a firm ball in cold water. Add nuts; spread mixture on wet pastry board. When *slightly* cooled, cut into diamond shapes. When completely cold, after about 2 hours, separate into pieces. Makes 18 pieces.

PASSOVER

"Mother, how many of us realize that Passover really marks the birth of a nation?"

"Passover has a double meaning, Hadassah. Firstly it is a spring farm festival; secondly it is the feast of freedom that commemorates the release of the Israelites from bondage.

"As you know, the Jews were originally farmers, and since Passover comes at the beginning of the grain harvest it was celebrated as an agricultural holiday. Every farmer brought an *omer* (measure) or sheaf of newly-cut barley as an offering of thanksgiving to God. There are seven weeks called the Period of the Omer which we observe today with special prayers in the synagogue, beginning with the second day of Passover and ending with Shavuot.

"The Passover *Seder* ceremony reminds us that Passover is the Festival of Freedom. It commemorates the sacrifice which every Jewish family offered on the night before they left Egypt.

"The Jews were bidden not to forget their emancipation from slavery. The celebration of Passover was ordained as a permanent holiday beginning on the eve of the 14th of Nisan and lasting eight days."

"There is no doubt that we Jews have kept faith throughout the ages in the celebration of Passover."

"Yes, Hadassah, for no other experience in its long history has impressed itself so deeply in the hearts and minds of the Jewish people as their freedom from slavery. The story of Passover is in the book of Exodus in the Bible and dates back some 3,500 years.

"The Israelites were a small tribe that wandered into the land of Egypt. Ahead of them came Joseph who, guided by Divine Providence, was able to give valuable advice to the pharoah of Egypt, and in this way the Israelites were favored and grew prosperous.

"After Joseph died and another pharaoh became the ruler, the Egyptians soon forgot all the good done for them by Joseph and became jealous of the wealth and comfort enjoyed by the Israelites. They confiscated their property and forced them into slave labor."

"Mother, why did the pharaoh order that all male children born to the Israelites be drowned?"

"According to the story, a sorcerer or fortuneteller in the pharaoh's court foretold that an Israelite child would be born who would one day free his people. In order to prevent this happening, the pharaoh issued this decree.

"To one of the Israelite families a male child was born and, in order to prevent the pharaoh's soldiers from finding him, Yochebed, his mother, wove a basketlike cradle, filled in the cracks with tar to keep it waterproof, placed the child in it and hid it among the reeds that grew along the banks of the Nile.

"When the pharaoh's daughter went to bathe, she heard the baby cry and ordered that he be brought to her. Impressed with his beauty, she decided to keep him and bring him up, giving him the name of Moses. Miriam, his sister, who had been told to watch over him, came up and asked the princess if she might get a Hebrew woman to act as his nurse. She suggested Yochebed. Fortunately, the princess agreed and Moses was nursed by his own mother.

"When Moses was three years old, the pharaoh's advisers noticed his character and wisdom and insisted that he be put to death because they feared that he would grow up to be the foretold leader who was to rise against the pharaoh's rule.

"According to legend, the infant Moses was tested for his wisdom and understanding and was given the choice of a piece of gold or a hot coal. The angel Gabriel directed his hand toward the hot coal. Moses put the hot coal into his mouth, and severely burned his tongue, making him forever tongue-tied, but his life was saved.

"When Moses grew to manhood, he saw the hardships that were being inflicted on the Israelites and he resolved to try to help them. One day he saw an Egyptian beating an Israelite. Enraged at the cruelty, he struck the Egyptian and killed him. Fearing that the pharaoh would find out about this deed and decree that he be put to death, Moses fled Egypt and settled in the land of Median, where he eventually married.

"It was while tending his flocks there that he came to Mount Horeb and saw a burning bush. Attracted to the flame, he came closer and was stopped by a voice coming from the burning bush. He was told that it was the presence of the Lord and he was commanded to return to Egypt and demand that the pharaoh set the Israelites free. When Moses doubted his own ability to act as the Lord's messenger he was told that his older brother Aaron would meet him in Egypt and act as his spokesman. God endowed Moses with the power of performing wondrous things to prove to the pharaoh that he was a true messenger of the Lord.

"Moses and Aaron came before the pharaoh and demanded that he free the Israelites, but he refused to allow them to go and continued to oppress them.

"Moses and Aaron appeared before the pharaoh again

and again, each time with a different sign until pestilence and plague, in the form of blood, frogs, vermin, murrain, boils, hail, locusts and darkness struck the Egyptian people who were oppressing the sons of Israel. Each of the plagues was removed upon the promise by the pharaoh that he would relent and allow the people to go. However, he did not live up to his promise and he continued to subjugate them to slavery more and more viciously. It was only after the tenth plague, when the Angel of Death had killed every first-born of man and beast belonging to the pharaoh and his people—sparing the first-born of the Israelites, who had been ordered by Moses to paint signs upon their doorposts with the blood of a slaughtered lamb—that the pharoah ordered the Israelites to leave Egypt immediately and take all their possessions.

"Having to leave so suddenly, they could not stop to prepare their food or to wait until the bread would leaven. They took their dough with them unleavened and baked it in the sun."

"I suppose that is why we eat matzos during the eight days of Passover, Mother?"

"Of course, matzo is a reminder of the unleavened bread which the Hebrews prepared in such haste when they fled from Egypt. It is now the symbol of liberty.

"You know, Hadassah, Passover as it is observed today, aside from the ritual, is one of the purest of Jewish holidays. All homes have a thorough going over to ensure that all leavened food or *chometz* is removed from every nook. On the night before Passover eve the ritual of *Bedikat Chometz* or the Search for Leaven is followed. In order to be certain that the home is ready for the holiday, the head of the house searches carefully in all the rooms for any remaining leaven. Since the house has been thoroughly cleaned he will probably not find any; therefore the mother places small pieces of bread in conspicuous places in each room. He goes from room to room, carrying a lighted candle, a wooden spoon and some feathers. The rest of the family, following, watch him sweep the bread into the spoon with the feathers."

"Mother, is there a special benediction at this time?"

"Before the search is commenced, a prayer is said: 'Blessed art Thou, O Lord our God, King of the Universe, who hast commanded us to remove all leaven.' After the search is completed another prayer is recited: 'All manner of leaven that is in my possession, which I have not seen nor removed, shall be null and accounted as the dust of the earth.' The following morning at ten o'clock this *chometz*, together with uneaten *chometz*, is burned and a blessing is said: 'All manner of leaven that is in my possession, which I have seen and which I have not seen, which I have re-moved and which I have not removed, shall be null and accounted as the dust of the earth.'

"After the burning of the *chometz* no leaven is eaten for the entire eight days. All cooking and eating utensils that we use all year are placed out of sight, and the Passover dishes are unpacked, washed and brought into use. These are kept from year to year for the Passover. If silverware that is used all year must be used it is permissible to kasher them. First it is polished and rinsed. Then it is tied to a long cord, each piece separated by a knot and dipped into boil-ing water into which one drops a very hot piece of iron or stone. After such kashering, they are considered fit for Passover. When all dishes and utensils are in place, the Pass-over groceries may be opened and used.

"The lunch on *Erev Pesach* is a simple one as no wine,

matzos or food prepared with matzo is eaten by Orthodox Jews until the *Seder* night."

"Mother, the *Seder* table is always so artistic, covered with our nicest white tablecloth, and freshly polished silverware, and the shining candlesticks placed in the center of the table. It is so beautiful and memorable."

"You know, of course, Hadassah, that the blessing for the lighting of the candles is recited both *Seder* nights and again on the last two nights of Passover."

"Yes, Mother, and the four intervening days are Chal Hamoed, just like during Succot. They are half holidays, are they not?"

"Well, Hadassah, all the laws of Passover apply to them except that work is permitted."

"Mother, with all the symbols on the *Seder* table and all the family gathered around it, each one of us participating in the ritual of the service, each following the story of the Exodus in the Haggadah, the Passover *Seder* is indeed a holiday for all of us to look forward to each year, with Father seated at the head of the table, reclining on a cushion."

"The cushion, too, is a symbol of freedom, Hadassah. Before Father comes to the table he places three matzos covered with a special cloth on a special matzo plate. A white napkin may be used as well. The three matzos represent the three divisions of Jews: Cohanim, Leviim and Israelim. On a platter are placed a roasted shankbone (the *zeroa*) reminiscent of the sacrifice of the lamb in Egypt; a roasted egg as a substitute for ancient holiday sacrifices which symbolizes in its smooth roundness that fate is variable; *maror* (root of horse-radish), a symbol of the bitterness endured in Egypt; *karpas* (sprig of parsley or watercress representing the sprig; a paste-like compound of ground apples, nuts, cinnamon and wine called *charoset*, to remind us of the clay from which our ancestors were forced to make bricks in building the two cities, Pithom and Raamses. A dish of salt water is reminiscent of the tears shed by an enslaved and captive race. Father pours a goblet or a glass of wine for each member of the family and will refill it until the *Arba Kosot* are drunk. He chants the *Kiddush* and then is followed by each male adult in chanting the *Kiddush*, while they drink the first of the four cups of wine required for the *Seder* service. The ritual of the washing of the hands is performed."

"Father always looks solemn when he lifts the plate of matzos and shows it to us, after which he breaks the third matzo."

"You know, Hadassah, it represents the food and the poor treatment which Jews received during the days of their bondage. 'Lo, this is the bread of affliction, which our ancestors ate in Egypt,' is recited at every *Seder*. Part of the broken matzo is the *afikomen*, and the children take delight in watching where it is hidden because the one who finds the *afikomen* is usually rewarded with a gift. The *afikomen* is eaten at the end of the meal. The children also take part in the *Seder* service."

"Yes, Mother, I still recall the thrill. I was the youngest at the *Seder* and asked the four questions. They are indelibly inscribed in my memory: 'Why on this night do we eat unleavened bread? Why do we eat *maror*? Why do we eat *charoset*? Why do we lean forward during the ceremony of the *Seder*?' We are all so proud when Father fills the second cup of wine and proceeds to answer the questions by telling the story of the Israelites in Egypt, of the Exodus led by Moses and how he brought the Israelites to the teachings of the one God. When the names of the ten plagues that God inflicted upon Egypt are repeated, each of us pours a drop from his goblet of wine."

"Hadassah, we all feel strongly the importance of the various symbols we prepare, as each is taken up in turn and its significance is explained. As each one of us tastes a little of each, saying the appropriate blessings, the whole story takes on a deeper meaning.

"A portion of *Hallel* is recited, a song from the psalms denoting joy in liberty. The reply closes with a benediction in which it is hoped that the holy Temple will be rebuilt, and the ancient rites restored.

"The hands are again washed because a benediction is pronounced over the matzos. Then the meal is served. The first course is traditionally a hard-boiled egg and potato in salt water.

"After the meal there are more rituals. After the search for the *afikomen*, each one receives a piece. In ancient times each person received a portion of the lamb for dessert. In memory of this, *afikomen* is eaten at the end of the meal. Then grace is chanted and the third cup of wine is drunk. A second part of the *Hallel* is sung, but before doing so, the door is opened, according to our old custom, to allow the prophet Elijah to enter. There is a special goblet filled with wine for him called *Kos shel Eliyahu*, and according to Jewish legend, he visits every *Seder* and at the end of days will bring the Messianic age."

"Mother, I recall the excitement of watching the goblet of wine to see whether any wine was being sipped by the prophet Elijah."

"We, too, each have our wine glasses filled for the fourth time; then, *Hallel* is continued. There are also several old Hebrew songs, Hadassah, I enjoy: *Addir Hu* and

Ki Lo Noe. The two the children most enjoy are *Echad Mi Yode'a* and *Chad Gadya.* That always brings the *Seder* to a close."

"I seem to remember that there are other customs observed for Passover."

"Yes, Hadassah, there is a very well-established tradition of distributing *moess hittin,* or baskets containing Passover food, to the needy so that they will be able to celebrate this holiday.

"Certain vegetables such as cabbage, peas and beans are not permitted during the Passover week.

"There is the law concerning the preparation of food on the festival for the Sabbath. It is called *erub tavshilin.* It is performed by taking some cooked or roasted food, which is eaten with bread, and pronouncing the blessing, 'Who hath sanctified us with his commandments and charged us with the observance of *erub?* By virtue of this *erub* be it permitted us to bake, cook, keep the victuals warm, light candles and do all the work that is necessary on the festival for the Sabbath.' If one does not understand Hebrew one may say it in any language one understands."

"Mother, is *erub tavshilin* made for any holiday or only for the Passover?"

"*Erub tavshilin* is made for other holidays, too. It also is made when the first *Seder* night falls on Thursday so that we may be permitted to prepare food on Passover for the Sabbath which follows. The blessing is made over meat, fish, egg or any food that may be eaten with bread. A whole matzo is used alongside of the food for Passover, whereas when it is not Passover a whole bread is used.

"During the week of Passover, prayers and appropriate portions of the Torah and Prophets are read in the synagogue. On the morning of the first day the *Tal* or Dew prayer is chanted asking for abundant dew in Israel during the summer months when no rain falls in that country. The *Hallel* is recited daily; it is a recitation of praise and thanksgiving compiled from the Psalms.

"On the last day of Passover, worshippers recall their departed kinfolk during *Yiskor*, or memorial service, for the dead."

"Mother, I have always felt that aside from the historical aspect of the celebration of Passover there is a broader meaning."

"You are right. It has been a symbol for men of all generations of their own search for freedom and their hope that the freedom they desire can be won. The pharaoh may be regarded as representative of all tyrants throughout human history. From his defeat we gain confidence that we can break all chains which enslave us. The fact that God had sent Moses on his mission assures us that it is the divine will that all mankind shall enjoy liberty. All freedom-loving people—no matter what their creed or race—have taken hope and courage from the Passover festival."

PASSOVER DINNER I (First Seder)

Wine   Matzo   Charoset

Bitter Herbs with Horse-radish

Hard-boiled Eggs   Salt Water

Onion Tops or Boiled Potatoes   Shank Bone

Gefilte Fish (see p. 39)   Horse-radish Sauce

Lettuce and Tomatoes

Chicken Soup (see p. 41)   Knadlech

Roast Chicken with Potato Stuffing

Roast Tongue   Harvard Beets   Fresh Asparagus

Sliced Fresh Pineapple   Sponge Cake   Tea

CHAROSET

½ apple, seeded   ½ teaspoon cinnamon
¼ cup ground walnuts   ½ teaspoon sugar
                              1 tablespoon red wine

Chop or coarsely grate the apple and mash well with other ingredients. When mixture is smooth, add wine and mix again. Makes ½ cup.

KNADLECH

2 eggs, separated   ½ teaspoon salt
½ cup matzo meal   1 or 2 tablespoons chicken fat
                              Boiling hot chicken soup or
                                    salted water

Beat the egg whites until stiff. Separately beat egg yolks, add to egg whites, then slowly add the matzo meal and salt, stirring constantly until soft dough is formed. Allow mixture to stand several minutes. Rub the palms of your hands with chicken fat, then form small balls of the matzo meal mixture and drop the balls into rapidly boiling soup or water. Cook, covered, 30 to 40 minutes. Makes about 6 large or 12 small.

POTATO STUFFING

4 medium potatoes	2 tablespoons chicken fat
1 carrot, grated	½ teaspoon salt
1 medium onion, grated	Dash of pepper
	3 eggs

Combine grated vegetables with chicken fat, salt and pepper. Beat in eggs one at a time, blending well. Use to fill neck and breast cavities, then truss with poultry skewers and lace up. Roast chicken in paper bag (en Papillote – see p. 41) or as for Rosh Hashanah menu (see p. 49). Makes enough stuffing for a 6-pound roasting chicken or capon.

ROAST TONGUE

1 beef tongue, 4 to 5 pounds	2 medium tomatoes, chopped
2 medium onions, diced	2 tablespoons chicken fat
1 green pepper, seeded and diced	Salt, pepper
	1 cup water

To remove skin from tongue, scald with boiling water, then dip in cold water and pull away skin with sharp knife. If skin does not come off easily, scald tongue a second time.

Sauté onion, green pepper and tomato in chicken fat until lightly browned. Season to taste. Add the cup of water. Pour this sauce over the skinned tongue in roasting pan and roast tongue in moderate (350°) oven until tender, about 2 hours. Slice tongue, serve with the sauce. Serves 6 to 8.

HARVARD BEETS

2 bunches fresh beets (2 cups diced cooked beets), or 1-pound can beets
1 cup beet juice

2 tablespoons potato starch
2 tablespoons sugar
2 tablespoons lemon juice or vinegar
Salt, pepper to taste

To cook fresh beets, remove tops, wash beets thoroughly, cook covered without peeling in salted water until tender, about 40 minutes. Drain, saving juice. (If canned beets are used, save canned juice, adding water if necessary to make 1 cup.)

Make a sauce of beet juice, starch, sugar, lemon juice or vinegar and salt and pepper. Cook over moderate heat in top of double boiler, stirring constantly until thickened. Remove skin from cooled fresh beets, dice beets, add to the sauce. Place over hot water in bottom of double boiler to keep warm until ready to serve. Makes 4 to 6 servings.

SPONGE CAKE I

6 eggs
1 cup sugar
1 tablespoon cold water
⅛ teaspoon salt

Juice and grated rind 1 lemon
⅔ cup Passover cake flour
⅓ cup potato starch

Beat eggs until light and foamy (do not separate); beat in sugar, water and salt, then the lemon juice and rind. Sift together flour and starch, slowly add to egg mixture, stirring lightly until very smooth. Very lightly grease or line with waxed paper 13 x 9-inch baking pan. Bake in 350° oven for 35 to 40 minutes or until cake springs back when pressed and can be drawn away from sides of pan. Sponge Cake II may be substituted.

SPONGE CAKE II

8 eggs, separated	½ cup potato flour
1½ cups sugar	2 tablespoons lemon juice
½ cup cake meal	¼ teaspoon salt

Beat egg yolks and sugar together until light and fluffy. Add cake meal and potato flour, which have been sifted together, beat until smooth, add lemon juice, blend well. Separately beat egg whites until stiff, adding salt. Fold egg whites into yolk mixture. Proceed as for Sponge Cake I.

PASSOVER DINNER II

Chopped Liver   Tomatoes and Lettuce

Beet Borsht   Boiled Potatoes

Roast Brisket of Beef   Potato Kugel

Applesauce (see p. 65)   Ingberlach

Glazed Carrots (see p. 100)

Fresh Fruit Salad on Sponge Cake

Tea

CHOPPED LIVER

½ pound beef liver	¼ teaspoon freshly ground
3 hard-boiled eggs	pepper
1 small onion, grated	2 to 3 tablespoons chicken
1 teaspoon salt	fat

Bake liver in moderate oven until tender, about 30 minutes. Put through food grinder with eggs. Add the onion, salt and pepper and enough chicken fat to make a smooth paste. Serves 6.

BEET BORSHT

1 pound brisket or flanken of beef	1 to 1½ tablespoons salt
1 marrow bone	2 tablespoons white or brown sugar or to taste
2 quarts water	⅓ cup lemon juice
10 large beets, grated	2 egg yolks, beaten
2 medium onions, peeled	2 potatoes, peeled, cooked, diced

Place beef and bone in water, bring to a boil, remove scum from top. Scrub beets thoroughly, grate raw beets and add to boiling water with whole onions and salt. Simmer 2 hours. Remove onions, if desired. Add sugar and lemon juice. Beat egg yolks, add a little of hot soup to yolks to blend, then stir yolks into soup, beating constantly. Just before serving, add cooked diced potatoes to soup. Serves 8.

ROAST BRISKET OF BEEF

4 pounds brisket of beef	¼ teaspoon pepper
1 or 2 tablespoons potato starch	2 tomatoes, sliced
	2 medium onions, chopped
2 to 3 teaspoons salt	1 green pepper, minced
	½ cup water

Sear the meat under a broiler flame or in heavy skillet on top of stove until surface is well browned on both sides. Combine potato starch, salt and pepper, sprinkle over meat. Place in roasting pan with tomato slices over top of meat. Place onions and green pepper around meat in pan. Add water, bake uncovered in 350° oven about 3 hours or until tender, basting frequently. Makes 8 servings.

POTATO KUGEL

5 large potatoes	½ cup melted fat
1 onion, grated	1 teaspoon salt
3 eggs	¼ teaspoon pepper
⅓ cup matzo meal	¼ teaspoon cinnamon (optional)

Grate potatoes on a fine grater, drain off most of the water. Add grated onion, eggs and other ingredients. Mix well. Pour into a well greased, heated pudding dish and bake in a hot oven, 400°, for about an hour or until a brown crust has formed on top. Makes 6 to 8 servings.

Note: To make the kugel lighter in texture and color, substitute one large cooked, mashed potato for one of the raw potatoes, and decrease the matzo meal to ¼ cup.

INGBERLACH (Ginger Squares)

1 pound (16 ounces) honey	¼ teaspoon powdered ginger
1 cup sugar	
3 cups matzo farfel	½ cup chopped nuts

Combine honey and sugar, heat and stir in saucepan over low heat until mixture comes to a boil. Combine matzo farfel and ginger, blending well; add slowly to honey mixture, continuing to cook until syrup is brown and thick. Moisten a pastry board, spread honey mixture over board. Sprinkle nuts over top. Chill. When firm, cut into squares.

FRESH FRUIT SALAD ON SPONGE CAKE

Make a fruit salad of any seasonable fruit and pile on slices of sponge cake. Top with meringue and garnish with chopped nuts.

PASSOVER DINNER III

Chopped Eggplant (see p. 71)

Tomatoes and Lettuce Salad

Meat Loaf with Hard-boiled Egg Center

Mashed Potatoes   Carrot Pudding   Sliced Beets

Deep Dish Apple Pie   Tea

MEAT LOAF

1 medium potato, peeled, grated | 1 teaspoon salt
1 large onion, grated | Dash of pepper
1½ pounds ground meat | ½ cup water
 | 4 hard-boiled eggs

Add grated raw potato and grated onion to meat, then work in seasonings and water, kneading to blend well. Heat a greased 9 x 5 x 3-inch loaf pan; press half the meat mixture in bottom of pan. Place shelled whole eggs in center. Cover with remaining meat, pressing around and over the eggs. Bake in oven at 350° for 1½ hours. Makes 6 servings.

CARROT PUDDING

1½ cups grated raw carrots | blanched almonds
8 eggs, separated | Grated rind ½ lemon
1 cup granulated sugar | 1 tablespoon sweet Passover
1 cup grated or ground | wine

Grease a 1½-quart baking dish or casserole. Combine grated carrots with well-beaten egg yolks, sugar, almonds, lemon rind and wine. Beat egg whites until stiff, fold into carrot mixture. Spoon into well-greased casserole. Bake uncovered for 1 hour at 325°. (May be baked at same time as meat, reducing oven heat from 350° to 325° after meat has been in oven for ¾ hour and increasing baking time for meat to 1¾ hours.) Serves 6.

DEEP DISH APPLE PIE

2 cups sliced apples
1 teaspoon allspice
½ teaspoon cinnamon

Place apples in 1½-quart casserole, sprinkle with sugar and cinnamon.

Pastry

2 eggs, beaten
½ cup sugar
3 tablespoons oil

1½ tablespoons potato flour
½ cup matzo meal
Pinch of salt

To make pastry, beat together eggs and sugar, add oil, flour, meal and salt. Mix thoroughly, spread over apples. Bake in oven preheated to 350° for 30 minutes. Serve warm or cold.

PASSOVER DINNER IV

Fruit Cocktail

Breaded Veal Chops   Potato Puffs

Diced Beets   Green Salad

Coconut Fruit Pudding   Tea   Cookies

BREADED VEAL CHOPS

Allow 1 chop per serving. Wash meat, pat dry with paper towel, then dip in beaten egg, then in matzo meal seasoned with salt and pepper. (Use ½ teaspoon salt to ½ cup meal.) Heat ¼ cup fat or oil in skillet, add chops, cook over moderate heat (300° on electric skillet) until well browned on each side.

POTATO PUFFS

4 large potatoes, cooked,
   mashed
3 egg yolks

¼ teaspoon salt
Dash of pepper
2 tablespoons chicken fat
3 egg whites, beaten stiff

121

Beat into mashed potatoes the egg yolks, salt, pepper and chicken fat. Fold in stiffly beaten egg whites. Grease baking sheet, drop mixture by spoonfuls on sheet, bake in hot oven (400°) until delicately browned, about 20 minutes. Makes 4 to 6 servings.

COCONUT FRUIT PUDDING

½ fresh coconut
2 apples, grated
¼ cup chopped walnuts
⅛ teaspoon salt

1½ to 2 tablespoons lemon juice
3 navel oranges, diced
⅓ cup sugar
2 eggs, beaten

Remove the white meat of the coconut and reserve the milk. Grate coconut meat or put through food grinder. Combine with remaining ingredients. Pour into 6 to 8 individual Pyrex baking dishes or custard cups, which have been well greased. Bake at 350° for 30 minutes or until firm (test by inserting knife blade in center). Cool before serving. Serves 6 to 8.

PASSOVER DINNER V

Giblet Fricassee

Broiled Spring Chicken (see p. 157)

Potato and Liver Blintzes

Glazed Carrots (see p. 100)   Tossed Salad

Raspberry Jam Torte   Tea

GIBLET FRICASSEE

1 pound mixed chicken giblets, necks and feet	2 tomatoes, chopped
4 tablespoons chicken fat	2 cups water
2 medium onions, chopped	2 tablespoons sugar
1 green pepper, minced	1 teaspoon salt
	¼ teaspoon pepper

Scald the giblets, neck and feet with boiling water, removing heavy skin from feet. Chop into small pieces. Melt chicken fat, sauté onions, green pepper and tomatoes until lightly browned, add water, sugar, salt and pepper. Add the chopped giblets, etc., simmer, covered, 2 hours.

Meat Balls

½ pound ground beef	1 small potato, peeled, grated
1 small onion, grated	½ teaspoon salt

Form small meat balls of the beef, onion, potato and salt. Add to the fricassee after first hour. Add more water if sauce cooks down too much. Makes 4 to 6 servings.

POTATO AND LIVER BLINTZES

Dough

3 eggs	½ teaspoon salt
1½ cups water	¾ cup cake meal

Beat eggs, add water and salt, then stir in cake meal until smooth. Drop by spoonfuls on lightly greased hot griddle to make very thin pancakes. As soon as brown on one side, turn out onto towel, browned side up.

123

Filling

3 medium potatoes	¼ pound beef liver, baked,
1 medium onion, sliced	minced
2 tablespoons chicken fat	Salt, pepper

Cook the potatoes, mash. Fry the onions in the chicken fat until lightly browned. Add onions and minced liver to potatoes. Season to taste. Place a spoonful of filling on each pancake, turn opposite sides in, roll up, place with over-lapped side down in baking pan or skillet. Fry or bake in oil or chicken fat until delicately browned. Makes about 18.

RASPBERRY JAM TORTE

8 eggs, separated	if stiff)
1½ cups sugar	¼ cup crushed walnuts
Juice and grated rind of	1 cup cake meal,
1 lemon	or ½ cup cake meal and
2 tablespoons raspberry	½ cup potato flour
jam or jelly (melted,	¼ teaspoon salt

Beat egg yolks and sugar together until light. Add lemon juice and rind, jam or jelly, half the walnuts and the cake meal. Separately beat egg whites until stiff, adding salt. Fold into batter. Line bottom of 9-inch-square cake pan with waxed paper, add batter, sprinkle remaining nuts over top. Bake in 325° oven for 1 hour.

Note: If preferred, instead of adding jam or jelly to the batter, place half the batter in pan, add a layer of jam or jelly, then remaining batter, with crushed nuts over the top.

PASSOVER DINNER VI

Petchah		Lettuce Salad
Broiled Steak	French Fried Potatoes (see p. 75)	
Celery	Radish Roses	Pickled Beets
Farfel Apple Pudding	Tea	Cookies

PETCHAH

Make a jellied stock by cooking 2 pounds veal knuckle or calves' feet, if available, in 4 quarts boiling water. To the stock, add 1 tablespoon salt, ¼ teaspoon black pepper, and a large onion, cut up. Simmer gently several hours until meat falls from bones and liquid has been reduced to ⅓.

Meanwhile, hard-boil 4 eggs, separate the cooked whites from the yolks. Strain stock, reserving meat and discarding bones. Chop meat with half the cooked egg whites, season with salt, pepper and a little minced onion. Except during Passover, 2 crushed or minced garlic cloves may also be added to chopped egg whites. Place this mixture in glass dish or mold, cover with 6 cups of the strained stock. Use ½ cup of the stock to blend with the mashed egg yolk. When first layer has started to set, cover with egg yolk mixture and decorate with rings of remaining egg whites. Chill until very firm, then cut into squares.

BROILED STEAK

Wipe a steak 1½ to 2 inches thick with damp cloth. Trim off fat. (Grease rack with fat scraps.) Have oven preheated to 500°. Place steak on rack in center of broiling oven 3 or 4 inches below flame. When steak is browned on one side, season with salt and pepper, then turn and brown on other side. Steak is done when browned on second side. Place on hot platter, season with salt and pepper, serve at once. It will take 20 to 30 minutes to broil a steak 1½ to 2 inches thick to serve well done. Reduce time for medium or rare.

PICKLED BEETS

Boil beets. When tender, peel while hot. Slice into bowl. Sprinkle with salt, pepper and sugar. Add a small onion, sliced. Pour boiling hot vinegar over beets, toss to blend with a fork. Chill and serve.

FARFEL APPLE PUDDING

3 cups farfel	3 tablespoons currant
4 eggs, beaten	or apple jelly
⅛ teaspoon salt	Sugar to taste, about ⅓ cup
3 or 4 tart apples	¼ cup chopped nuts (optional)

Cover farfel with boiling water, let stand about 10 minutes. Drain; add cold water just to cover. Stir in eggs and salt, mix well. Add remaining ingredients, except nuts. Spoon into greased shallow baking dish. Sprinkle nuts over top. Bake at 350° until delicately browned on top. Serves 6.

PASSOVER DINNER VII

Stuffed Green Peppers

Chicken Soup (see p. 41) with Passover Noodles

Broiled Liver Smothered in Onions

Baked Potatoes   Broiled Tomatoes

Baked Apples   Matzo Spice Cake   Tea

STUFFED GREEN PEPPERS

6 large green peppers	2 tablespoons cold water
½ pound ground beef	1 large onion, chopped
1 tablespoon grated onion	2 tomatoes, chopped
1 medium potato, grated	2 tablespoons fat
1 teaspoon salt	Salt, pepper to taste
¼ teaspoon pepper	1 cup hot water

Remove tops and seeds from peppers. Cut a very thin slice off bottom of each so that they will stand upright in baking dish. Combine beef, grated onion, grated potato, salt, pepper and 2 tablespoons cold water. Stuff peppers with this mixture. Place upright in baking dish. Arrange chopped onion and tomato around peppers in dish, dot top of peppers with some of fat, add remaining fat to vegetables in pan. Sprinkle with salt and pepper from shakers. Add hot water. Bake covered in 350° oven for 45 minutes, uncover, baste peppers with sauce in baking dish, bake 15 minutes longer. Makes 6 servings.

PASSOVER NOODLES

Beat 2 eggs until foamy, add 2 tablespoons fine matzo meal. Heat 1 teaspoon chicken fat in skillet. Pour in the thin batter as for pancakes (see p. 143); as soon as firm, turn over with spatula. When brown on both sides, turn out on board. When cold, cut into noodles.

BROILED LIVER SMOTHERED IN ONIONS

Buy calves' liver or beef liver steaks cut 1 inch thick. Wash and wipe dry. Sprinkle with salt. Broil in preheated oven 3 inches from unit for 2 minutes on each side. Remove, wash under cold water quickly. Meanwhile, fry sliced onion in chicken fat until golden, add liver, cook covered for 5 minutes. (If desired, a little chopped green pepper may be added to the onion, as well.)

BROILED TOMATOES

Wash, but do not peel, medium-sized firm tomatoes. Roll in matzo meal, seasoned with salt and pepper. Dot each tomato with a little fat. Broil a few minutes at about 500° and serve immediately.

127

BAKED APPLES

Select tart apples; wash and core. Place in baking dish, fill center with sugar. Sprinkle with cinnamon if desired. Cover bottom of dish with boiling water; bake in hot oven until soft. Baste often. Serve hot or cold.

MATZO SPICE CAKE

6 eggs, separated	Pinch of salt
1 cup sugar	¼ cup sweet Passover wine
½ teaspoon cinnamon	¾ cup cake meal
	½ cup chopped nuts

Beat egg whites until stiff, set aside. Beat yolks until light and fluffy, add sugar gradually, then the remaining ingredients. Fold in stiffly beaten whites. Bake in 13 x 9 x 2-inch pan lined with waxed paper for 45 minutes at 325°.

PASSOVER DINNER VIII

Black Radish Salad

Stuffed Squash

Stuffed Veal Brisket

Roasted Potatoes   Carrots

Pineapple Pudding   Tea

BLACK RADISH SALAD

Cut into large pieces lettuce, tomatoes, cucumbers, spring onions, celery and green pepper. Add a large black radish, grated. Season with salt, pepper, oil.

STUFFED SQUASH

1 large cocozelle or
marrow squash,* about
10 inches long
1 pound ground beef
1 small onion, grated
or 3 soda crackers, soaked

1 medium potato, grated
1 teaspoon salt
½ cup cold water
1 large onion, sliced
3 tomatoes, chopped
2 tablespoons fat
2 tablespoons sugar

Scrape outside of squash; cut off a slice lengthwise, scoop out all seeds, leaving ¼- to ½-inch shell. Combine meat, grated onion and potato, salt and cold water. Stuff squash with this mixture. Place in shallow roasting pan or casserole.

Meanwhile, fry sliced onion and tomatoes in fat until lightly browned, place around squash in pan. Add boiling water enough to fill pan to depth of 1 inch. Cover pan with its own cover or foil, bake at 350° for 1 hour. Halfway through baking add sugar and sprinkle with salt and pepper. When cooked, cut into 1-inch slices, serve with sauce. Serves 4 to 6.

* Cocozelle looks like an overgrown zucchini. However, any soft-rind squash can be prepared in the same way. If only smaller squashes are available, use 2 6- to 8-inch squashes, with same amount of filling.

STUFFED VEAL BRISKET

5 pounds brisket of veal*
2½ teaspoons salt
½ teaspoon pepper
¼ teaspoon ginger

¼ cup potato flour
2 tablespoons chicken fat
1 onion, diced
½ cup boiling water

* Veal breast may be used in place of brisket, filled with the same stuffing.

Have butcher make pocket in center of brisket. Fill with stuffing (see instructions below). Close opening with toothpicks or poultry skewers, dredge outside of meat with mixture of seasonings and potato flour. Place in roasting pan in oven preheated to 500°, with chicken fat spread over top. Sear until meat starts to brown, then reduce heat to 300°, add diced onion and boiling water, cover tightly and cook until meat is very tender, about 3 hours. Makes 8 to 10 servings.

Stuffing

4 matzos, crumbled	2 tablespoons chicken fat
½ cup water	1 teaspoon salt
3 eggs, beaten	¼ teaspoon pepper
1 tablespoon chopped parsley	¼ teaspoon ginger
	2 tablespoons chopped onion

Sprinkle crumbled matzos with water, add remaining stuffing ingredients, blending well. Force into pocket cut in center of brisket.

ROASTED POTATOES

Peel small potatoes. Place in Pyrex casserole; sprinkle with salt, pepper and paprika. Add 1 large onion cut fine, and 3 tablespoons chicken fat, or other shortening. Cover; bake in oven until potatoes are done. Remove cover, baste frequently to brown.

PINEAPPLE PUDDING

4 eggs, separated	Grated rind ½ lemon
⅔ cup granulated sugar	or ½ orange
2 cups drained crushed pineapple (1 large can)	½ cup matzo meal
	½ cup chopped nuts

Beat egg whites until stiff. Separately beat egg yolks until thick, add sugar, well-drained pineapple, grated rind and matzo meal. Fold in beaten egg whites, spoon into greased 1½-quart casserole. Sprinkle nuts over top and, if desired, sprinkle with a little additional sugar. Bake at 350° for 45 minutes, until top is delicately browned. Makes 6 servings.

PASSOVER DAIRY MEAL I

Baked Oranges

Fresh Fish Patties   Mashed Potatoes

Vegetable Salad

Cheese Blintzes   Sour Cream

Chocolate Sponge Cake   Tea

BAKED ORANGES

3 oranges	6 tablespoons sugar
1½ tablespoons butter	or honey
	Juice of 1 lemon

Place oranges, which have been cut in halves, in a casserole. Sprinkle each orange with sugar and cover with the butter and sprinkle with lemon juice. Bake in moderate oven about 1 hour.

FISH PATTIES

1 pound fillets of haddock or sole	1 teaspoon sugar
	¾ teaspoon salt
1 medium onion, quartered	⅛ teaspoon pepper
1 medium potato, cooked	¼ cup potato stock
1 carrot, grated	Matzo meal
1 tablespoon minced parsley	Deep fat or oil for frying
1 egg, beaten	

Put raw fish through food grinder with the quartered onion. Cook the potato, saving ¼ cup of the liquid or stock in which the potato cooks. Mash the potato, add to fish mixture with grated onion, parsley, egg, sugar, salt and pepper, and the ¼ cup potato stock. Form into patties, rub each patty in matzo meal. Heat fat or oil (should be 1½ to 2 inches deep) to 370° in electric skillet or deep-fat fryer. Drop patties into fat, fry until golden. Serve at once. Makes 4 servings.

CHEESE BLINTZES

3 eggs
½ teaspoon salt

1½ cups water
¾ cup cake meal

Dough
Beat eggs, add water and salt. Stir in cake meal until smooth. This makes a very thin batter. Fry thin sheets on hot, slightly greased pan. Turn out on clean cloth or towel.

Filling
Mix together 1 pound pot cheese or farmer cheese, 2 eggs, ½ teaspoon salt, 2 tablespoons sour cream and, if desired, a tablespoon of sugar. Mix well until of smooth consistency. Place a spoonful on each sheet of dough. Roll up and fry or bake in butter. Serve with sour cream. Makes about 16.

CHOCOLATE SPONGE CAKE

6 eggs, separated
1 cup sugar
½ cup cake meal
3 tablespoons Passover cocoa

2 tablespoons water
½ cup chopped nuts
1 tablespoon orange juice

Beat egg whites stiff; then gradually beat in the sugar. Beat egg yolks until thick and smooth; then fold into whites and sugar. Sift together cake meal and cocoa and fold into egg mixture, a little at a time. Add water slowly, fold in nuts, add orange juice. Bake in pan (13 x 9 x 2 inches) lined with waxed paper for 45 minutes at 325° or until top springs back when touched.

PASSOVER DAIRY MEAL II
Potato Soup
Baked Gefilte Fish Mold
Fresh Vegetable Salad   Horse-radish Sauce
Jelly Roll   Tea   Coffee

POTATO SOUP

3 large potatoes, peeled, quartered	4 cups water
1 onion, quartered	1 teaspoon salt
2 carrots, diced	1 tablespoon butter
4 stalks celery with green tops, chopped	1 tablespoon potato starch
	2 cups hot milk

Place vegetables in pot with water and salt, cook until very tender, then force through coarse sieve or strainer. Melt butter, blend with potato starch, slowly add 1 cup of the hot milk, then the strained vegetable stock. Adjust seasoning to taste, add remaining cup milk. Makes 6 servings.

BAKED GEFILTE FISH MOLD

2 pounds fish fillets: whitefish, pike, or mixed fish	Dash of pepper
	2 eggs
2 onions, chopped	½ cup cold water
1 carrot, grated	2 tablespoons melted butter or oil
1 teaspoon oil	Green pepper rings
1 tablespoon sugar	Small slices of onion
1 teaspoon salt	

Put fish through food grinder with chopped onion; add grated carrot, oil, sugar, salt, pepper, beaten eggs and cold water. Blend well.

Brush butter over bottom of Pyrex loaf pan (9 x 5 x 3 inches). Place green pepper rings across bottom of pan, then slices of onion inside each green pepper ring. Spoon fish mixture over pepper rings. Bake 1 hour at 350°, uncovered. Remove from oven, turn out upside down on platter. Slice, serve hot or cold. Makes 6 to 8 servings.

JELLY ROLL

6 eggs, separated	¼ cup potato starch
⅛ teaspoon salt	½ cup sifted cake flour.
¾ cup sugar	1 cup jelly
2 teaspoons lemon juice	Confectioners' sugar

Beat egg whites stiff, add salt. Beat in ½ of the sugar. Add balance of sugar to the well-beaten yolks. Fold yolks and whites together. Fold in lemon juice, then potato starch and cake flour, sifted together. Line a 13 x 9 x 2-inch pan with waxed paper, pour in batter, bake 20 minutes at 350°. Turn out onto cold wet towel, wrung as dry as possible. Spread immediately with jelly and roll up. Dust top with sifted confectioners' sugar.

PASSOVER DAIRY MEAL III

Vegetable Soup

Omelet   Cottage Potatoes (see p. 58)

Lettuce and Tomatoes

Strawberry Refrigerator Cake

Tea or Coffee

VEGETABLE SOUP

2 medium onions, chopped
2 stalks celery, chopped
2 carrots, diced fine
½ green pepper, minced
2 quarts water
1 tablespoon salt,
   or to taste

1 medium potato, diced
3 or 4 tomatoes, peeled,
   chopped; or 1-pound
   can peeled tomatoes
½ teaspoon sugar
2 tablespoons butter
3 tablespoons Passover
   egg barley

Cook onions, celery, carrots and green pepper in salted water ½ hour; add potato and tomatoes, continue to cook at lowest heat until vegetables are very soft. Add remaining ingredients, continue to cook slowly. Total cooking time should be 1 hour. Makes 8 servings.

OMELET

3 eggs, separated
3 tablespoons water

1 tablespoon butter
Salt and pepper to taste

Beat yolks, salt and pepper until thick. Add water and mix well. Beat whites until stiff and fold into yolks. Melt butter in 8-inch skillet, spread mixture evenly and bake in moderate oven (350°) about 10 minutes or until omelet is just firm but still moist. Serves 2.

STRAWBERRY REFRIGERATOR CAKE

1 quart strawberries
1 cup granulated sugar
3 eggs, well beaten

1 cup heavy cream,
   whipped
Sponge cake strips

135

Wash, stem and crush the berries, holding out a few for garnish. Add sugar to berries, let stand at room temperature an hour or longer. Drain juice, blend this with beaten eggs, then cook over lowest heat, stirring constantly, until thickened. Cool, fold in the whipped cream and the berries. Line a rectangular Pyrex dish or shallow casserole with strips of stale sponge cake, add half the berry mixture, then more cake, and remaining berry mixture, top with layer of cake. Let stand in refrigerator at least 12 hours. Serve garnished with whole berries. Makes 10 to 12 servings.

PASSOVER DAIRY MEAL IV

Cold Beet Borsht (see p. 154)   Diced Cucumbers

Broiled Fresh Salmon

Baked Potatoes   Fresh Salad Bowl

Cream Puffs   Tea or Coffee

BROILED SALMON

Place slices of salmon, 1 inch thick, in shallow dish. Sprinkle with salt and pepper and dot with butter. Broil in preheated oven 4 inches from heat until lightly browned on 1 side, approximately 10 minutes. Turn over, squeeze lemon juice over the salmon. Baste with melted butter and continue to broil about 5 to 8 minutes. One-pound salmon serves 2 or 3.

CREAM PUFFS

Pastry

1 cup water	1 cup matzo meal
⅓ cup fat	Pinch of salt
	4 eggs

Bring water and fat to boil, then pour in meal and salt and continue to cook, and stir, until dough no longer sticks to pot. Remove from fire, add unbeaten eggs, 1 at a time, beating in each one thoroughly. Drop by tablespoons on greased baking sheet and bake for 25 minutes at 450°, then for about another 45 minutes at 325° or until crisp and golden. Cut off tops when cool, spoon in filling, replace tops.

Filling

2 eggs	1 tablespoon potato flour
¾ cup sugar	1 lemon
	1 cup water

Beat eggs well. Mix sugar and flour, then add to eggs, beating in slowly. Add lemon juice and water. Cook in double boiler over hot water until thickened and smooth. When cool, spoon filling into shells. (If filling is forced into puffs through a small opening with a pastry tube, double the recipe, as the shells hold more when not slit.) Makes 8 large cream puffs.

PASSOVER DAIRY MEAL V

Grapefruit Halves

Baked Fillets of Sole	Potato Stuffing
Buttered Beets	Spring Salad
Prune Whip Macaroons	Tea or Coffee

FILLETS OF SOLE WITH POTATO STUFFING

4 small fillets of sole (1 pound)	1 egg, beaten
4 medium potatoes	1 cup milk
2 onions, sliced	¾ teaspoon salt
4 to 5 tablespoons butter	1 large tomato, sliced (optional)

137

Cook potatoes, drain, mash. Fry the sliced onion in 3 table-spoons of the butter until soft; add half the onion to the mashed potato with the egg and ¼ teaspoon salt. Blend well. Place ¼ the potato mixture in each fillet, roll up and secure with toothpick. Place remaining onion in bottom of baking dish, with rolled-up fillets over the onion. Add the milk, dot with remaining butter, sprinkle with remaining salt. Place slices of tomato over top, if desired, sprinkling these with salt and butter. Bake at 350° for 30 minutes. Serves 4.

SPRING SALAD

1½ cups chopped cucumber	onion
1 cup chopped green	½ cup diced celery
	½ cup grated raw carrot

Mix vegetables together; season with salt, oil and vinegar. Serve on lettuce leaf.

PRUNE WHIP

Sweeten 2 cups of drained stewed prunes to taste. Mash through a sieve. For 1½ cups of prune pulp, fold in an equal amount of whipped cream or stiffly beaten egg whites. Pile in sherbets and chill.

COCONUT MACAROONS

3 egg whites	½ cup sugar
1/16 teaspoon salt	½ teaspoon lemon juice
	2½ cups shredded coconut

Beat egg whites stiff, add pinch of salt, then gradually add sugar. Beat again. Add lemon juice and coconut. Mix well. Drop from teaspoon onto greased baking sheet. Bake 15 minutes at 350°, or until light golden brown. Makes 24.

PASSOVER DAIRY MEAL VI

Cream of Celery Soup

Fish Chowder of Fresh Salmon or Halibut

Tossed Salad

Chremsel   Tea or Coffee

CREAM OF CELERY SOUP

5 stalks celery, chopped
1 medium onion,
  quartered
4 cups milk
2½ tablespoons butter

2½ tablespoons potato
  starch
1 cup cream
2 teaspoons salt,
  or to taste

Cook celery and onion in 2 cups milk for 20 minutes. Discard onion. Melt butter, blend with potato starch, slowly add remaining 2 cups milk. Simmer until smooth. Add celery-milk mixture, the cream, and salt to taste. Reheat slowly just before serving, without permitting it to come to a boil. Makes 8 servings.

FISH CHOWDER

1½ pounds fresh salmon
  or halibut
2 medium onions
2 carrots

2 stalks celery with tops
3 potatoes
Salt, pepper

Slice onion and carrots; dice celery; cut potatoes in cubes. Cook the vegetables for 10 minutes in approximately 1 cup water, which has been seasoned with salt and pepper to taste.

Place fish in pot, either in 1 piece or in serving portions, add 1 cup milk, continue cooking over low heat for 20 to 30 minutes, until the fish flakes easily. Serves 4.

CHREMSEL

6 eggs, beaten	¼ teaspoon powdered
1½ cups matzo meal	ginger
6 tablespoons cold water	1 cup shelled walnuts
3 tablespoons softened	or almonds, ground
butter	⅓ cup cold sweetened tea
1 teaspoon salt	Melted butter, about 3
½ cup chopped, well-	tablespoons
drained pickled beets	Syrup of 6 tablespoons each
⅓ cup honey	honey and butter

Combine eggs, meal, water, butter and salt, forming into a dough. Let stand ½ hour. Meantime, combine beets, ⅓ cup honey, ginger and nuts in skillet; place over heat, cook, stirring until mixture is thick. Remove from heat, add tea. Take small pieces of the dough, with fingers form into triangular pieces ¼ inch thick, place on greased baking sheet. Spoon a little of the beet mixture over each triangle of dough, top with another triangle of dough to fit, so that beet mixture forms a filling. Brush melted butter over top of each. Bake in oven preheated to 400° for ½ hour. Turn after 15 minutes so that they will brown evenly on each side. Heat syrup of 6 tablespoons honey and 6 tablespoons butter in skillet; when filled chremsel are browned, place in syrup to glaze on each side. Serve hot or cold. Makes about 36.

PASSOVER DAIRY MEAL VII

Grapefruit Juice

Baked Stuffed Pike   Scalloped Potatoes

Cucumber Salad

Fruit Salad with Cheese Balls

Cookies   Tea or Coffee

BAKED STUFFED PIKE

2½-pound pike*
6 matzos
4 tablespoons chopped parsley
2 tablespoons grated onion
1 onion, minced
¼ teaspoon red pepper
¼ teaspoon black pepper

2½ teaspoons salt
Matzo meal
5 tablespoons butter
1 tablespoon potato flour
2 cups water
2 cups fresh tomatoes, cut up
2 tablespoons chopped green pepper

Scale and clean fish, sprinkle with salt inside and out. Soak matzos in water until soft; squeeze as dry as possible. Add 2 tablespoons of the parsley, half the grated onion, half of the red and black pepper and 1½ teaspoons salt. Stuff fish with this mixture. Pin edges of fish together by inserting toothpicks in holes pierced about 1½ inches apart; then lace string around the toothpicks. Dredge stuffed fish with matzo meal, salt and pepper and put 5 tablespoons butter on top of fish. Place fish on strip of cheesecloth or heavy aluminum foil in bottom of baking pan. (The cloth facilitates the removal of fish when done.) Bake uncovered in 350° oven for ½ hour. Mix together potato flour, water, tomatoes, minced green pepper and remaining onion, 2 remaining tablespoons parsley, 1 teaspoon salt, and remainder of red and black pepper. Pour sauce over fish and continue baking another 30 minutes at 325°, basting frequently with sauce. Lift fish from pan by holding ends of cloth; place on platter and gently ease cloth from under fish. Makes 6 servings.

* Perch or sea bass may be prepared the same way.

141

SCALLOPED POTATOES

4 medium potatoes
1 tablespoon potato flour

4 tablespoons butter
Salt, paprika
2 cups milk

Peel potatoes, cut in thin crosswise slices. Put a layer of potatoes in a buttered baking dish. Sprinkle each layer very lightly with potato flour, salt and paprika. Dot with bits of butter, about 1 tablespoon to each layer. Repeat until potatoes are all used. Add milk, and pour over all, barely to cover. Bake in oven at 350° for 45 minutes, covered. Uncover, and bake until soft, tender and browned on top, about 15 minutes longer. Serves 6.

FRUIT SALAD WITH CHEESE BALLS

Arrange any desired fresh fruit, cut in pieces and sweetened to taste, on a lettuce leaf. Mix pot or farmer cheese with some of the fruit juice, form small balls the size of walnuts, roll in chopped nuts and place on salad.

PASSOVER DAIRY MEAL VIII

Fruit Cup
Fried Fillet of Sole or Haddock
Creamed Mashed Potatoes   Buttered Beets and Carrots
Matzo Meal Pancakes
Strawberry Shortcake   Tea or Coffee

FRUIT CUP

3 navel oranges
½ pound seedless grapes
½ cup cut-up fresh
  pineapple

Juice of 1 lemon
Sugar to taste
¼ cup chopped walnuts
  (optional)
3 bananas, sliced

142

Cut oranges in half crosswise, reserving the outer skin to use as salad cups. Remove fruit from each orange half; dice fruit and mix with grapes and pineapple. Sprinkle with sugar, add lemon juice and let stand in cool place for several hours. Before serving, add sliced bananas and chopped walnuts, if desired. Fill orange shells with fruit. Serves 6.

FRIED FILLETS

Fresh fillets of either haddock or sole may be used. Cut fish into portions and wash. Sprinkle with salt. Dip into beaten egg, then in matzo meal, to which salt and pepper have been added. Fry in deep fat (370°) until golden brown on both sides. Drain on absorbent paper.

CREAMED MASHED POTATOES

Boil 6 potatoes and 1 small onion in water, to which salt and pepper have been added. When tender, drain off remaining water. Add butter and 2 or 3 tablespoons heated milk. Beat until creamy and fluffy.

MATZO MEAL PANCAKES

3 eggs, separated	½ cup cold water
½ cup matzo meal	½ teaspoon salt

Beat egg yolks and salt, stir in matzo meal. Beat egg whites until stiff, fold into matzo meal mixture. Drop mixture by spoonfuls onto well greased griddle. Fry until brown on both sides. Serve with sugar or jam, if desired. Makes 12.

143

STRAWBERRY SHORTCAKE

4 eggs, separated
¾ cup sugar
Juice and grated rind of ½
  lemon

¼ teaspoon salt
½ cup sifted cake flour
1 quart strawberries
½ pint whipped cream

Beat egg yolks and sugar together until very light. Add lemon juice and rind, salt and sifted cake flour. Fold in stiffly beaten egg whites. Bake in 2 pie pans or round layer cake pans at 375° until golden, about 12 minutes. Remove from oven, let cool completely. Meantime, wash, trim, slice and sugar berries to taste, saving a few whole berries for garnish. Place the sugared berries mixed with a little of the whipped cream on 1 cake layer, add second layer, cover this with sweetened whipped cream. Decorate with whole berries. Serves 6.

LAG B'OMER

"Is that you, Hadassah?"

"Yes, Mother, I met cousin Ruth. She is quite busy with the preparations for her wedding. As a matter of fact, she says it is scheduled for Lag b'Omer eve. It seems that the invitations have to be changed because of a mistake. Only after they were printed did they think of daylight saving time and that the ceremony cannot take place until one hour later so that it will be after sundown when Lag b'Omer begins."

"Lag b'Omer is a perfect day for us to celebrate with festivities, especially weddings. It recalls a chapter in the long and eventful history of the Jewish people and is the youngest of Jewish festivals. It is connected with an attempt of our ancestors to regain independence as a nation. About sixty years after the Temple in Jerusalem had been burned by the Romans, or about 1,900 years ago, Palestine lay in ruins. Tens of thousands had lost their lives in the long wars with the Romans.

"But our ancestors did not give up hope. They began to rebuild then, as our brave men and women do even today. Farmers went back to the fields and orchards, and artisans to their work benches. Scholars established schools to carry on Jewish learning and the observance of Jewish law. Synagogues took the place of the Temple in Jerusalem and prayer was substituted for sacrifice.

"The leaders then were Bar Cochba and Rabbi Akiba, one an able general, the other a great scholar. They were successful at first, the Romans being driven from a large part of the country and Judea was declared an independent nation. New coins with Bar Cochba's name were put into circulation as a sign of independence. A large army sent by Rome to suppress the uprising was defeated. Rome, however, 'was too mighty and eventually the fall of the city of Bethar—which Bar Cochba held for many months—and the death of Bar Cochba himself put an end to this attempt by the Jews to rebuild their nation in Palestine.

"As usual, the Roman victory on the battlefield was followed with cruel persecution intended to wipe out the Jewish religion and culture. Laws were decreed forbidding circumcision, the observance of the Sabbath and teaching of the Torah. Death was the penalty for observing these commandments."

"How dreadful, Mother! What trials we Jews have had to go through!"

"Yes, to be sure, Hadassah, and even our great scholars, the great Akiba and nine other foremost scholars of the day, were tortured to death. But no amount of persecution or torture could force the Jews to give up their religion and Torah. They continued to live in accordance with Jewish law despite the threat of death. And that is why our Jewish faith has survived through all persecutions.

"Did you know, Hadassah, that the name Lag b'Omer is really the calendar date of this festival?

"*Lag* is made up of Hebrew letters which have a numerical value of thirty-three. *Omer* is the Hebrew word for a measure of grain. In those days the Jews, an agricultural people, celebrated the beginning of the harvest by bringing

146

an *omer* or measure of grain on the second day of Passover as an offering of thanksgiving. They counted seven weeks from that day, celebrating Shavuot on the fiftieth day. These forty-nine days came to be known as *omer* or *sephirah* days, which means 'counting.' Lag b'Omer is observed on the thirty-third day or on the 18th of Iyar.

"During the Bar Cochba revolt, tradition tells us, a terrible epidemic struck the students of Akiba in the *omer* season, and thousands of lives were lost. On Lag b'Omer the epidemic suddenly stopped. As Akiba and his students were so highly regarded by the people, the *omer* weeks were declared a period of semimourning during which no weddings or celebrations were permitted. Only on Lag b'Omer proper is festivity allowed, and it came to be known as 'Scholar's Day'."

"Now I understand why one has to watch the Jewish calendar before making arrangements for a wedding or other festivities. What else of importance is there about this period, Mother?"

"Well, Hadassah, Simeon Bar Yohai, another great teacher of that period, is also linked with this day. He refused to obey the Roman decree against the study of the Torah and continued to teach his pupils despite their cruel decree. Finally, he escaped to a cave in the mountains of Galilee where he lived for thirteen years and where each year on Lag b'Omer he was visited by his students. When he died on Lag b'Omer he requested that his death be observed by celebration rather than by mourning.

"Two other important events are said to have occurred on that day. Manna, eaten by the Israelites in the desert on their journey from Egypt to Palestine, came down for the first time on the 18th of Iyar. The second event was the

147

beginning of Haman's downfall, when he led Mordecai through the streets of Shushan on the 18th of Iyar.

"There are no special prayers or blessings for this festival. Thus the story of Lag b'Omer lives on in its customs.

"In Palestine, Meron is said to be Bar Yohai's burial place. There Lag b'Omer is celebrated more joyfully than anywhere else in the world. It is near Safed where hundreds of pious Hassidim from all parts of Palestine and from other countries come to honor the great teacher and scholar and the ideals for which he stood. They chant psalms, sing Hassidic songs and study the Zohar, the holy book ascribed to Bar Yohai."

LAG B'OMER TEA MENU

Pineapple Basket Salad

Cheese Straws   Toasted Raisin Bread

Cake   Cookies   Nuts   Candies

Tea or Coffee

PINEAPPLE BASKET SALAD

Cut pineapples into halves, lengthwise, leaving green stems. Scoop out the pulp in cubes or balls. Mix with other fruit such as diced oranges and peaches and pile in pineapple baskets. Serve topped with mayonnaise or whipped cream.

CHEESE STRAWS

1 cup flour
¼ pound butter

1 3-ounce package cream cheese
1 cup grated American cheese

Knead together flour, butter and cream cheese until well blended. Roll out and sprinkle with a little of the grated American cheese. Fold over and roll out again. Sprinkle with more cheese and continue in this manner until all the cheese has been absorbed. Roll into ball and chill until very firm. Roll out on lightly floured board to ½ inch thick and cut in strips ½ inch wide and 2 inches long. Twist and bake in hot oven (450°) until golden, 8 to 10 minutes.

TOASTED RAISIN BREAD

1 pint (2 cups) milk	½ cup sugar
¾ cup (12 tablespoons) butter	1 teaspoon salt
	½ cup seedless raisins
1 cake compressed yeast or 1 envelope active dry yeast	1 whole egg, beaten
	8 cups sifted all-purpose flour
	1 egg yolk

Heat milk to scalding. Pour 1½ cups hot milk over butter in large mixing bowl. Cool remaining milk to lukewarm, add sugar and salt, then yeast; stir to dissolve. To the butter mixture add the raisins, egg, and 1 cup flour. Mix well, add dissolved yeast and continue adding flour until a stiff dough is formed. Let rise until doubled in warm place free from drafts (80°). Turn out on lightly floured board, knead until smooth and elastic. Form into 2 loaves, place in greased loaf pans. Brush each with the egg yolk, let rise again until doubled. Bake in oven preheated to 350° for 1 hour until top is crusty and golden. Makes 2 loaves.

Note: If preferred, 1 loaf may be frozen to be served later. After baking and after bread has cooled completely, wrap securely in plastic and store in freezer. When ready to use, allow 3 hours to defrost.

SHAVUOT

"I have often heard Shavuot referred to as the Feast of Weeks, Mother."

"The word *shavuot* means weeks. In the early days, Hadassah, the exact date of Shavuot was figured by counting for seven weeks from the second day of Passover. It was celebrated on the fiftieth day. It is also known as Pentecost, the Greek word meaning the fiftieth day. During these seven weeks no festivities are permitted. When a fixed calendar was adopted, the sixth day of Sivan was specified as the date. Shavuot is also known as the Festival of Harvest and the Season of the Giving of the Law.

"Shavuot was originally observed as an agricultural festival which marked the beginning of the wheat harvest. At this season the first of the fruits of the soil were offered to God. Customarily, no cereal offering of the new crop was made before Shavuot. When Shavuot arrived every housewife ground fresh flour from the new grain and baked bread and cakes for the family feast. In the Temple at Jerusalem a special cereal sacrifice was offered of two loaves of bread baked from the new crop. Each man brought the first of his crop of barley, wheat, grapes, figs, olive oil, dates and pomegranates, the 'seven varieties' for which Palestine was famous. This token reminded the Israelites that everything belonged to the Lord, that they were merely the custodians of these products. They were enjoined to share the harvest with the poor and the stranger. One who had many possessions was responsible for alleviating the suffering of those who were less fortunate. Shavuot today is a reminder of the social obligations of man to man.

"The festival is associated with the great historical event, the giving of the Ten Commandments through Moses on Mount Sinai."

"Just think, Mother, after the Exodus of our people from Egypt a way of life was evolved that seems to be followed by righteous people throughout the world."

"Since the Ten Commandments are the guiding principles by which we live, we ought to review them more frequently in our own minds for guidance in our everyday life. How many of us really know the Ten Commandments? Hadassah, do you know them?"

"Let me think now, we did memorize them so well in one class that I believe I can still recite them. They are:

Thou shalt have no other gods before me.

Thou shalt not make unto thee any graven images.

Thou shalt not take the name of the Lord thy God in vain.

Remember the Sabbath to keep it holy.

Honor thy father and thy mother.

Thou shalt not kill.

Thou shalt not commit adultery.

Thou shalt not steal.

Thou shalt not bear false witness against thy neighbor.

Thou shalt not covet anything that is thy neighbor's."

"Splendid, Hadassah! On Shavuot the Ten Commandments are recited in the synagogue, as are other appropriate selections from the Torah. The *Akdamot*, a most beautiful Shavuot prayer, tells of God's love, of Israel's devotion to the Torah, and of the hope for the Messiah when goodness will reign in the world."

"Speaking of the Torah reminds me of a few lines one of our teachers in Hebrew school taught us:

The more Torah the more life,

The more schooling the more wisdom

The Torah is a tree of life

And happy are those who guide themselves by it.

"Shavuot marks the birthday of Israel's religion, just as Passover is the birthday of Israel's nationhood. The presentation of the Decalogue has proven to be of the utmost importance both to Israel and to the world, since it has become the basis of modern civilization. Since the exile from Palestine, the Torah has been the single tie that bound the Jewish people together.

"The Book of Ruth is read in the synagogue on Shavuot because the story of Ruth embracing Judaism is compared with the acceptance of the Torah by all Israel. During a famine in Palestine, a Jewish family from Bethlehem went to the land of Moab, where living conditions were more favorable. The family consisted of Elimelech, his wife Naomi and their two sons, Mahlom and Chilion. The two sons married two Moabite maidens, Orpah and Ruth. After some years the men died in Moab, leaving the three women widowed. Naomi wished to return to the land of her fathers and she suggested that, since her daughters-in-law were not of the same faith as she, they return to their own homes. Orpah did as she suggested but Ruth, who had found much happiness in her association with Naomi, insisted on accompanying her wherever she went, declaring, 'Whither thou goest I will go and where thou lodgest I will lodge; thy people shall be my people and thy God my God.' This declaration became the pattern of loyalty in the family relationship which has come down through the centuries, and today is often quoted as the ideal in close human associations.

"In Bethlehem, Ruth lived up to this principle by providing the aged Naomi with the necessities of life by working in the fields and conducting herself in accordance with the Hebrew precepts. Eventually Ruth remarried and history tells us that King David was her direct descendant and was born on Shavuot.

"The story gives a vivid description of the agricultural life in ancient Palestine, particularly of the poor who gleaned in the fields at harvest time. It tells how the poor were allowed to pick up the fallen ears of grain and the forgotten sheaves and also to cut the grain left for them in the corners of the field, all in accordance with carefully prescribed Jewish law.

"Some Jews pass the entire night of Shavuot in reciting *Tikun Lail Shavuot*, a collection of excerpts from the Bible and from rabbinic literature, in appreciation for the gift of the Torah.

"The spirit of this joyous holiday is heightened by the decorating of the home and the synagogue with flowers and green branches and plants and fruits. Dairy dishes are usually prepared, with milk and honey. Delicacies such as bagels, blintzes and honey cakes are particularly popular. The honey and milk represent the Torah and learning, the Torah being spiritually as sweet as honey and as nourishing as milk. The flowers and fruits represent the land and crops. They also commemorate the harvest festivals as it is believed to be the judgment day for the thriving of the fruits of trees. It is customary to bring plants and flowers or fruits when visiting friends or relatives on Shavuot."

"Mother, why do we serve dairy meals on Shavuot?"

"There is a legend, Hadassah, that prior to Shavuot there was no *kashrut;* the laws given that day through Moses included that of kashering meat. When the children of Israel returned to their tents there was no time to prepare any meat dishes; therefore a quick dairy meal was prepared. Most of us carry on the tradition of serving dairy foods.

"It is obvious, Hadassah, that it is by the observance of these holidays and customs in our homes that we have been able to retain the religion and traditions of our heritage."

SHAVUOT DINNER I

Grilled Grapefruit Halves
Cold Beet Borsht
Celery   Olives   Pickles
Baked Stuffed Whitefish   Stewed Tomatoes
Cauliflower au Gratin
Green Beans   Lettuce Hearts
Cheese Knishes with Sour Cream
Tea or Coffee   Cookies

GRILLED GRAPEFRUIT HALVES

Prepare grapefruit. Sprinkle each half with 1 teaspoon brown or white sugar, dot with butter. If desired, each half may also be sprinkled with one dessertspoon wine or brandy. Place on broiling rack, 3 inches below flame. Broil about 10 to 15 minutes.

COLD BEET BORSHT

2 bunches beets	⅓ cup sugar
2 quarts water	2 teaspoons salt, or to taste
Juice of 2 lemons	Sour cream
	Diced cucumbers

Peel and grate raw beets; dice red stalks. Boil in water until tender. Add lemon juice, sugar and salt, continue cooking ½ hour longer. Cool. When cold, strain, serve topped with sour cream and diced cucumbers. Makes 8 servings.

BAKED STUFFED WHITEFISH

3-pound whitefish, dressed	½ teaspoon pepper
1½ cups stale bread crumbs	½ teaspoon summer savory
2 tablespoons butter	2 eggs, beaten
1 small onion, chopped	Seasoned flour
1 teaspoon salt	Melted butter, about ¼ cup

Have backbone of fish removed. Sprinkle inside and out with salt. Make stuffing of bread crumbs, 2 tablespoons butter, onion, salt, pepper, savory and beaten eggs. Stuff cavity of fish, fasten with toothpicks, sew up with thread. Dredge in seasoned flour. Place in baking dish, brush with melted butter, cover (use foil if dish has no cover), and bake at 350° for ½ hour or until flesh is lightly browned and firm to the touch. Makes 4 to 6 servings.

CAULIFLOWER AU GRATIN

Separate cauliflower into small pieces. Boil in salted water. When tender, drain off water and place in Pyrex baking dish. Make a white sauce as follows: Blend 2 tablespoons butter and 2 tablespoons flour, slowly add 1½ cups milk and ½ teaspoon salt. Cook slowly, stirring constantly, until thickened and smooth. Add 1½ cups grated cheese. Pour sauce over cauliflower and sprinkle bread crumbs over cheese sauce. Dot with butter and bake until crumbs are golden brown in a moderate oven (350°).

CHEESE KNISHES

Filling

1 pound pot or farmer cheese

2 eggs, beaten

¼ teaspoon salt

½ of 8-ounce package (4 ounces) cream cheese, softened

⅛ teaspoon pepper

Combine cheese, half of 8-ounce package cream cheese, eggs and seasonings for filling.

Pastry

3 cups sifted all-purpose flour

½ teaspoon baking powder

½ teaspoon salt

4 tablespoons cream cheese

½ cup melted butter

½ teaspoon salt

Combine flour, baking powder and salt, work in softened cream cheese and melted butter to make firm dough. Separate into 6 pieces. Roll out each very thin (⅛-inch thick). Brush melted butter over surface. Place about 3 tablespoons filling on each, spreading along 1 edge. Roll up, pressing edges together. Place in baking pan, not too close together. Bake in oven preheated to 375° for 30 minutes or until golden brown. Slice, serve with thick sour cream. Makes 18 knishes.

SHAVUOT DINNER II

Chicken Livers and Mushrooms

Lima Bean and Barley Soup

Broiled Spring Chicken

Varnishkes

Asparagus

Beet Mold

Rhubarb and Strawberry Pie

Tea

CHICKEN LIVERS AND MUSHROOMS

1 medium onion, sliced	2 tablespoons chicken fat
½ pound mushrooms, sliced	1 pound chicken livers, cut in pieces
	Salt, pepper to taste

Fry onion and mushrooms in chicken fat until lightly browned. Add livers, simmer about 10 minutes. Season to taste. Makes 6 appetizer servings.

Note: Beef liver may be used instead of chicken liver, but should be baked or broiled before adding to onions.

LIMA BEAN AND BARLEY SOUP

2 pounds soup bones	½ cup barley
2 quarts cold water	½ cup dried lima beans
1 onion	1 tablespoon chopped parsley
2 carrots	
3 stalks celery	Salt and pepper to taste

Cover soup bones with cold water. Bring to boil and skim. Add vegetables, beans, barley, parsley, salt and pepper. Simmer slowly about 2 hours. Makes 6 to 8 servings.

BROILED SPRING CHICKEN

Allow 1 broiler for each 2 to 4 persons. Cut each in halves or quarters. Rub a cut lemon, grated onion and garlic salt, if desired, over skin of chicken. Sprinkle all pieces with paprika or powdered ginger. Let stand in refrigerator several hours. To broil, place on aluminum foil in broiler pan 4 to 6 inches from heat in preheated oven. Turn frequently until crisply brown, basting each time with drippings, allowing 20 to 30 minutes' cooking time. Serve at once.

VARNISHKES

½ pound medium kasha
1 egg, beaten
Salt to taste

2 to 3 tablespoons chicken
fat or oil
Boiling water
½ pound noodle bows

Place kasha in shallow pan, add egg, stir to mix well, and toast over low heat, stirring constantly, until egg is absorbed. Cover with 2 cups boiling water and cook in saucepan over moderate heat for 15 minutes. Separately, in another pan, cook the noodle bows in boiling salted water until tender, about 15 minutes; drain, add to kasha with chicken fat or oil. Adjust seasoning, serve hot. Serves 6–8.

BEET MOLD

1 can (16 ounces) shoe-
string beets
1 can (20 ounces) crushed
pineapple

1 bottle (6 ounces) pre-
pared horse-radish
2 packages kosher lemon-
flavored gelatin
1 teaspoon salt

Drain juice from beets and pineapple, combine with liquid drained from horse-radish. Measure liquid, add water if necessary to make 2½ cups. Heat combined liquid, add to gelatin, stir to dissolve. Chill. When starting to set, add beets, pineapple, horse-radish and salt. Pour into 8 individual molds or 1½-quart mold. Chill until firm. Unmold by dipping in hot water and pulling gelatin away from edges with fingers. Serve topped with mayonnaise, if desired. Makes 8 servings.

RHUBARB AND STRAWBERRY PIE

Crust

2 cups sifted all-purpose flour

¾ cup vegetable shortening

3 tablespoons cold water

1 tablespoon vinegar

¼ teaspoon salt

Cut shortening into flour with 2 knives or pastry blender. Add water and vinegar; mix lightly. Put this mixture on wax paper, fold and pat the paper together; then divide dough into 2 portions, roll out each on lightly floured board to fit 9-inch pie pan.

Filling

1½ cups rhubarb

1½ cups strawberries

1 egg, slightly beaten

2 tablespoons cornstarch

1½ cups sugar

Line pie plate with crust. Cut rhubarb in ¼-inch pieces, add berries; sprinkle with cornstarch. Add egg and sugar, mix well; turn into lined pie plate. Cover with top crust or pastry strips, sealing edges. Bake in hot oven for 20 minutes at 425°, then reduce the heat to 325° and bake 25 minutes longer or until crust is golden and the filling bubbling.

THREE WEEKS and TISHA B'AV

"Mother, I heard you discussing the approach of the Three Weeks. What is the significance of this period?"

"You know that because of the ancient customs and observances of our people we should consult the Jewish calendar closely when we plan weddings or other festivities. No weddings are solemnized during the Three Weeks. That is something every Jew should know. The Three Weeks are from the 17th of Tamuz to the 9th of Av. The 17th of Tamuz is observed as a fast day; the 9th of Av is called Tisha b'Av and is also a fast day. It commemorates the destruction of the first and second Temples, and the first and second commonwealths in Palestine. This day, so heavy with the tragedy that befell the Jewish people, is one of mourning and fasting, of grief and sorrow, yet also of confident hope proclaimed by Scripture and cherished throughout Jewish history for the restoration of Zion with God's help.

"I am sure, Hadassah, that you are interested in knowing something of the historic background of this observance.

"The building of the first Temple was begun in the fourth year of King Solomon's reign, some 3,000 years ago. It was destroyed by Nebuzaradan, commander of King Nebuchadnezzar's armies, 2,536 years ago. The second Temple was built after the return from the Babylonian exile 2,466 years ago. It was destroyed by the Romans under

Titus in the year 68. Both the first and second Temples were destroyed on the 9th of Av (Tisha b'Av). Thousands of Jews were exiled from their native land, the kingdom of Judea ended, and with it the political independence of our forefathers. Other nations and faiths died when the lands where they had flourished fell to the conquerors and when the people were sent away into slavery. But such was not our fate.

"Fortunately, after seventy years of exile in Babylon, the Jews received permission to return to Palestine and to rebuild their Temple. This enabled them to resume their life as a people on their own soil, to strengthen and develop their religious, ethical and cultural heritage. During the following six hundred years Judaism grew to maturity in the Holy Land, largely achieving its present form of thought and religious ideals."

"But how did our special home observances in connection with these periods originate, Mother?"

"Well, Hadassah, since the final acts of the destruction of the Temple were in each instance preceded by periods of warfare and siege, it is the general practice of Jews to begin the observance of the mourning period three weeks before Tisha b'Av, to be exact, from the 17th of Tamuz. During the last nine days of this period, except for the Sabbath, Jews abstain from eating meat and drinking wine. Nor are marriages solemnized. The Sabbath immediately preceding Tisha b'Av is known as Shabbat Chazon, because the prophetic reading of the Haphtorah is the chapter *The Vision of Isaiah*, beginning with the word *Chazon*. In this chapter the prophet points with great sternness to the punishment which must follow sin, and says that after the punishment will come the restoration of Zion, with justice.

161

The Sabbath following Tisha b'Av, is known as Sabbath Nachamu because the Haphtorah read on that day begins with *Nachamu, nachamu ami* (Comfort thee, comfort thee, my people), in which the same prophet holds out the promise of comfort and hope to his people."

"Mother, Tisha b'Av is a fast day, is it not?"

"Yes, Hadassah, it begins as all Jewish holy days and festivals, at sundown and continues until the following sunset. A twenty-four-hour fast is observed; signs of mourning are displayed in the synagogue where the curtain is removed from the ark. The congregation sit barefoot on the floor or on low benches and chant the elegies of the Book of Lamentations. Departing from the usual practice as a sign of mourning, the men do not wear the *tallis* or *tephillin* at the morning service but wear them at the afternoon service.

"Jewish tradition ascribes the Book of Lamentations to the prophet Jeremiah who witnessed the destruction of the first Temple. Its passionate poetry expresses the grief of Israel over the catastrophe. In the course of the centuries many *kinnot* or dirges were composed and added to the liturgy of Tisha b'Av. These dirges bewail the loss of the Temple and the land of Israel and voice the universal Jewish hope that the Messiah will come speedily to redeem Israel from its exile.

"The Jew rises from his observance of Tisha b'Av with high confidence in the future of Israel and mankind, and certainty that the Jews who wish to return to Israel will be able to live in peace and freedom; that Israel will be restored to dignity and liberty; that the family of mankind will come to live in peace, and that brotherhood shall prevail among mankind."

MISCELLANEOUS RECIPES

BISCUITS

2 cups sifted all-purpose flour
4 teaspoons baking powder
½ teaspoon salt
2 tablespoons butter
¾ cup cold milk

Sift together flour, baking powder and salt. Cut chilled butter into flour mixture until the size of peas. Now add the chilled liquid to make a soft dough. Knead lightly. Toss onto a floured board and do not handle more than is necessary. Roll out lightly about 1 inch thick. Cut with a floured biscuit cutter. Bake on a buttered cookie sheet in a hot oven (450°), 12 to 15 minutes. Makes 12.

BRAN MUFFINS

¾ cup bran
1¼ cups flour
3 tablespoons sugar
½ teaspoon salt
4 teaspoons baking powder
1 egg
4 tablespoons butter, melted
¾ cup milk

Mix all dry ingredients together, add egg, melted butter and milk to make a soft batter. Beat well until thoroughly mixed. Grease 12 muffin tins. Half fill muffin tins and bake in oven preheated to 425° 15 to 20 minutes until golden and firm. Makes 12.

CORN MUFFINS

1¼ cups flour
¾ cup corn meal
3 teaspoons baking powder
2 tablespoons sugar
½ teaspoon salt
1 cup milk
1 egg, beaten
4 tablespoons butter, melted

Sift together dry ingredients, add milk, egg and melted butter. Mix well, half fill 12 well-greased muffin tins and bake in oven preheated to 400° about 20 minutes until golden and firm. Makes 12.

SOUTHERN SCONES

2 cups sifted all-purpose flour	¼ cup butter
3 teaspoons baking powder	2 eggs
2 tablespoons sugar	⅓ cup sweet cream
½ teaspoon salt	2 tablespoons brown sugar
	½ teaspoon cinnamon

Sift together flour, baking powder, sugar and salt. Add butter, cut into flour mixture with knife or pastry blender until the size of peas. Separate 1 of the eggs, set aside the white. Beat together the yolk with the other whole egg, add to flour mixture with the cream. Knead until smooth. Toss dough on a floured board, pat and roll to ¾-inch thickness. Cut in diamonds about 2 inches across, brush with the reserved egg white, sprinkle with brown sugar and cinnamon and bake in oven preheated to 400° for 15 minutes.

ALMOND FINGERS

2 cups sifted all-purpose flour	¼ teaspoon salt
2 tablespoons sugar	1 egg, beaten
½ teaspoon baking powder	½ cup butter, melted
	Almond Topping

Sift together dry ingredients, add egg and butter. Knead to form a smooth dough. Roll out on lightly floured board to ¼ inch thick. Spread with Almond Topping, cut in strips ½ inch by 2½ inches. Place on greased baking sheet and bake in oven preheated to 375° until lightly browned, about 12 minutes. Makes about 24.

Almond Topping

Beat 1 egg white until stiff, fold in ½ cup sugar and ½ cup chopped shelled almonds.

APPLE SQUARES

4 cups sifted all-purpose flour	2 eggs, beaten
⅛ teaspoon salt	5 or 6 apples, pared, grated
1 teaspoon baking powder	¾ cup granulated sugar
6 tablespoons butter	1 teaspoon cinnamon
	Confectioners' sugar

Sift together flour, salt and baking powder. Cut in butter with knife or pastry blender until size of peas. Add beaten eggs. Knead into smooth dough; divide in half, pat ½ in well-greased 13 x 9 x 2-inch baking pan. Blend together grated apples, sugar and cinnamon; spread mixture over dough. Cover with remaining dough. Place in oven pre-heated to 350° and bake 45 to 50 minutes until golden brown. As soon as pan is removed from oven, sprinkle sifted confectioners' sugar over the top. When cool, cut into squares. Makes 12 to 16.

FRIED APPLE TWISTS

Pastry

2 cups sifted all-purpose flour	⅔ cups shortening
	5 tablespoons water
¼ teaspoon salt	2 tablespoons butter

Filling

3 medium apples, peeled and cut in sixths	¼ cup sugar
	½ teaspoon cinnamon

165

Sift flour and salt; cut in the shortening and mix with water. Knead to form smooth dough. Roll out into a rectangle ½ inch thick; dot with 2 tablespoons butter. Roll up as for Jelly Roll (see page 134); roll out again into a rectangle. Fold sides toward center, making 3 layers; fold from ends to center, making 9 layers in all. Wrap in waxed paper and chill thoroughly. Roll out to rectangle about 18 by 11 inches; cut into 18 1-inch strips. Wind strips of dough around a wedge of apple, pinching ends together. Fry in deep fat, 375°, about 10 minutes, or until golden brown. Remove from fat and drain on absorbent paper. Shake the twists in a paper bag containing a mixture of sugar and cinnamon.

BANANA CAKE

2¼ cups sifted cake flour	1 cup mashed ripe bananas
2½ teaspoons baking powder	½ cup shortening
½ teaspoon baking soda	1 cup white sugar
½ teaspoon salt	2 eggs
1 teaspoon vanilla	¼ cup sour milk or buttermilk

Sift flour, baking powder, salt and soda once. Cream shortening with sugar until fluffy. Add eggs to shortening, 1 at a time, beating after each addition. Stir in vanilla. Combine mashed bananas with sour milk or buttermilk, and add to creamed mixture alternately with the sifted dry ingredients, a little at a time. Beat until smooth and pour into 2 greased 8- or 9-inch layer cake pans. Bake in oven preheated to 375°, about 25 to 30 minutes, until cake springs back when pressed. Spread layers with chocolate or white frosting.

BANBURY TARTS
Pastry

3 cups sifted all-purpose flour	1 cup vegetable shortening
½ teaspoon salt	½ cup cold water
	1 tablespoon vinegar

Combine flour and salt, cut in vegetable shortening with knife or pastry blender until the size of peas. Add water and vinegar; blend well but do not knead. Chill thoroughly, at least 1 hour. Roll out on lightly floured board to ¼ inch thick. Cut into 4-inch rounds and place inside muffin or patty pans. Fill each half-full with Banbury Filling. Bake in oven preheated to 375° until crust is golden and filling swelled and firm, about 35 minutes. Cool before removing from pans.

Banbury Filling

1 egg, beaten	Grated rind and juice of ½ lemon
¾ cup granulated sugar	
2 tablespoons melted butter	¾ cup mixed raisins and currants
¼ cup milk	¼ cup chopped nuts
Pinch of salt	½ teaspoon almond flavoring

Combine all ingredients, blend well, spoon into the unbaked tart shells. Makes 12 to 16.

TUTTI-FRUTTI TARTS

Make pastry for tart shells as in Banbury Tarts but bake shells first by placing over inverted muffin tins or patty pans. Prick all over with tines of fork, bake in oven preheated to 425° for 15 to 20 minutes until golden. Cool before removing from pans. When cold, fill with Tutti-Frutti Filling.

Tutti-Frutti Filling

1 pint heavy cream, whipped	1 cup strawberries, mashed and stemmed
¼ cup sifted confectioners' sugar	½ cup chopped walnuts or pecans

Whip sugar into the cream, when stiff fold in berries and nuts. Fill shells with mixture. Makes 16.

BUTTERSCOTCH ROLLS

4 tablespoons butter, softened	flour
	6 teaspoons baking powder
4 tablespoons sugar	⅛ teaspoon salt
2 eggs, beaten	1 cup sour cream
3 cups sifted all-purpose	Butterscotch Filling

Cream together butter and sugar until fluffy. Add eggs 1 at a time, beating after each. Sift together dry ingredients, add to butter mixture alternately with sour cream, blending well. Chill in refrigerator 20 minutes. Roll out half the dough at a time on lightly floured board to ¼ inch thick, cut into 2 rectangles and spread each with Butterscotch Filling. Roll up as for Jelly Roll (see p. 134), cut into 1-inch slices and place cut side down in well-greased muffin tins lined with paper cups. Bake in oven preheated to 425° for 15 minutes or until golden. Remove immediately from tins. Makes 24.

Butterscotch Filling

Combine ¼ pound butter, melted, with 2 cups brown sugar and ¼ cup crushed nuts.

CHEESE CAKE I

Cake

½ cup butter, softened	flour
½ cup sugar	⅛ teaspoon salt
1 egg, beaten	Cheese Filling
5 tablespoons all-purpose	Meringue

Cream butter and sugar until fluffy, beat in egg, then the flour and salt. Spread mixture in greased 13 x 9 x 2-inch pan and bake in oven preheated to 375° for 15 minutes. Spread with Cheese Filling, return to oven for 15 minutes, then remove from oven, top with meringue, and again replace in oven until meringue is lightly browned.

Cheese Filling

1½ pounds pot or farmer cheese	Juice of ½ lemon
4 egg yolks	½ cup sugar, or to taste

Combine ingredients, beat to blend well.

Meringue

Beat 4 egg whites until stiff, fold in 4 tablespoons sugar.

CHEESE CAKE II

Cake

2 cups corn flakes, crushed fine	½ teaspoon baking soda
1½ cups flour	¼ teaspoon salt
	¼ pound butter, melted
	1 cup brown sugar

Mix all ingredients together well. Put aside 1½ cups of mixture for topping. Pat remainder in base of buttered spring-form mold.

Cheese Filling

4 eggs, beaten
1 cup sugar
2 pounds pot or farmer cheese
1 cup sour cream
1 teaspoon vanilla
2 tablespoons flour
Grated rind of 1 lemon

Mix all ingredients in order given. Spread filling over cake mixture, top with reserved cake mixture. Bake in 325° oven for 1 hour.

CHEESE SQUARES

½ pound butter, melted
1 cup brown sugar, firmly packed
1¾ cups sifted all-purpose
flour
½ teaspoon baking soda
2 cups corn flakes, crushed
Cheese Topping
½ cup chopped nuts

Combine melted butter, sugar, flour, baking soda and corn flakes, beating to blend thoroughly. Spread over bottom of buttered 9-inch-square pan. Cover with Cheese Topping and nuts. Bake in oven preheated to 375° for 40 minutes. After cake is cool, cut into squares.

Cheese Topping

1 pound (16 ounces) pot or farmer cheese
½ teaspoon salt
1 cup sugar
4 teaspoons flour
2 eggs, beaten
1 teaspoon vanilla
Juice of 1 lemon

Combine all ingredients, blending well.

CHINESE CHEWS

¾ cup sifted all-purpose flour
1 teaspoon baking powder
⅛ teaspoon salt
¾ cup sugar
1 cup dates, pitted and chopped
1 cup chopped walnuts
2 eggs, beaten
¼ cup butter, melted

Sift together flour, baking powder and salt; add sugar, dates and nuts, then the eggs and butter. Beat to blend well. Spread in well-greased 13 x 9 x 2-inch pan. Bake in 325° oven for 30 minutes until golden. Cool in pan, cut into squares or bars, then roll in confectioners' sugar.

CHERRY CUSTARD CAKE

Cake

2 eggs, beaten	2 teaspoons baking
½ cup sugar	powder
½ cup oil	⅛ teaspoon salt
2½ cups sifted all-purpose	1 teaspoon vanilla
flour	

Beat eggs until foamy, beat in sugar, then the oil. Sift together flour, baking powder and salt, add to the egg mixture, then beat in vanilla until batter is smooth. Pat ⅔ of dough into ungreased spring-form pan, covering bottom and partway up the sides.

Filling

1 package vanilla pudding	red cherries, drained
mix, cooked as directed	¾ cup cherry juice
on package	1½ tablespoons cornstarch
1 can (1 pound) pitted tart	½ cup sugar

Spread cooked vanilla pudding over the dough, then the drained cherries over the pudding. Roll out remaining cake dough on lightly floured board, cut into long thin strips and form in overlapping lattice strips above the cherries. Make a syrup of the reserved cherry juice, the cornstarch and sugar, boiling until thickened and smooth. Pour this over the cake. Bake in oven preheated to 350° for 45 minutes.

CHOCOLATE CREAM LAYER CAKE

½ cup shortening
1 cup sugar
⅛ teaspoon salt
1 teaspoon vanilla
2 eggs, beaten

2 cups sifted cake flour
2½ teaspoons baking powder
¾ cup milk
Soft Chocolate Frosting

Cream shortening until fluffy, beat in sugar, then salt, vanilla and eggs, 1 at a time. Sift together flour and baking powder, add to shortening mixture alternately with milk until batter is very smooth. Grease or line with waxed paper 2 8-inch round cake pans. Divide batter into the two pans. Bake in oven preheated to 375° for 25 to 30 minutes until cake springs back when pressed. Cool in pan 10 minutes, then turn out on cake racks. When cold, split each layer in half, making 4 layers. Spread layers with frosting.

Soft Chocolate Frosting

⅓ cup unsweetened cocoa
3 tablespoons cornstarch
1⅓ cups sugar

⅛ teaspoon salt
1½ cups milk
1 teaspoon butter
1 teaspoon vanilla

Combine cocoa, cornstarch, sugar and salt. Slowly stir in milk, cook over low heat until it comes to a boil and is thickened, stirring constantly. Remove from stove, add butter and vanilla. Cool slightly, then spread over cake layers.

CHOCOLATE FUDGE CAKE

⅓ cup softened butter
1 cup sugar
1 egg, well beaten
2 cups sifted cake flour
3 teaspoons baking powder

¼ teaspoon salt
½ cup sour cream
½ cup hot coffee
2½ tablespoons cocoa
1 teaspoon baking soda

Cream together butter and sugar. Add beaten egg, then the flour, salt and baking powder (sifted together) alternately with sour cream. Dissolve cocoa and baking soda in coffee, stir into batter, mixing well. Bake in 2 greased 8- or 9-inch layer pans in oven preheated to 350° for 30 minutes. When cake is cold, spread layers with chocolate frosting.

CHOCOLATE FUDGE SQUARES

¼ pound butter, softened
1 cup sugar
2 squares unsweetened chocolate, melted
2 eggs, beaten
⅔ cups sifted all-purpose flour
⅛ teaspoon salt
¼ cup milk
1 teaspoon vanilla
1 cup chopped nuts

Cream butter and sugar, add melted chocolate and beaten eggs. Sift the flour and salt, and add alternately with the milk. Add vanilla and nuts. Bake in greased 8 x 8-inch pan, at 350°, for 30 minutes. Top with Chocolate Frosting.

Chocolate Frosting

1 tablespoon softened butter
1 teaspoon vanilla
2 squares unsweetened chocolate, melted
1 cup sifted confectioners' sugar
1 egg

Cream butter, add vanilla, melted chocolate, and sugar. Add egg and beat mixture until creamy. Spread on cake. When cold, cut in squares.

CHOCOLATE ROLL

2 eggs, separated
1½ tablespoons unsweetened cocoa
½ cup sifted confectioners' sugar
½ teaspoon vanilla

Beat egg yolks until thick, add cocoa, sugar and vanilla, blending well. Beat egg whites until stiff, fold into yolk mixture. Line 9 x 12 shallow baking pan with waxed paper, spread paper with soft butter. Spread chocolate mixture over paper. Bake in oven preheated to 300° for 10 minutes. Turn out on dampened towel. When cold, spread with sweetened whipped cream and roll up like Jelly Roll (see p. 134). Cut in 1-inch slices to serve.

CHOCOLATE SQUARES

½ cup softened butter	1 teaspoon baking powder
¾ cup white granulated sugar	½ teaspoon salt
2 egg yolks	3 squares unsweetened chocolate, grated
1½ cups sifted cake flour	Meringue

Beat butter and sugar until fluffy. Sift together flour, baking powder and salt, add to butter to make a stiff batter. Spread over buttered 9-inch square cake pan. Sprinkle grated chocolate over batter. Spread with Meringue. Bake in 350° oven for 35 minutes.

Meringue
Beat 2 egg whites until stiff, gradually beat in ¾ cup brown sugar and ½ teaspoon vanilla.

CHOCOLATE TORTE

½ cup softened butter	4 eggs, separated
1½ cups sifted confectioners' sugar	4 squares unsweetened chocolate, melted
	1 cup chopped walnuts

Cream butter and sugar. Beat egg yolks until thick, add to butter mixture. Stir in melted chocolate and walnuts. Beat egg whites until stiff, fold in. Divide mixture in thirds, place ⅓ of the mixture in refrigerator, and bake the balance in 2 layer cake pans for 20 minutes at 350°. When layers have cooled, spread chilled mixture between them. Sprinkle top with confectioners' sugar.

DELICATE COCONUT CAKE

1 cup sugar	2 cups sifted cake flour
¼ cup butter, softened	3 teaspoons baking powder
½ teaspoon almond flavoring	½ teaspoon salt
	3 egg whites, beaten stiff
½ teaspoon lemon flavoring	¾ cup shredded or flaked
⅔ cup milk	coconut

Cream together sugar and butter; add flavoring. Sift together dry ingredients and add to first mixture alternately with milk. Fold in stiffly beaten egg whites. Stir in half cup coconut, pour batter into 9-inch tube or spring-form pan. Sprinkle remaining coconut over batter. (No icing required.) Bake in moderate oven (350°) for 45 minutes or until cake springs back when pressed.

COCONUT SQUARES

½ cup shortening	2 eggs
1½ cups brown sugar	1 cup chopped walnuts
1¼ cups sifted flour	1½ cups shredded
¼ teaspoon salt	or flaked coconut
1 teaspoon vanilla	

Cream shortening; add ½ cup of the sugar, 1 cup of the flour and ¼ teaspoon salt. Mix well. Pat into greased pan, 9 x 13 inches. Bake at 375° for 10 minutes. Mix remaining ingredients together. Spread over baked mixture in pan and bake 20 minutes longer. When cool, cut into squares.

CORN FLAKE MACAROONS

2 egg whites

⅛ teaspoon salt

1 cup sugar, brown or white

2 cups corn flakes, crushed

1 cup chopped nuts

1 cup shredded or flaked coconut

½ teaspoon vanilla

Beat egg whites and salt until stiff. Gradually fold in sugar. Fold in corn flakes, nuts, coconut and vanilla. Drop by spoonfuls on greased cooky sheet. Bake at 350° for 15 to 20 minutes.

DATE ALMOND SQUARES

1 cup chopped pitted dates

½ cup water

6 tablespoons softened butter

½ cup sugar

2 eggs, separated

1 teaspoon vanilla

1½ cups sifted all-purpose flour

1 teaspoon baking powder

¼ teaspoon salt

¾ cup firmly packed brown sugar

½ cup chopped almonds

Cook together until thick, dates and water; set aside. Cream butter and sugar; add well-beaten egg yolks and vanilla. Add dry ingredients, which have been sifted together. This makes a stiff dough and it is necessary to use the hands to work dough together well. Press the dough into a greased pan 9 inches square, making the layer about ⅓ inch thick. Spread the date paste over dough. Beat the egg whites stiff and beat in gradually the salt and brown sugar. Spread Meringue (see p. 169) over dates and sprinkle thickly with chopped almonds. Bake in a moderate oven, 350°, about 50 minutes. Cut into squares when cold.

MERINGUE KISSES

2 egg whites

8 tablespoons brown sugar
½ pound almonds, crushed

Beat egg whites until stiff, add sugar a spoonful at a time, beating until glossy. Fold in almonds. Drop by spoonfuls on waxed paper over baking sheet, bake 1 hour in oven at 250°. Remove meringues from baking sheet while hot.

DATE AND NUT REFRIGERATOR COOKIES

½ cup shortening
1 cup brown sugar, well packed
½ teaspoon vanilla
1 egg, beaten

1¾ cups sifted all-purpose flour
½ teaspoon salt
¼ teaspoon soda
½ cup chopped dates
½ cup chopped nuts

Cream shortening; add sugar, vanilla and egg; beat until light. Add sifted dry ingredients, dates and nuts. Mix well. Shape dough into 2-inch roll; wrap in waxed paper; chill overnight. Slice ⅛-inch thick and bake on greased cooky sheets in a 375° oven for 8 or 10 minutes.

DATE AND ORANGE CAKE

½ cup softened butter
1 cup sugar
1 egg
1 cup pitted and chopped dates
½ cup chopped walnuts
Grated rind of 1 orange

1 cup sour milk
2 cups sifted cake flour
1 teaspoon baking powder
1 teaspoon baking soda, dissolved in 1 tablespoon lukewarm water

Cream butter and sugar; add egg and beat well. Add dates, nuts and grated orange rind. Add sour milk alternately with sifted flour and baking powder. Stir in the baking soda, dissolved in water, beat to blend well. Turn into greased 9-inch-square baking dish and bake in moderate oven (350°) for 30 to 35 minutes. This cake does not have to be iced. When you take the cake from the oven, and while still warm, spread with Orange Topping.

Orange Topping

Mix well together the juice of 1 orange and ½ cup sugar, and spread over cake.

DATE PINWHEELS

Pastry

½ cup softened butter	2 cups sifted all-purpose flour
1 cup brown sugar	
2 eggs	1 teaspoon baking powder
	¼ teaspoon salt

Cream butter, add sugar, beaten eggs and beat until smooth. Add dry ingredients, which have been sifted together. Knead into a stiff dough. Chill several hours. Roll out ¼ inch thick. Spread with date filling. Wet edges, roll up and chill well. Slice ¼ inch thick and bake cut side down in hot oven (400°) for 15 minutes.

Filling

1 cup chopped dates	½ cup water
½ cup white sugar	½ cup chopped nuts

Cook dates with sugar and water for 10 minutes over low heat. Add chopped nuts; cool.

DAY AND NIGHT CAKE

Dough

3 tablespoons sugar	1 cup sifted flour
3 tablespoons oil	1 teaspoon baking powder
3 egg yolks	¼ teaspoon salt

Beat together sugar, oil and egg yolks. Add flour, baking powder and salt. Mix well; divide into 3 portions. Roll out each to fit 9-inch-square pan. Grease pan, add first layer of dough, cover with Walnut Filling; add second layer of dough; then the Almond Filling. Cover with the third layer of dough. Bake at 325° for 1 hour. Cool in pan. Cut into small squares before serving.

Walnut Filling

¼ cup chopped walnuts	1 tablespoon water
¼ cup sugar	4 tablespoons of mixture of
1½ tablespoons	3 egg whites, beaten stiff,
unsweetened cocoa	blended with ¾ cup sugar

Almond Filling

½ cup chopped almonds	Remaining egg white
	mixture

DARK FRUIT CAKE

1 pound raisins	½ teaspoon cloves
1½ cups water	½ teaspoon allspice
1½ cups sugar	1 teaspoon baking
¼ cup butter	powder
or shortening	1 teaspoon baking soda
2½ cups sifted all-purpose	½ cup citron peel, cut
flour	in pieces
½ teaspoon salt	½ cup chopped nuts
1 teaspoon cinnamon	2 eggs

Wash raisins and cook them with the water and sugar for 5 minutes. Add butter, and set aside to cool. Sift together the flour, salt, spices, baking powder and baking soda. Add citron peel and nuts to sifted dry ingredients. Beat eggs until light, add to cooled raisin mixture, then to flour mixture. Beat vigorously to blend well. Pour into well-greased loaf pans (9 x 5 x 3 inches) lined with waxed paper. Bake at 325° for 1½ to 2 hours until toothpick inserted in center comes out clean and top is firm, with cake pulling away from side of pans.

APPLE ROLL

4 medium apples, pared, chopped	1 teaspoon cinnamon
1½ cups sugar	½ cup raisins (optional)
2 cups water	4 tablespoons confectioners' sugar
Biscuit Dough	2 tablespoons butter

Set chopped apples aside. Make syrup of sugar and water, cooking slowly until thickened. Meanwhile, make Biscuit Dough, roll out into rectangle ½ inch thick. Spread with chopped apple, sprinkle ½ teaspoon cinnamon and the raisins over apples. Roll up, cut into 1½- to 2-inch slices. Pour syrup into 13 x 9 x 2-inch pan, place slices with cut side down in the syrup. Sprinkle remaining cinnamon, the confectioners' sugar and dots of butter over each slice. Bake in oven preheated to 400° until crust is golden and apples bubbling. Cool slightly, then invert on platter. Serve warm or cold, with heavy cream or Hot Fruit Sauce (see p. 73).

Biscuit Dough

2 cups sifted all-purpose
  flour
½ teaspoon salt
2 tablespoons sugar

4 teaspoons baking powder
3 tablespoons vegetable
  shortening
1 egg, beaten
½ cup milk

Sift together dry ingredients, chop in shortening, add egg and milk to form a soft dough. Knead lightly, then turn out on lightly floured board and roll to rectangle ½-inch thick.

Note: For pareve menu, use orange juice in place of milk in Biscuit Dough.

FUDGE BARS

1 cup white sugar
1 cup brown sugar
¾ cup milk
2 tablespoons light corn
  syrup
2 squares unsweetened

chocolate
3 tablespoons butter
1 teaspoon vanilla
¾ cup chopped nuts
  (optional) or ⅓ cup
  peanut butter

Combine the 2 sugars, milk and corn syrup, cook slowly until thickened; add chocolate cut in small pieces, stir until mixture comes to a boil. Continue to cook and stir until a little of mixture dropped from teaspoon into cup of cold water forms a soft ball. Remove pan from fire, add butter, cool to lukewarm. Add vanilla, beat vigorously until mixture thickens and loses its gloss. Add nuts, if desired. Pour into 9-inch-square pan. Cool. When cold, cut into bars. (If peanut butter is used, add at same time as butter.)

GINGERBREAD

¾ cup shortening	2½ cups sifted all-purpose flour
1 cup brown sugar	
¾ cup molasses	2 teaspoons baking powder
1 cup boiling water	
¾ teaspoon baking soda	2 teaspoons powdered ginger
2 eggs, beaten	

Cream shortening and sugar until fluffy. Add molasses, then the boiling water, in which the soda has been dissolved. Beat in eggs 1 at a time, then gradually add remaining ingredients, which have been sifted together. Grease or line with waxed paper a 9-inch-square pan, pour batter into pan, bake in oven preheated to 375° for ½ hour or until cake springs back when pressed. Serve warm or cold, with applesauce or whipped topping.

REFRIGERATOR COOKIES

½ pound softened butter	½ pint sour cream
3 cups sifted flour	Pinch of salt

Cream butter, add flour, sour cream and salt. Knead well, wrap dough in waxed paper and leave in refrigerator overnight. Next day roll about ¼ of the dough at a time, spread with jam, sprinkle with sugar and roll up like Jelly Roll (see p. 134). Slice ¼ inch thick and place on greased baking sheet. Bake 15 or 20 minutes in oven preheated to 375°.

JAM SQUARES

Cake

¼ cup butter, melted	2 egg yolks
½ cup mixed brown and white sugar	1¼ cups sifted all-purpose flour
1 teaspoon vanilla	½ teaspoon baking soda
	⅛ teaspoon salt

Combine ingredients and spread in 9-inch-square greased pan. Cover with Jam Topping and Meringue as directed below.

Jam Topping and Meringue

1 cup damson plum jam	1 cup chopped walnuts
Grated rind of 1 lemon	2 egg whites, beaten stiff
1 teaspoon lemon juice	2 tablespoons confectioners' sugar

Combine jam with grated rind and juice of lemon. Spread this mixture over cake base. Sprinkle with ½ the nuts. Spread the beaten egg whites over nuts, sprinkle with confectioners' sugar and remaining nuts. Bake in 350° oven for 25 to 30 minutes.

KICHEL

3 eggs	3 teaspoons sugar
½ cup oil	⅞ cup sifted all-purpose flour

Beat eggs, oil, sugar and flour for 20 minutes. Drop ½ teaspoon at a time, on well-greased baking sheet, far apart. Bake 15 to 20 minutes in oven preheated to 375°.

MANDELBROIT

3 eggs, beaten
1 cup sugar
½ cup oil
3 cups all-purpose flour, sifted
3 teaspoons baking powder
¼ teaspoon salt

1½ cups slivered almonds
1 teaspoon almond flavoring
1 teaspoon vanilla
½ teaspoon cinnamon
2 tablespoons orange juice, and grated rind of 1 orange

Beat eggs well, add sugar gradually. Add other ingredients in order given, beating constantly to blend well. Divide into 5 portions, form into rolls and place in slightly greased roasting pan or baking sheet. Bake in a 400° oven for 25 minutes until golden. While hot, cut into slices, and return to oven reduced to 350° for 10 minutes until crisp.

MOTHER'S SWEIBEC

4 eggs, well beaten
1 cup oil

1 cup sugar
3 cups sifted cake flour
1 cup shelled almonds

Beat eggs until fluffy; add oil slowly while beating. Add sugar, then flour and almonds. Form into long rolls. Bake in a shallow pan in oven set at 350° approximately ½ hour. When top is browned, remove from oven. Cut in slices and put back in oven to brown slowly.

MERINGUE CAKE

Batter

½ cup softened butter
½ cup sugar
4 egg yolks
1 cup sifted cake flour

2 teaspoons baking powder
⅛ teaspoon salt
Grated rind and juice of ½ lemon
¼ cup milk

Cream butter, add sugar gradually and continue beating until light and fluffy. Add egg yolks and beat until well blended. Add sifted dry ingredients alternately with milk. Add lemon juice and rind. Pour batter into 2 greased spring-form or 8-inch layer cake pans. Spread Meringue over top of each and bake in slow oven (325°) for 40 minutes. Allow about 10 minutes to cool in oven after heat is turned off, leaving oven door open. Meringue should be dry and light brown.

Meringue

4 egg whites	¼ teaspoon baking powder
½ teaspoon salt	1 cup sugar
	½ cup chopped nuts

Beat egg whites with salt and baking powder until almost stiff. Add sugar gradually, beating constantly until all sugar is thoroughly combined with egg whites. Divide Meringue in half and spread over top of each cake batter. Sprinkle with nuts.

Filling

1¾ cups sugar	⅛ teaspoon salt
5 tablespoons cornstarch	2 eggs, beaten
2 cups scalded milk	½ teaspoon lemon juice

Put all ingredients in double boiler and cook, stirring constantly, until thick. Cool; just before serving, spread filling over top of 1 cake layer; top with second cake layer.

NUT BUTTER BALLS

2 cups sifted all-purpose flour	1 cup softened butter
	2 teaspoons vanilla
¼ cup sugar	2½ cups finely chopped nuts*
½ teaspoon salt	

* Pecans, walnuts, almonds or filberts may be used.

185

Sift flour, sugar and salt together; work in butter and vanilla. Add 2 cups of the nuts and mix well. Shape into ½-inch balls. Roll ½ the balls in remaining nuts. Place all the balls on greased cooky sheets; bake in moderate oven 350°, about 40 minutes. Roll balls in confectioners' sugar while warm.

RUM BALLS

2 cups finely sifted graham cracker crumbs
1 cup crushed nuts
2 tablespoons cocoa
1 cup sifted confectioners'
sugar
⅛ teaspoon salt
1½ tablespoons honey
¼ cup dark sweet rum
Confectioners' sugar

Combine crumbs, nuts, cocoa, sugar and salt. Slowly add honey, which has been blended with rum. Form into small balls with fingers. Roll the balls in confectioners' sugar. Put away in cool place to ripen for 12 hours.

CHERRY BALLS

2 squares unsweetened chocolate
2 squares semisweet chocolate
1 can (15 ounce) condensed milk
18 graham crackers, crushed

Melt chocolate in top of double boiler over hot water. Add condensed milk, cook 10 minutes; remove from heat. Add cracker crumbs. Form into small balls. Place a maraschino cherry in center of each, then roll balls in crushed nuts or shredded coconut.

SWISS PASTRY

¼ pound butter (1 stick)
¼ cup brown sugar, firmly packed
1 egg yolk
1 unbeaten egg white
1 cup sifted all-purpose flour
¼ cup crushed nuts

Cream butter and sugar, until fluffy. Add egg yolk, then flour. Form into balls, dip in egg white, then roll in nuts. Chill.

OATMEAL COOKIES

1 cup butter, softened
1½ cups brown sugar
2 eggs, beaten
1½ cups sifted all-purpose flour
2 tablespoons baking powder
¼ teaspoon salt
½ teaspoon vanilla
1¼ cups quick-cooking oats
1 cup flaked coconut
Maraschino cherries, quartered

Cream butter, add sugar and beat until light. Add well-beaten eggs; then the flour, baking powder and salt, which have been sifted together. Add the vanilla, rolled oats and coconut. Mix thoroughly; place in refrigerator, until well chilled. Roll in tiny balls in palm of hand, place in ungreased pan, press down with fork and place cherry in center of each. Bake in oven preheated to 375° 10 to 12 minutes until golden.

CRISP OATMEAL COOKIES

1½ cups brown sugar, firmly packed
¾ cup melted shortening
6 tablespoons sour milk
½ teaspoon salt
¾ teaspoon vanilla
1½ cups sifted flour
¾ teaspoon soda
3 cups quick-cooking rolled oats

Combine ingredients in order given, mixing thoroughly. Shape into small balls, about 1 inch in diameter, and place on greased cooky sheets. Flatten each cookie to ⅛-inch thickness by pressing with a fork. Bake in a preheated 375° oven for 10 to 12 minutes.

PINEAPPLE CHEESECAKE

Biscuit Dough (see
  p. 181)
½ can crushed drained
  pineapple
1 pound (2 8-ounce

packages) cream cheese
½ cup granulated sugar
1 tablespoon cornstarch
3 eggs, well beaten
½ cup light cream

Line a spring-form pan with Biscuit Dough. Spread the pineapple over the dough. Cream together cream cheese, sugar and cornstarch, add eggs and cream, beat until light. Pour over pineapple. Bake in oven preheated to 350° for 45 minutes. Open oven door, turn off heat, leave cheese-cake in oven until cool. Serves 8.

PINEAPPLE COOKIES

½ cup shortening
½ cup white sugar
½ cup brown sugar, firmly
  packed
1 egg
2 cups sifted all-purpose

flour
1 teaspoon baking powder
½ teaspoon salt
½ cup chopped walnuts
1 cup undrained crushed
  pineapple

Cream shortening; add sugars and the egg, beat until light. Add sifted dry ingredients combined with nuts, alternately with the pineapple. Mix well. Drop from teaspoon 2 inches apart, onto greased cooky sheets. Bake at 350° for 15 to 20 minutes.

PINEAPPLE SQUARES I

Cake

¼ pound butter, softened
½ cup sugar
2 egg yolks, beaten
2 cups sifted all-purpose

flour
1 teaspoon baking powder
3 to 4 tablespoons sweet
  cream
⅛ teaspoon salt

Cream together butter and sugar, add eggs, then the flour,

baking powder and salt, and finally the cream. Knead to blend well, then press into pan 9 x 9 inches square. Bake in 350° oven until a delicate brown, about 25 minutes.

Pineapple Topping

3 ounces semisweet chocolate bits
1 cup crushed pineapple, drained
2 egg whites
½ cup sugar
½ cup coconut

Sprinkle chocolate over baked cake. Spread pineapple on chocolate. Beat egg whites until stiff with ½ cup sugar. Spread on pineapple. Sprinkle with coconut. Bake in a 325° oven until golden, about 20 minutes.

PINEAPPLE SQUARES II

Cake

½ cup softened butter
1 cup sugar
1 egg, beaten
1 cup chopped walnuts
2 teaspoons vanilla
2 squares unsweetened chocolate, grated
2 cups sifted flour

Cream butter, add sugar and egg, beating until light and fluffy. Add walnuts, vanilla, chocolate and sifted flour. This mixture is quite stiff. Pat ¾ of this mixture into a 9-inch-square Pyrex baking dish. Reserve ¼ of the mixture for latticework over Pineapple Topping.

Pineapple Topping

2 eggs
1 cup sugar
1 cup drained crushed pineapple
2½ tablespoons flour

Beat eggs, add sugar, pineapple and flour. Pour over base. Take remainder of base mixture and roll between floured palm of hands, forming thin strips. Arrange these in lattice formation over top. Bake in moderate oven (350°) for 30 to 35 minutes.

PINWHEEL COOKIES

½ cup softened butter
½ cup sugar
1 egg, beaten
3 tablespoons milk
1 teaspoon vanilla
1½ cups sifted all-purpose flour

1 teaspoon baking powder
⅛ teaspoon salt
1-ounce envelope baking chocolate, or 1 ounce unsweetened chocolate, melted

Cream butter and sugar until fluffy, beat in egg, then milk and vanilla. Combine flour, baking powder and salt, work into butter mixture, kneading until smooth. Divide dough in half. To 1 part add chocolate. Chill ½ hour. Roll out each on lightly floured board into thin, oblong sheets. Place chocolate dough over white dough. Roll up as for Jelly Roll (see p. 134). Place in refrigerator until firm. Cut in slices, bake at 325° for 20 minutes or until delicately browned.

PIRISHKES (Turnovers)

Mix 1-pound can pitted tart red cherries, drained, with 2-tablespoons cornstarch and ¾ to 1 cup sugar thoroughly blended.

Dough

½ cup shortening
½ cup sugar
2 eggs
2 cups sifted all-purpose flour

2 teaspoons baking powder
¼ teaspoon salt
1 to 2 tablespoons water

Cream together shortening and sugar, beat in eggs, then add the flour sifted with baking powder and salt. Add 1 tablespoon water at a time to make a soft dough. Roll out on lightly floured board to ¼ inch thick. Cut into 3-inch circles. Place a spoonful of cherry mixture in each. Close up the circles into triangles, pressing together. Bake on greased baking sheet in oven preheated to 375° for 15 minutes or until golden.

POPPY SEED COOKIES I

3 eggs
1 cup sugar
¾ cup oil
Grated rind and juice
  of 1 orange

4 cups sifted all-purpose flour
2 teaspoons baking powder
½ teaspoon salt
¼ cup poppy seeds

Beat eggs, add sugar, oil, orange rind and juice. Add dry ingredients blended with poppy seeds. Roll out thin and cut into desired shapes. Bake in moderate oven (350°) until lightly browned, 12 to 15 minutes.

POPPY SEED COOKIES II

1 cup sugar
½ cup butter
2 eggs
Grated rind and juice
  of 1 lemon

½ cup poppy seeds
3 cups sifted all-purpose flour
3 teaspoons baking powder

Cream sugar and butter until light and fluffy; add eggs and mix well; add lemon rind and juice and the poppy seeds. Add sifted dry ingredients. Roll out on floured board and cut into desired shapes; sprinkle with granulated sugar and bake in a moderate oven, about 350°, for 15 or 20 minutes.

PRUNE TORTE

16 prunes, cooked, pitted, cut in small pieces
2 tablespoons lemon juice
2 tablespoons chopped almonds
2 tablespoons citron, cut fine
9 eggs

1¾ cups sugar
3 tablespoons grated unsweetened chocolate
1 teaspoon cinnamon
1 teaspoon allspice
1¼ cups crushed cracker crumbs

Rub the prunes to a smooth paste with the lemon juice. Add almonds and citron. Beat 2 whole eggs and 7 egg yolks, add sugar, beat again and add prune mixture, chocolate, spices and cracker crumbs. Stir well. Beat the 7 remaining egg whites until stiff, fold in gently. Bake in springform pan for 1 hour at 350°. To serve, garnish with whipped cream and, if desired, chocolate or bits of cherries.

SCOTCH CURLS

2 cups sifted flour	⅔ cup milk
4 teaspoons baking powder	1 egg
¼ teaspoon salt	4 tablespoons creamed butter
4 tablespoons firm butter	½ cup brown sugar
	½ cup chopped walnuts

Sift together flour, baking powder and salt. Cut in butter, add milk and egg. Mix to make soft dough. Roll out ¼-inch thick; spread with creamed butter; sprinkle with brown sugar and nuts. Roll as for Jelly Roll (see p. 134) and cut in slices about 1 inch thick. Place cut side down in greased muffin tins. Bake ½ hour in hot oven, 400°.

SMETENE TORTE (Sour Cream)
Dough

½ pound butter, softened	1 teaspoon baking powder
¾ cup sugar	2 cups sifted all-purpose flour
1 egg	

Cream butter and sugar, add egg and beat well. Add dry ingredients, forming a soft dough. Divide in 3 portions, roll out to fit 9-inch-square pans. Bake simultaneously in moderate oven, 350°, until golden brown, about 25 minutes.

Filling

1 pint sour cream	½ cup crushed nuts
1 cup confectioners' sugar	1 teaspoon vanilla

Mix in order given. Pour ⅓ of filling on first layer. Cover with second layer, add second ⅓ of filling; cover with last layer and remainder of filling. Place in refrigerator overnight. Remove from refrigerator 1 hour before serving. Cut in squares.

SHORTBREAD WITH CHOCOLATE BITS

10 ounces butter (1 stick plus 2 tablespoons)
¾ cup sugar
3 cups all-purpose flour
Pinch of salt

Work above ingredients with hands. When well blended, spread over a baking sheet. Pat down well. Sprinkle with semisweet chocolate bits and bake in a 375° oven for 30 minutes. Cut in squares immediately.

SKI JUMPERS

1 cup shortening
1 cup brown sugar
¾ cup sour milk
2 cups flour
1 teaspoon baking soda
2 cups rolled oats
½ teaspoon salt

Mix all ingredients together, forming a soft dough. Roll out ¼ inch thick; cut in oblongs or rounds. Bake in hot oven (400°) about 15 minutes; while hot spread with date filling or thick plum jam. Make sandwiches by pressing 2 cookies together. Roll in confectioners' sugar.

SOUR CREAM COFFEE CAKE

¼ pound butter, softened
1 cup sugar
2 eggs
1 cup sour cream
½ teaspoon baking soda
1½ cups flour
2 teaspoons baking powder
1 cup raisins
¼ teaspoon cinnamon

Cream butter and sugar well; add eggs, beat well. Dissolve baking soda in sour cream and add alternately with sifted dry ingredients. Put half of this batter in a buttered square cake pan, cover with raisins, sprinkle with cinnamon; add remainder of batter. Cover with the Crumb Topping.

Crumb Topping

Mix together ¼ cup flour, ½ cup brown sugar, 1 tablespoon butter, and ½ teaspoon cinnamon. Sprinkle over batter. Bake in a 350° oven for about 1 hour.

SPRITZ COOKIES

1 cup softened butter	½ teaspoon baking
¾ cup sugar	powder
1 egg or 3 yolks	¼ teaspoon salt
2½ cups flour	1 teaspoon almond extract

Cream butter, add sugar gradually. Add egg or egg yolks, unbeaten. Sift flour, measure, add baking powder and salt and sift 3 times. Add almond flavoring. Force through cooky press onto cooky sheet and bake in a 400° oven, 10 to 12 minutes.

Cookies in 2 colors: Divide pastry into 2 parts. Add red food coloring to 1 part and green coloring to the other. Put into cooky press in layers.

STRUDEL

Ingredients for Dough

1½ cups flour   Pinch of salt   ¾ cup warm water

Other required ingredients

A little flour	confection)
⅓ cup oil	4 to 5 tablespoons powdered
Turkish delight (jellylike	sugar

Sift flour and salt on a pastry board, make a well in center, into which add a little water. Work in flour with finger tips, adding remaining warm water. This results in a very sticky mass, so keep on ½ of board. Now beat dough with palm of hand, raising hand in slapping motions. Continue until palm and board are clean and free of dough.

On unused portion of board, sprinkle 1 tablespoon flour. Lift doughy mass, placing it on this floured portion of board. Turn dough until well but lightly covered with flour. Knead lightly to a round ball-like form.

Put 1 tablespoon oil on a plate, place dough on this, first 1 side, then the other, so that the entire ball is covered with oil. Place a bowl over plate to make it airtight and allow to stand for 1 to 1½ hours in a warm room. While waiting for dough to become of right consistency and elasticity for stretching and pulling, prepare the filling.

Filling

½ pound walnuts	(no crusts)
½ pound white sultana raisins	1 teaspoon vanilla
1 cup sugar	Grated rind and juice of medium lemon
1 cup chalah crumbs	

Crush walnuts with rolling pin, to small pieces, but not to a powder. Wash and dry 1 cup raisins, put through fine blade of food grinder. Mix raisins, crumbs, lemon juice and rind, and vanilla, thoroughly, to free from any lumpy masses. Now, with 2 forks, lift mixture, adding walnuts until very well blended, but do not crush nuts. (This would result in a pasty mixture, because of the release of the oil from the nuts.) Prepare Turkish delight in rolls ½ inch thick.

Dough Stretching

The room must be warm and free from drafts. Spread on a table 1½ yards long by 32 to 36 inches wide, a single bed sheet. Sprinkle on table portion a generous amount of flour. Thoroughly rub and work into cloth. Drain off oil from plate containing strudel dough. Allow dough to fall from plate onto this well-floured cloth. Roll dough with rolling pin to ¼-inch thickness. Cover this dough with a small tea towel or corner of sheet spread on table. Allow to stand for 15 to 20 minutes. Now commence to pull and stretch dough gently, but firmly, taking care to have a greater overlap on 1 long side of the table. Continue this stretching until dough is of tissue-paper thinness. Trim off edge all around. On long side where there is shorter overhanging dough, place the Turkish delight rolls close to the edge along the entire length. Sprinkle entire dough that is on the table surface with oil, by allowing it to drop from spoon or pastry brush. Now, quickly scatter the filling. Cover the Turkish delight with about 1 inch of the overhanging dough. Now, gather up sheet to edge of table on side where Turkish delight has been placed and roll evenly and firmly as a Jelly Roll (see p. 134) until ½ has been rolled up. Pull sheet so that portion of dough that has been over-hanging is now brought up to the table surface, that is, toward the side where you are standing. Sprinkle powdered sugar on this portion of dough and finish rolling. Cut strips the length of a cooky sheet that has been well (but not excessively) oiled, and place each strip on this baking sheet. Bake in slow oven (300° to 325°) for approximately 20 minutes. Remove from oven. Allow to cool and cut in slices with very sharp knife, about 1 inch wide, as required. Strudel must be handled very carefully when baked. It will retain its freshness for some time and actually improves as it ripens. It is wholesome, economical, and not, once the trick of stretching the dough is mastered, difficult to make.

FILLED TEIGLACH

Dough

½ cup oil	2½ to 3 cups sifted
½ cup sugar	all-purpose flour
2 eggs	Pinch of salt
1 teaspoon vanilla	2 teaspoons baking powder

Beat oil, sugar and eggs. Add vanilla and sifted dry ingredients. Use enough flour to make smooth pliable dough. Roll out ¼ inch thick; cut into rounds with glass and put some filling on each piece of dough. Fold over and pinch edges tightly. Bake in a 350° oven for 30 minutes.

Filling

½ pound prunes, pitted	¼ cup sugar
½ pound raisins	Grated rind and juice ½
½ cup nuts	lemon

Put fruit and nuts through food grinder, add sugar, juice and rind, and mix together.

Coconut Glaze

When baked, the teiglach are then dropped into a pot containing ½ cup honey and ¼ cup sugar that has been brought to a boil. Boil the teiglach for 5 minutes, with not more than 12 at 1 time in syrup. Remove from honey and roll in shredded coconut. Makes about 36.

THIMBLE COOKIES

½ cup shortening	¼ teaspoon almond extract
¼ cup sugar	1 cup sifted flour
1 egg	Chopped nuts or coconut
½ teaspoon lemon extract	Jam or jelly

197

Cream shortening and sugar, and beat in the egg. Beat well, add flavoring and flour. Roll into small balls. Roll in coconut or chopped nuts and make a hollow in the center with a thimble. Place on greased baking sheet and fill the hollow with jelly or smooth jam. Bake in a moderate oven, 350°, for 12 to 15 minutes.

TROPIC AROMA CAKE

½ cup shortening	¼ teaspoon salt
1¾ cups sugar	1 teaspoon nutmeg
2 eggs	1 teaspoon cinnamon
2½ cups sifted cake flour	1 cup milk
4 teaspoons baking powder	1 tablespoon cocoa
	1 tablespoon boiling water

Cream shortening; add sugar and beaten eggs. Mix well. Sift together the dry ingredients. Add ½ to the egg mixture, then add milk and the remainder of dry ingredients. Bake ⅔ of this batter in 2 greased layer cake pans; to remaining ⅓ of batter, add 1 tablespoon cocoa, which has been mixed with 1 tablespoon boiling water. Bake the 3 layers in hot oven (400°) for 15 to 20 minutes.

Mocha Filling

3 tablespoons softened butter	5 tablespoons unsweetened cocoa
3 cups sifted confectioners' sugar	1 teaspoon vanilla
	5 tablespoons strong coffee

Cream butter; add sugar and cocoa very slowly, beating until light and fluffy. Add vanilla and coffee a few drops at a time, making soft enough to spread.

TURKISH DELIGHT ROLLS

½ pound butter
½ pound cream cheese
2 cups sifted flour
1 pound Turkish delight
  (jellylike confection),

red or green
1 egg white, slightly
  beaten
¼ cup crushed nuts

Cream butter and cheese thoroughly. Add flour, mix well and place in refrigerator overnight. Roll about ¼ of the dough at a time very thin, about ⅛ inch, into oblong shape. Place rolled Turkish delight on edge of dough and roll over 3 times. Brush outside of roll with beaten egg white and sprinkle with crushed nuts. Bake at 350° for about 25 to 30 minutes. Remove from pan, and when cool, cut in slices about 1 inch thick.

Note: Individual rolls may be made by cutting dough in circles, with cooky cutter or glass, and placing a small piece of Turkish delight rolled in each round of dough.

TURKISH DELIGHT SQUARES

Dough

¼ pound butter, softened
3 tablespoons sugar

2 egg yolks
1½ cups flour
Juice of ½ lemon

Mix these ingredients in order given and place in refrigerator overnight until very firm and hard.

Filling

5 pieces Turkish delight
  (red) cut in small pieces
½ cup brown sugar
1 orange, grated coarsely

½ cup Brazil nuts,
  cut in pieces
3 tablespoons strawberry
  jam
2 egg whites, beaten stiff

199

Grate a little more than half the dough on coarse side of grater, into a square baking dish. Spread on filling evenly. Grate the remaining dough to cover. Bake in a 350° oven for 40 to 50 minutes. Cut in squares when cool.

UPSIDE-DOWN CAKE

¼ cup brown sugar
4 slices pineapple, drained
Maraschino cherries
¼ cup shortening
½ cup white sugar
1 teaspoon grated orange
rind
1 egg, well beaten
1 cup flour, sifted
¼ teaspoon salt
1½ teaspoons baking powder
¼ cup orange juice

Spread bottom of well-greased 8- or 9-inch round pan with brown sugar and the pineapple ring slices, with a cherry inside each pineapple ring. Cream shortening, sugar and rind. Add egg and sifted dry ingredients, alternately with juice. Mix well; pour over fruit. Bake 45 minutes at 350°.

WALNUT SQUARES

2 eggs, separated
¼ cup (½ stick) softened butter
1¼ cups firmly packed brown sugar
1 cup sifted all-purpose flour
½ teaspoon baking powder
1 cup chopped walnuts

Combine the egg yolks with butter, ¼ cup of the brown sugar, flour and baking powder. Beat to blend well. Pat well into greased 8-inch-square pan. Beat the egg whites until stiff, fold in remaining 1 cup brown sugar and the walnuts. Spread this over the first mixture. Bake in oven preheated to 350° for 20 minutes or until meringue topping is golden. Remove from oven, cool. When completely cold, cut into squares. Makes 16 to 18 squares.

YEAST DELIGHTS

Dough

½ pound (2 sticks) butter, softened (or half butter, half shortening)	2 egg yolks
	1 cake compressed yeast or 1 envelope active dry yeast
2 cups sifted all-purpose flour	½ cup lukewarm milk
2 tablespoons sugar	⅛ teaspoon salt

Cut butter into flour until size of peas. Make a well in the center, place 2 tablespoons of the sugar and the egg yolks in the well, work together with fingers until smooth. Dissolve the yeast in the milk, add the salt and remaining 1 tablespoon sugar. Blend yeast mixture with dough. Chill overnight in refrigerator. Roll out on lightly floured board to rectangular shape ¼ inch thick. Spread with filling, roll up as for Jelly Roll (see p. 134).

Filling

4 tablespoons light brown sugar	2 egg whites, beaten slightly
1 teaspoon cinnamon	½ cup seedless raisins

Blend together the sugar and cinnamon, fold into the stiffly beaten egg whites, then fold in raisins.

When dough has been rolled up, cut in 1-inch slices, place on greased baking sheet 2 inches apart. Let rise in warm place (80°) free from draft for 15 minutes or until half again as large. Preheat oven to 375°; bake at this temperature for 25 minutes until golden and firm. Makes about 2½ dozen.

If preferred, half the buns may be frozen to be reheated later. After buns are thoroughly cold, wrap securely with plastic, sealing shut, place in freezer. Defrost partially before reheating.

RAISIN-FILLED CRESCENTS

3 cups sifted all-purpose flour

3 tablespoons sugar

½ teaspoon salt

1 cup (½ pound) butter

1 cake compressed yeast, or 1 envelope active dry yeast

½ cup lukewarm milk

2 eggs, well beaten

4 tablespoons softened butter

¼ cup sugar

1 cup raisins

Cinnamon-sugar blend

Combine flour, 3 tablespoons sugar and salt. Chop in butter until size of peas, using knife or pastry blender. Dissolve the yeast in milk; add eggs, gradually add flour mixture, beating until smooth. Cover mixing bowl with waxed paper, store in refrigerator overnight. Next day divide dough in 2 parts. Roll out each into a circle on lightly floured board to ¼ inch thick. Spread each with softened butter, sprinkle with sugar, cut into 8 pie-shaped wedges. Place about 2 tablespoons raisins over each wedge, roll up, beginning at wide side. Place with overlapped side down in shallow greased pans, sprinkling cinnamon-sugar mixture over each. Allow to rise in warm place (80°) free from draft, until doubled. Preheat oven to 350°, then place rolls in oven; bake 15 minutes or until golden brown. Makes 24 crescents. If preferred, freeze half to be reheated later.

BRAZIL NUT SLICES

2 squares unsweetened chocolate, melted

2 tablespoons butter

2 cups granulated sugar

1 cup maple syrup

½ cup milk

¼ cup slivered Brazil nuts

Put all ingredients, except nuts, into a saucepan and cook slowly without stirring until a small amount of the mixture dropped from a teaspoon into a glass of cold water forms a soft ball. Remove from fire; allow to cool until mixture can be handled with fingers. Spread nuts on board, place candy over nuts, roll up and slice immediately, using small sharp knife. Chill until ready to serve.

CANDIED FRUIT PEEL

Cut into strips the peel of 2 grapefruits, 3 oranges and 1 lemon. Cover with cold water, soak 24 hours, drain. Add fresh water, bring slowly to a boil. Remove from stove, drain well. Repeat, adding fresh water 3 or 4 times, each time bringing to a boil, then draining. Make a syrup of 2 cups sugar and 1 cup water, add the fruit peel, cook slowly until all syrup is absorbed, shaking pan frequently to prevent sticking. Pour onto plates to cool, then roll in additional granulated sugar. When thoroughly dried, spoon into sterilized jars; seal.

QUICK AND EASY FUDGE

2 eggs, separated	unsweetened chocolate,
½ pound (2 cups sifted)	melted
confectioners' sugar	¼ pound shelled nuts
⅛ teaspoon salt	(almonds, pecans, or
1 teaspoon vanilla	walnuts), chopped,
3 squares (3 ounces)	about 1 cup

Beat egg whites until stiff, fold in sugar. Beat egg yolks until smooth and thick, fold into stiffly beaten whites, then add salt, vanilla, the melted chocolate, and the nuts. Beat to blend well. Spread into buttered 8- or 9-inch-square pan. Chill. Cut into 1-inch squares to serve.

MAPLE FUDGE

1 pound brown sugar	1 teaspoon vanilla
½ cup milk	1 tablespoon butter
Pinch of salt	½ cup nuts (optional)

Put sugar, milk and salt into a saucepan and bring to a boil slowly. Continue cooking, stirring constantly, until a little of the mixture dropped from a spoon into cold water forms a soft ball. Add vanilla and butter. Remove from fire and add nuts. Beat with rotary beater or electric mixer for 3 minutes. Pat into buttered 8- or 9-inch baking pan and cut into squares. Chill.

CHEESE BAGELECH

Strudel Dough (see p. 194) ⅓ cup butter, melted

Filling

1 pound creamed pot or farmer cheese
1 egg, well beaten
½ cup granulated sugar

⅓ cup sifted all-purpose flour
2 tablespoons sweet or sour cream
1 teaspoon salt

Brush or spoon melted butter over Strudel Dough; combine ingredients for filling, beat to blend well, spread over dough, roll up. Place rolls of filled bagelech on greased baking sheet 2 inches apart. Bake in oven preheated to 350° for 25 minutes until pastry is golden and crisp. Serve warm with sour cream. Makes 12 large or 16 to 18 medium portions.

CHEESE KNADLECH

1 pound (2 cups) pot or farmer cheese
2 eggs, beaten
½ cup matzo meal

4 tablespoons flour
1 teaspoon quick-cooking tapioca
¼ teaspoon salt
Freshly ground pepper

Combine all ingredients, beat to blend into doughlike mixture. Form into 1-inch balls, drop into kettle of rapidly boiling salted water. Boil 20 minutes or until they rise to top. Lift out one at a time with slotted spoon. Serve hot, topped with melted butter (about ¼ cup—4 tablespoons) and, if desired, sour cream. Makes about 18.

CHEESE SOUFFLÉ

2 tablespoons butter	¼ teaspoon salt
1 tablespoon flour	4 eggs, separated
1½ cups milk	¾ cup grated cheese

Melt butter, stir in flour, then gradually add milk and salt. Cook until thickened and smooth. Beat egg yolks until thick, beat in a little of the hot sauce, then combine with remaining sauce. Stir in grated cheese and the egg whites which have been beaten until stiff. Pour into 1½- or 2-quart soufflé dish, place dish in pan of water. Bake at 450° for 10 minutes; reduce heat to 375°, bake 25 minutes longer until golden. Serve immediately.   Serves 4.

NOODLE AND CHEESE RING

1 package broad noodles	¼ pound butter, melted
1 pound pot or farmer cheese	Grated rind and juice of 1 orange
2 eggs	⅛ teaspoon cinnamon
1 cup raisins	(optional)
¾ cup sugar	

Boil noodles in boiling salted water; drain. Mix cheese with the eggs, raisins, sugar, butter, orange rind and juice and the cinnamon. Add noodles and beat well. Butter oven-proof casserole or 1-quart ring mold, heat in 350° oven a few minutes before adding noodle mixture. Bake until golden brown. Makes 6 to 8 servings.

CHEESE PANCAKES

2 cups (1 pound) pot or farmer cheese
2 tablespoons sour cream
2 eggs, beaten
1 tablespoon sugar
2 tablespoons flour
Sour cream or confectioners' sugar
¼ teaspoon salt
⅓ cup filberts, finely chopped
¼ cup butter

Rub cheese through a sieve and add sour cream, eggs, sugar, salt, filberts and flour, and mix lightly. Melt butter in heavy skillet; drop batter from teaspoon and fry each pancake until a golden brown on both sides. Serve with sour cream or sprinkle with sugar. Makes 18 to 24 pancakes.

TURKISH PILAF

2 tablespoons butter
½ cup uncooked short-grain rice
1 cup hot water
2 cups canned tomatoes
¾ teaspoon salt
⅛ teaspoon pepper
2 cups grated cheese

Melt butter in top of double boiler. Add rice a little at a time and stir over direct heat for 3 or 4 minutes. Add hot water and cook until water is absorbed. Add tomatoes, salt and pepper and steam covered in double boiler without stirring for 15 minutes. Pour into buttered 7-inch-square baking dish 1½ inches high. Cover with cheese and bake until cheese is melted. Makes 4 servings.

APPLE CRISP I

5 or 6 medium tart apples, peeled, sliced
3 tablespoons sugar
½ teaspoon cinnamon
½ cup sugar
½ cup oil
1 egg
½ cup all-purpose flour
½ teaspoon baking powder
¹⁄₁₆ teaspoon salt
1 teaspoon vanilla

Place apples in 1½-quart baking dish. Sprinkle with mixture of 3 tablespoons sugar and the cinnamon. Combine remaining ingredients, spread over apple mixture. Bake in 350° oven approximately 30 minutes until top is crisp and apples bubbling. Makes 6 to 8 servings.

MAPLE ICE CREAM

⅔ cup sweetened condensed milk
½ cup water
1½ teaspoons maple extract
1 cup heavy cream
¼ cup chopped nuts

Combine milk, water and maple extract. Chill. Whip cream to custardlike consistency and fold into chilled mixture. Pour into freezing tray, place in refrigerator until crystals form around edges. Scrape from tray, beat until smooth, add nuts and replace in freezing tray, freeze until firm. Makes 4 servings.

OLD-FASHIONED RICE PUDDING

1 cup uncooked rice
2 cups water
1 teaspoon salt
2 eggs, well beaten
2 cups milk
½ cup sugar
1 cup raisins
1 apple, grated
1 teaspoon vanilla or almond extract
1 tablespoon butter
Nutmeg

Cook rice in boiling salted water until soft; drain, rinse immediately with cold water. Add eggs, milk, sugar, raisins, apple and vanilla. Pour into 1½-quart baking dish. Dot top with butter, sprinkle with nutmeg. Bake in 350° oven until firm (knife inserted in center should come out clean) and top golden. Makes 6 to 8 servings. Serve warm or cold with cream.

JELLY AND SOUR CREAM DESSERT

3 packages kosher fruit-flavored gelatin (3 ounces each)
3 cups hot water
3 cups cold water
2 cups cut-up fruit*
1 cup crushed graham crackers
1 pint sour cream

Dissolve flavored gelatin in hot water, add cold water. Pour half the gelatin in a 13 x 9 x 2-inch Pyrex dish. Place in refrigerator until it starts to set (consistency of unbeaten egg white). Stir in 1 cup of the fruit. Return to the refrigerator until almost firm. Cover this layer with the crushed graham crackers and spread the sour cream over the cracker crumbs. Add remaining jelly blended with the fruit (while standing it should have jelled enough to hold the fruit in suspension); pour over the sour cream, chill until very firm. When firm, cut into squares. Makes about 12 servings.

* Any combination of fresh or canned fruit may be used except fresh pineapple.

STRAWBERRY WHIP

1 egg white
1¼ cups hulled strawberries, sliced
¼ cup sifted confectioners' sugar
Few drops lemon juice

Beat egg white until foamy, add strawberries, beat steadily until egg white begins to hold its shape, then add sugar gradually, beating until it forms peaks. Stir in lemon juice, pile into sherbet glasses, chill; will hold its shape for several hours. Makes 6 servings.

ANTIPASTO

Place lettuce on each plate. Place on the lettuce a slice each of tomato, cucumber, hard-boiled egg, and salami. Add 3 stuffed anchovies and 1 tablespoon diced beets.

GREEK SALAD

Cut the following ingredients in small pieces: lettuce, tomatoes, cucumber, radishes, spring onions, green pepper, celery, black olives and salt or schmaltz herring. For 4 to 6 cups salad, add 3 tablespoons vinegar and 2 tablespoons oil, toss to blend.

SALMON ROLLS

Dough

2 cups sifted all-purpose flour	½ teaspoon salt
	¼ cup butter
2 teaspoons baking powder	¾ cup milk

Sift dry ingredients together. Cut butter into dry ingredients. Add milk slowly, for a stiff dough. Turn onto floured board and roll out to ¼ inch thick.

Filling

½ cup celery, diced fine	6-ounce can salmon, drained
1 small onion, diced fine	1 cup canned green peas, drained
¼ pound mushrooms, cut in pieces	2 tablespoons chopped pimiento
2 tablespoons butter	1 egg, beaten

Fry celery, onion and mushrooms in butter until golden brown. Add salmon, green peas, pimiento, and egg. Spread on pastry and roll up as in Jelly Roll (see p. 134). Slice into 8 portions. Place overlapped side down in buttered baking dish. Bake in a 350° oven, about 30 minutes, or until golden brown. Serve with Cheese Sauce. Makes 6.

Cheese Sauce

2½ tablespoons butter	¼ teaspoon paprika
2½ tablespoons flour	1½ cups milk
½ teaspoon salt	½ cup grated cheese

Melt butter, add flour, salt and paprika. Stir until well blended. Add the milk, stirring constantly. Just before removing from stove, add the cheese. Serve hot.

WHOLE CRANBERRY SAUCE

Wash 4 cups cranberries. Put in pot with 2 cups boiling water, and boil for 20 minutes. Rub through sieve; return to saucepan and cook 3 minutes longer. Add 2 cups sugar and cook another 2 minutes. Turn into mold and chill.

CONCORD GRAPE JELLY

Wash and stem grapes. Place in kettle and cook over low heat until skins break. Force grapes through strainer. Put juice into a cheesecloth bag and allow to drain overnight. Next day measure ¾ cup of sugar for every cup of strained juice. Heat sugar in kettle over a low heat, stirring constantly until thoroughly warmed. Add juice and cook until it forms a jelly when a little is dropped into cold water. Pour into hot sterilized glasses and seal.

PEACH MARMALADE

24 peaches	10 maraschino cherries,
4 oranges	sliced (optional)
	1 lemon

Scald peaches, remove skins and slice fruit very thin. Grate rind of oranges and lemon. Cut off white pulp and throw away. Cut fruit of oranges and lemon into very small pieces. Measure fruit; for each heaping cup of fruit use 1 scant cup of sugar. Pour sugar over fruit and let stand overnight. Bring to a boil and boil hard for 15 minutes; then boil slowly over very low heat for about 1 hour. Pour into sterilized jelly glasses. Cool slightly, then cover with melted paraffin.

QUICK STRAWBERRY JAM

Hull and wash berries. Measure fruit. For each cup of fruit, measure ¾ cup sugar. Put sugar into shallow pot. Heat very slowly, stirring constantly, over low heat until sugar begins to melt. Add berries and cook slowly on low heat until syrup reaches a boil. Cook quickly for 3 minutes, no longer. Do not stir while cooking. Turn off heat, remove scum. Place in sterilized jars and seal with paraffin.

CHICKEN PIE

Filling

1½ to 2 cups diced cooked chicken

4 large potatoes, cooked, diced

2 carrots, cooked, diced

1 cup chicken gravy (or soup thickened with 2 tablespoons flour)

1 cup boiling water

Salt, pepper to taste

In a 1½-quart baking dish, place the chicken, potatoes, and carrots. Combine gravy and water, taste to determine if added seasoning is needed. Pour this over chicken and vegetables.

Pastry

½ cup shortening

2 cups sifted all-purpose flour

¼ teaspoon salt

3 tablespoons cold water

1 tablespoon vinegar

Make the pastry exactly as for any other pie crust: cut shortening into flour, work in salt, add water a tablespoon at a time, then vinegar. Form stiff dough with fingers, roll out on floured board to ⅛ inch thick. Place over top of baking dish so edges are sealed by pressing to sides of dish. Cut a slash in center of pastry for escape of steam. Bake in oven preheated to 375° until crust is golden, about 45 minutes. Makes 4 to 6 servings.

BEEF PIE

Prepare exactly as above, using 1½ to 2 cups cooked left-over beef in place of chicken and leftover beef gravy in place of chicken gravy.

SPAGHETTI AND MEAT SAUCE

1 large onion, minced
2 tablespoons chicken fat
1 pound ground meat
1 garlic clove, minced or crushed
1 6-ounce can tomato paste
1½ cups water
½ teaspoon crushed red peppers, or 1 whole red pepper from pickling spice, broken into small pieces
Salt, pepper to taste
1 pound spaghetti, cooked, drained

Sauté onion in chicken fat, add meat and onion, stir until meat has lost its pink color. Add tomato paste, water, salt and black pepper to taste and the crushed red pepper. Simmer 30 minutes. Meanwhile, cook spaghetti in boiling salted water until tender, drain in colander, rinse immediately with boiling water. Serve spaghetti topped with meat sauce. Makes 6 to 8 servings.

SHEPHERD'S PIE

6 medium potatoes
2 eggs
4 tablespoons chicken fat
Salt, pepper to taste
3 tablespoons matzo meal
½ pound beef or calf's liver, broiled, chopped
1 sliced onion, fried separately in chicken fat

Peel and cook potatoes until tender; drain, mash while hot. Beat in eggs, chicken fat and salt and pepper. Place half the potato mixture in 1½-quart greased casserole. Combine

212

the chopped cooked liver with the fried onion; place this over potatoes, top with remaining potatoes. Bake in oven preheated to 350° until top is golden brown, about ½ hour. Turn out on platter, serve hot. Makes 6 servings.

Note: Instead of liver, ¾ to 1 cup any chopped cooked meat, such as that from leftover roast, may be used.

MOCK SALMON PATTIES

3 large carrots, grated	1 20-ounce can (2½ cups)
2 eggs, beaten	tomato juice
¼ teaspoon salt	5 cups water
1 tablespoon matzo meal	1 large onion, minced
1 tablespoon chopped	2 stalks celery, chopped
parsley	½ teaspoon salt
2 to 3 tablespoons fat	Dash of pepper

Blend together grated carrots, eggs, ¼ teaspoon salt, matzo meal and parsley. Form into 2-inch patties. Heat together tomato juice, water, onion, celery, ½ teaspoon salt and pepper; when boiling, add patties, lower heat, cook ½ hour until liquid has been reduced to half. Makes 4 to 6 servings.

APPLE CRISP II

3 cups sliced apples	¼ cup butter
½ cup flour	1 teaspoon cinnamon
1 cup brown sugar	⅓ cup chopped nuts

Place sliced apples in greased 1½-quart baking dish. Mix flour and brown sugar, cut in the butter to pieces the size of peas. Add chopped nuts and cinnamon. Sprinkle this mixture over the apples. Bake at 375° for 45 minutes. Serve with cream if desired. Makes 6 servings.

213

BUTTERSCOTCH PIE

1 cup brown sugar
1 tablespoon butter or
  shortening
2 tablespoons water
1 cup milk
2 tablespoons cornstarch
1 egg yolk

½ teaspoon vanilla
1 egg white, beaten stiff
1 tablespoon
  confectioners' sugar
Baked 9-inch pie shell
¼ cup chopped nuts
  (optional)

Combine brown sugar, butter and water, heat, stirring, until sugar is dissolved. Mix milk, cornstarch and beaten egg yolk together and add to the sugar mixture. Cook, stirring constantly, over hot water until thick. Add vanilla. Pour into baked pie or tart shells. When cool, top with meringue of confectioners' sugar and egg white. Sprinkle with crushed nuts, if desired. Bake in 325° oven until golden, about 20 minutes.

APPLE PIE

Pastry

9 tablespoons sifted
  all-purpose flour
Pinch of salt
1 teaspoon sugar
1 teaspoon baking powder
3 tablespoons vegetable

shortening
3 tablespoons cold water; or
  1 tablespoon lemon juice
  or vinegar and 2 table-
  spoons water

Blend together flour, salt, sugar and baking powder. Chop in vegetable shortening. Add water, or lemon juice and water, a tablespoon at a time, blending well. Knead until smooth, roll out ½ at a time to ⅛ inch thick on floured board. Fit into 9-inch pie pan, trimming edges.

Filling

6 to 8 medium apples   ⅔ cup sugar   1 teaspoon cinnamon

Place apples in bottom crust, sprinkling with sugar and cinnamon. Top with upper crust, cutting slashes in center. Press edges of pastry together to seal. Bake in oven preheated to 425° for 10 minutes, reduce heat to 350°, bake 20 to 30 minutes longer (1 hour altogether) until crust is golden and filling is bubbly.

LEMON PIE

Pastry for 1-crust pie

½ cup vegetable shortening   1½ cup flour
½ teaspoon salt   ¼ cup water
                                         1 teaspoon vinegar

Combine as for pastry for Apple Pie (see p. 214).

Pastry for 1-crust pie
4½ tablespoons cornstarch
1 cup sugar
Pinch of salt
1½ cups boiling water
3 egg yolks
6 tablespoons lemon juice

2 teaspoons grated lemon rind
1 tablespoon butter or margarine
3 egg whites, beaten stiff
3 tablespoons sifted confectioners' sugar

Roll out pastry to fit 9-inch pie pan to ⅛ inch thick. Prick bottom and sides with fork. Flute edges between fingers. Chill in freezer 15 minutes, then place in oven preheated to 450° for 10 to 15 minutes until golden. (Prechilling prevents crust from shrinking). Cool before adding filling.

To make filling, combine cornstarch, sugar and salt, blending well. Add boiling water, cook and stir in top of double boiler, over hot water, 15 minutes. Add a little of this hot mixture to egg yolks, then add egg yolks, lemon juice and rind to cornstarch mixture. Cook 3 minutes longer. Remove from heat, add butter or margarine.

215

Cool slightly, pour into baked pie shell. Top with meringue of stiffly beaten egg whites blended with sugar, bake at 350° for 10 to 15 minutes until golden.

STRAWBERRY TARTS
Pastry

½ pound (1 cup) butter

2 cups sifted all-purpose flour

1 teaspoon vanilla

3 tablespoons confectioners' sugar

To make pastry, chop butter into flour, add vanilla and sugar, blend into stiff dough. Chill. Roll out to ⅛ inch thick, cut into round 2½ inches in diameter. Fit into small muffin tins. Bake in oven preheated to 375° until golden. Remove, cool. Makes 18 shells, 2½ inches each.

Filling

1 package vanilla pudding and pie filling mix, cooked as directed

1 pint strawberries, washed and hulled

Make vanilla pudding as directed on package, divide tart shells. Place whole strawberries over the pudding.

Glaze

1 cup water

½ cup sugar

1 tablespoon cornstarch

Few drops red food coloring

Prepare glaze by boiling together water, sugar and cornstarch until thickened. Add food coloring. Spoon over strawberries. Makes 18 tarts.

BREAD AND BUTTER PICKLES
Pickles

6 cucumbers

2 onions

1 small bunch celery

Salt

Cut vegetables in thin slices, salt generously and allow to stand overnight.

Syrup

2 cups brown sugar

2 tablespoons celery seed

2 tablespoons mustard seed

1 teaspoon cinnamon

½ teaspoon ginger

2 cups vinegar

½ cup water

Combine sugar and spices, add the cut-up vegetables, vinegar and water. Bring to a boil and cook slowly for 5 minutes. When cool, pack in sterilized jars and seal.

CHILI SAUCE

12 tomatoes, peeled, chopped

6 apples, cored, peeled, diced

12 stalks celery, diced

2 sweet red peppers, seeded, chopped

1¾ cups sugar

1 teaspoon ginger

1 onion, chopped

2 green peppers, seeded, chopped

3 cups vinegar

3 teaspoons cinnamon

½ teaspoon allspice

1 tablespoon salt

Combine all ingredients, bring to a boil, lower heat, simmer uncovered 1½ hours. Store in sterilized jars, seal when cold.

MUSTARD PICKLES

3 heads cauliflower

2 quarts small onions

6 stalks celery, diced

2 cucumbers, sliced

1 dozen sweet red peppers, seeded

1 package pickling spices

1 dozen hot red peppers, seeded

3 quarts vinegar

4 cups brown sugar

½ ounce turmeric powder

½ pound mustard

1 cup flour

217

Cut up and trim cauliflower, celery and cucumbers. With the onions, this should make 9 quarts. Soak in salted water for 12 hours. Put peppers through food mincer and set aside. Bring to a boil 2 quarts of the vinegar with the brown sugar, add mixed spices in a cotton bag so that they can be removed later. Add the cauliflower, boil for 10 minutes. Add cucumbers, and boil 5 minutes. Add onions, celery and minced peppers. In another bowl, mix until smooth the 1 quart of remaining vinegar with turmeric powder, mustard and flour. Pour into boiled mixture; cook together a few minutes until mixture thickens. Remove bag of spices. Pour into sterilized jars. Seal when cold.

SCHAV OR SPINACH BORSHT

Wash 1 pound spinach or schav (sour grass). Chop or cut into small pieces. Pour 1 quart boiling water over schav and bring just to a boil. Remove from fire and cool. Put ¾ cup sour cream in a bowl, add salt to taste, cut up 1 or 2 cucumbers and 2 or 3 shallots. Pour in schav slowly, stirring constantly. Chill and serve.

BREAD STUFFING FOR FOWL

Soak ¼ loaf chalah in cold water. Remove crusts, squeeze out water. Mix together with 2 eggs, 1 small grated onion, 2 tablespoons chicken fat, chopped parsley, salt and pepper to taste. Add ¼ teaspoon thyme. Mix thoroughly and stuff fowl. Enough for 6-pound bird.

BROWNED RICE

1½ cups uncooked rice	2 tablespoons salt
4 tablespoons butter or fat	3½ cups boiling water

Brown rice in fat in frying pan and keep turning until all the rice is brown; add salt. Add boiling water slowly. Turn into casserole and cover. Place in moderate oven for 25 minutes. Each grain of rice will be separate. Serve with meat, chicken or fish. Makes 6 servings.

NAHIT WITH RICE

1 pound dried chick peas
1 cup uncooked rice
½ cup butter, melted
½ cup honey

Wash, pick over peas; cover with cold water and allow to soak overnight. Drain, cover with fresh cold water; add 2 teaspoons salt and cook slowly for 45 minutes, or until tender. Drain. Cook rice separately in boiling salted water until tender. Drain and mix with hot chick peas. Add butter and honey. More or less honey may be used, according to taste. (To serve with a meat meal, substitute chicken fat for butter.) After mixing with rice, fat and honey, mixture can be placed in a casserole in the oven to brown.

VEGETABLE HALISHKES

1 large cabbage
1 pound spinach, washed thoroughly, chopped fine
2 large onions, chopped
2 tablespoons butter
1 teaspoon salt
2 large carrots, grated
1 pound fresh green peas, shelled, or ½ pound (10-ounce package) frozen peas
1 large parsnip, grated
2 tablespoons minced parsley
10 to 12 stalks celery, chopped
½ cup matzo meal
1 egg, beaten
1 can (10½ ounces) condensed tomato soup
¼ pound butter
½ cup sugar
Juice 2 lemons

Remove core from head of cabbage, place cabbage in pot, cover with boiling water, cover tightly, allow to cool. This makes cabbage leaves easy to separate. Drain well. Lay out leaves to be filled.

Sauté onions in butter, add salt. Add spinach, carrots, parsnip, peas, parsley, celery, matzo meal and egg. Blend thoroughly. Place about 2 tablespoons this filling on each cabbage leaf, roll up, tucking in ends. Place with overlapped side down in heavy pot. Combine soup, butter, sugar and lemon juice. Cook covered 1½ hours. Serve hot. Serves 10 to 12.

SOUR CREAM REFRIGERATOR CAKE

1 pint dairy sour cream
¾ cup sugar
10 graham crackers, crushed

4 bananas, sliced
½ cup sliced maraschino cherries

Chill cream thoroughly, beat in sugar. Place layer of crushed graham crackers over bottom of 9-inch square glass baking dish, add layer of sweetened cream, then bananas. Repeat until all ingredients are used with layer of cracker crumbs on top. Decorate with cherries. Chill in refrigerator 4 hours. Serves 8.

PASSOVER BAGEL

Boil together 1½ cups water and ¾ cup oil. Add 2½ cups matzo meal, 4 tablespoons sugar and ¼ teaspoon salt. Mix well. Add 6 egg yolks, and 6 whites, well beaten. Roll into balls. Place on well-greased pan and make a hole in center of each. Bake one hour in a 400° oven until golden brown.

PASSOVER STUFFING

Pour hot water over 2 matzos. Let stand 10 minutes. Drain.
Pour cold water over matzos. Drain thoroughly and squeeze
out excess moisture. Add a large grated potato, a grated
onion and a grated carrot, 2 eggs, 5 tablespoons matzo meal,
2 stalks celery cut in pieces, and 2 tablespoons chicken fat.
Season with salt and pepper to taste. Mix well.

PASSOVER FARFEL COOKIES

2 eggs	1 cup matzo farfel
¾ cup sugar	½ teaspoon cinnamon
⅓ cup oil	½ cup raisins
1 cup matzo meal	½ cup walnuts
	Pinch of salt

Beat eggs, add sugar and oil. Add matzo meal, farfel and
other ingredients. Drop from teaspoon onto oiled baking
sheet. Bake in 350° oven for 30 minutes.

PASSOVER REFRIGERATOR COOKIES

¼ pound butter, or ½ cup oil	1 cup cake meal
	½ cup chopped nuts
1 cup sugar	Juice of 1 lemon
2 eggs	Pinch of salt

Cream butter or oil with sugar. Add eggs, cake meal, nuts
and lemon juice. Mix well and form into 1 or 2 long rolls.
Wrap in waxed paper and chill overnight. Cut in slices and
bake in a 350° oven for 20 to 25 minutes.

INGBERLACH (Ginger Sticks) FOR PASSOVER

1 pound honey	1 heaping teaspoon cinnamon
1 pound sugar	
1 heaping teaspoon ginger	Matzo meal

221

Cook honey and sugar together about 3 minutes, stirring constantly to avoid burning. Add ginger and cinnamon while stirring. Remove pan from fire and set on board. Stir in enough matzo meal until thick enough to be able to handle. Let stand awhile. Wet hands with cold water. Roll mixture into ropelike rolls; cut into 2- or 3-inch pieces. Glaze with a little honey. Put on clean cloth to harden. (If mixture should become too cold to roll easily, set pan over very low flame to soften.)

MACAROONS

3 egg whites, unbeaten
2 cups shredded coconut or 1 cup each coconut and chopped nuts
Pinch of salt
1 cup granulated sugar
Maraschino cherries, chopped (optional)
1 tablespoon potato starch

Beat egg whites in a bowl until stiff but not dry. Add salt, gradually beat in sugar, add coconut, chopped nuts and potato starch. Put above mixture in double boiler. Cook over hot water for 10 minutes or until mixture stiffens around the edges. Drop by teaspoons on a greased cooky sheet; garnish with pieces of cherries, if desired. Bake in slow oven, 300°, until firm and golden, about 10 minutes.

PASSOVER COOKIES

2 eggs
¾ cup sugar
½ cup oil
½ cup chopped nuts
2 tablespoons potato flour
1 cup cake meal

Beat eggs with sugar. Add oil and nuts, then potato flour and cake meal, which have been sifted together. Let stand 1½ hours in cool place. Form small balls, roll in crushed nuts. Place on greased baking sheet, bake in moderate oven (350°) about 20 minutes.

WINE CAKE

12 eggs, separated
1 cup sugar
1 cup wine

1 cup cake meal
½ teaspoon salt
1 teaspoon cinnamon
1 cup ground walnuts

Beat together egg yolks and sugar until very light. Add wine, cake meal, salt, cinnamon and nuts. Fold in stiffly beaten whites of eggs. Pour into 10-inch tube pan. Bake in moderate oven (325°) for 1½ hours. Invert pan and cool before removing.

APPLE FRITTERS

3 tart apples, peeled, sliced
1 cup matzo meal
2 tablespoons chicken fat or oil

3 eggs
½ teaspoon salt
½ cup water
Deep fat for frying

Peel apples and slice as thin as possible. Beat together other ingredients. Add apples. Drop by spoonfuls into fat, preheated to 370°. Fry until golden brown. Drain on brown paper, sprinkle with sugar and cinnamon, if desired.

CARROT CANDY FOR PASSOVER

Scrape and grate on the fine side of grater, 1 pound large carrots. Mix with 1 pound sugar and cook over low heat, stirring often to prevent burning. Cook until very thick. This takes well over 1 hour and the candy must be stirred almost constantly. When almost done, add ½ pound chopped almonds or walnuts and ¼ teaspoon ginger. When done, spread on wet cooky sheet. Cool for 1 hour, then cut in diamond shapes.

223

STRAWBERRY DESSERT FOR PASSOVER

Line a 7-inch baking dish or shallow casserole with crushed macaroons. Sprinkle with ¼ cup white or red wine. Spread 1 quart hulled, sliced strawberries over the macaroons. Beat 4 egg yolks, ¾ cup sugar, grated rind of 1 lemon and juice of ½ lemon until thick. Separately beat 2 egg whites until stiff. Fold the beaten whites into the yolk mixture, and pour the batter over the strawberries. Bake in a 350° oven about 30 minutes or until the egg mixture is firm. To the remaining 2 egg whites, add 2 tablespoons sugar, and beat until stiff. Spread over top of pudding and return to oven with heat reduced to 325°; bake until the meringue is light brown. Chill and serve with cream, plain or whipped.

EGG AND POTATO APPETIZER

2 potatoes, boiled and mashed
3 hard-boiled eggs, chopped
1 small onion, chopped fine
Chicken fat, just enough to hold mixture together
Salt and pepper to taste

Mix all ingredients together and serve scoops of it on lettuce leaves, garnished with tomato slices and parsley.

MARMALADE FOR PASSOVER

Peel half a grapefruit, 2 oranges and 2 lemons. Remove and discard seeds. Put fruit through food chopper. Add 4 cups water, cook over low heat 1 hour. Add 5 cups sugar, cook slowly for another ½ hour.

224

PINEAPPLE MARMALADE FOR PASSOVER

Peel 4 pineapples and put through food chopper, or grate on coarse grater. Cook slowly until juice simmers. Add juice and rind of 2 lemons. Add 1 cup sugar for each cup of pineapple pulp. Cook 1 hour or until thick and jellied. (If desired, very thin slices of orange and lemon may be added before pulp is measured.)

BAKED MATZO AND CHEESE

4 matzos	½ pound (1 cup) pot or
1 cup warm milk	farmer cheese
2 eggs, well beaten	1 teaspoon sugar
½ teaspoon salt	½ teaspoon cinnamon
	⅓ cup butter

Cut matzos with sharp knife, place in a bowl and cover with warm milk. Let soak 5 minutes, then drain. Beat eggs in a separate bowl, until whites and yolks are blended. Add cheese and seasonings and mix well. Butter a baking dish and arrange a layer of drained matzos, a layer of cheese, dots of butter. Repeat layers until all ingredients are used. If any milk remains in bowl, pour over top layer. Dot with remaining butter. Bake in a moderate oven (350°) about 30 minutes, or until firm in the center and light brown on top. Serve from baking dish.

MAYINA (Liver Pie) FOR PASSOVER

Filling

½ pound liver, baked	5 eggs, beaten
2 large onions, fried in	Salt and pepper to taste
chicken fat	¾ cup cake meal

Put liver, onions and fat through food chopper. Add beaten eggs, salt and pepper. Fold in cake meal.

225

Batter

Beat together 3 eggs and 2 tablespoons water. Add 1 table-spoon potato starch and salt to taste. This mixture makes 3 large pancakes. Grease large frying pan. Heat; pour ⅓ of the batter on hot pan and fry quickly. Turn out onto clean towel. Make 2 more pancakes the same way. Put 1 pancake in casserole; add ½ the liver mixture; cover with second pancake, add the balance of liver and then the third pan-cake. Bake in slow oven until golden brown.

ORANGE AND LEMON KEZEL

Bring 1 large sweet, juicy orange and 1 large lemon to boil in water. Pour off water; refill pan with water; bring to a boil and pour off the water again. Add water a third time and boil fruit until tender. Drain. Open fruit, and allow to stand until cool. Remove any seeds or stems. Mash fruit, rind and pulp thoroughly. Beat 4 eggs, ⅔ cup sugar, and 4 tablespoons matzo meal until foamy. Add fruit pulp. If desired, ½ cup chopped nuts may also be added. Bake 45 to 50 minutes in a moderate oven.

PRUNE TSIMES

6 medium potatoes (3 pounds)	½ pound fat meat or brisket bone
¾ pound prunes, pitted	2 cups water
1 teaspoon salt	¾ cup sugar

Peel and slice potatoes. Put a layer each of potatoes and prunes into pan. Place meat in center. Add remaining potatoes and prunes. Cover with salt and water; cook 15 minutes. Add sugar, place in oven preheated to 350°. Continue baking until water is absorbed and the tsimes nicely browned. Serves 6.

SWEET POTATO PUDDING FOR PASSOVER

½ pound prunes
½ cup sugar
1 cup water
6 sweet potatoes

¼ cup sugar
½ cup matzo meal
3 eggs
3 tablespoons chicken fat

Cook prunes with ¼ cup sugar and 1 cup water, until soft. When cool, remove pits. Cook potatoes in jackets in salted water. When done, drain off water. Peel and mash potatoes, add sugar, matzo meal and eggs, 1 at a time. Add chicken fat and mix well together. Heat a greased tube pan. Place half of the potatoes in pan, put prunes on top and cover with balance of potatoes. Bake in 350° oven until golden brown. Turn upside down on platter and place vegetables of contrasting color in center. Serves 6 to 8.

LIVER VARENIKES

Chop or grind ½ pound broiled liver. Add diced onion, which has been fried golden brown in chicken fat. Add salt and pepper to taste. Mash 6 boiled white potatoes, add 2 beaten eggs, ½ cup flour and salt and pepper to taste. Mix well. Shape into patties, place a tablespoon of the liver filling on each patty, and cover with another patty. Place in heated, well-greased baking pan and bake in a moderate oven until golden brown. Serves 6.

CIRCUMCISION, PIDYON HA-BEN, BAR MITZVAH

"I am glad you are home early, Hadassah."

"Why, of course, Mother, I hurried so that you would have time to read your paper to me before you present it to the Mother's Club at their meeting."

"I am beginning to get stage fright before I get near the platform."

"That is good, Mother. It means that you'll be perfectly at ease when you do get up to speak there, and it will be clear sailing once you get started. Your paper is on the Jewish tradition of circumcision, Pidyon Ha-Ben and Bar Mitzvah. I can't think how many times I've heard you answering questions of friends and neighbors on those matters. All you are really doing when you give your paper is to answer all the questions of a group of friends and neighbors."

"I feel better already, Hadassah. It does seem silly to feel uncertain about something as simple as just talking to a large group of friends. I will read the paper now and you can interrupt whenever you wish to make a suggestion."

CIRCUMCISION (Brith Milah)

"Circumcision is the one religious rite to which all Jews have adhered most faithfully throughout the centuries. It is also known as *Brith Milah*, the Hebrew term meaning a covenant. It is known, too, as the Covenant of Abraham, since Abraham adopted it as a sign of a covenant between

God and the newborn son. We read in Genesis, 'And ye shall be circumcised in the flesh of your foreskin, and it shall be a token of a covenant betwixt Me and you.' Circumcision must take place on the eighth day after the birth of a boy, and is the initiatory rite of adherence to Judaism. The Jewish philosopher Philo associated circumcision with cleanliness and health, as well as with spiritual purification. Modern medical authorities have accepted this theory of a safeguard to cleanliness and health, and it is now practiced among many Christians."

"Mother, did you remember to explain the exceptions to this arrangement?"

"Of course, I have it right here as an example of how meticulous our forefathers were in safeguarding us even in the carrying out of our religious rites. Circumcision is never permitted under any conditions that might endanger a child's life. In case of illness the rite may be postponed.

"If possible the ceremony takes place in the presence of ten men, a *minyan*. It must take place between sunrise and sunset. The *kwater*, who is the godfather, takes the baby from the mother and carries it to the room where the ceremony is to be performed. Here the *sandek*, a wise counsellor, takes the child, since he has been given the honor and privilege of holding the child during the operation.

"Some people place the baby on a chair called Elijah's chair, before the operation. The *mohel*, while doing so, says, 'This is the throne of Elijah, may he be remembered for good. For Thy salvation, O Lord, have I waited." This procedure is based on a legend that the prophet Elijah once complained to God that Israel was neglecting this covenant. As a consequence God ordered him to be present at each circumcision to witness Israel's loyalty to this covenant. The *mohel* performs the operation of circumcision in much the same manner as it has been performed for centuries.

"When circumcision is over, the father says, 'Praised art Thou, O Lord our God, King of the Universe, Who has sanctified us with His Commandments and enjoined upon us the rite of circumcision.'

"The company present responds with the traditional wishes for the boy who has just been admitted to the community of Israel: 'As he has entered the covenant so may he be permitted to enter the study of law (Torah), the state of marriage (*chuppah*), and the practice of good deeds (*Mitzvoth*).' The *mohel* concludes the ceremony by reciting the blessings over wine, which is afterwards offered to the godfather, announcing the baby's name and offering a prayer for the baby and for its mother. The baby is then returned to its mother. After the ceremony, wine and cakes are usually offered to the company."

"Are you going to say anything about the naming of a girl, Mother?"

"Now I know that you were listening very carefully, Hadassah. I have a short paragraph on that right here: In the case of the birth of a girl, the father is called to the synagogue ark during the reading of the Torah; the reader announces the name given to the baby girl and makes a benediction for the child and parents. The child can be named the first day of the reading of the law (Torah) after the day of birth. The Torah is read on Monday, Thursday and Saturday."

PIDYON HA-BEN

"The ceremony known as Pidyon Ha-Ben (Redemption of the Son) takes place only when the boy is the first-born of his mother. It commemorates the tenth plague which befell Egypt in which the first-born male of every Egyptian home was slain though the first-born males of the Hebrews were saved. This ceremony takes place on the thirty-first day after the boy's birth, but since money is exchanged it is delayed if it falls on the Sabbath or on a religious holiday."

"Here I am again, Mother. As I remember it, aren't the descendants of Aaron (Cohanim) and Levite families exempt from this particular ceremony?"

"Of course, but I didn't think it necessary to make a point of that since it is common knowledge among Jews."

"I doubt that, Mother. I think you should explain that rather fully. As with the Elijah legend, I think that the reason for these exemptions will add interest to what you are saying."

"You are probably right, Hadassah. I will put that in right now.

"If the father or mother is a member of a Cohanim or Levite family, this ceremony does not take place because the members served in the Temple. In ancient days the Jews redeemed their first-born from Temple service by payment of money. According to the Book of Numbers, the child must be redeemed by a payment of five shekels or an equivalent substitute. This money can only be paid to a descendant of the family of Aaron, a Cohen.

"The father presents the child to this Cohen saying, 'This, my first-born, is the first-born of his mother, and the Holy One, blessed be He, has commanded me to redeem him, etc.'

"A member of the tribe of Aaron then asks, 'Which do you prefer, to give me thy first-born son, for God's service, the first-born of his mother, or to redeem him for five shekels which you are by law required to give?' The father replies, 'I prefer to redeem my son. Here is the value of his redemption which I am by law obliged to give.' The redemption money is accepted by the Cohen and the child is returned to the father, who says, 'Praised be Thou, O Lord our God, King of the Universe, who has sanctified us with His Commandments, and enjoined upon us the redemption of the son.'

"The Cohen holds the redemption money over the child's head and declares, 'This is instead of that. This is in exchange for that. This is in remission of that. May it be the will of God that as this child has entered the period of redemption, the child may be spared to enter the study of the law, the state of marriage and the practice of good deeds. Amen.' The redemption money is usually given to charity. The Cohen then puts his hand on the baby's head, reciting a blessing which concludes, 'The Lord shall guard thee against all evil. He will guard thy life. Amen.'

"There is one other exception. If the child is of Caesarian birth a Pidyon Ha-Ben does not take place.

"The Pidyon Ha-Ben ceremony is usually the occasion for a gathering of friends and relatives and at the conclusion of the ceremony there is a feast."

BAR MITZVAH

"Now, what did you say about Bar Mitzvah, Mother?"

"At the *brith* a boy is accepted as a Jew, but his parents speak for him. However, at the age of thirteen, after studying the history and religion of his people, he knows what it means to be a Jew, and according to custom has attained his religious majority. His thirteenth birthday is, therefore, one of the most important dates in the life of a boy, and is celebrated by him and his family in the synagogue and the home.

"Before his thirteenth birthday a boy has received

instruction, particularly in the section of the Torah which is read on the Sabbath following his thirteenth birthday, according to the Jewish calendar, and the corresponding portion in the Prophets. He is also taught to lay phylacteries, or *tephillin*, a small square box containing a parchment upon which four sections of the *Shema* are inscribed. The *tephillin* are worn upon the forehead and left arm for morning prayers daily except on Saturdays and holidays.

"The father is responsible for the education of his son and for all childhood violations of religious duties; but when the boy becomes a Bar Mitzvah the father is freed from further responsibility for the child's transgression of our law.

"The ceremony of introducing the Bar Mitzvah to the congregation usually takes place on the Sabbath following his thirteenth birthday. In the synagogue the boy is called to the *bimah* at the reading of the Torah. The Bar Mitzvah is given the honor of reading the Maftir, which consists of the last part of the weekly Torah reading and the entire reading from the Prophets, which follows the reading of the Torah. In some instances the boy may also deliver an address to the assembled congregation.

"When the synagogue service is over, the event is usually celebrated by a reception or dinner."

"Did you explain why the age of thirteen was selected?"

"No, Hadassah, I omitted that deliberately because there are so many different reasons given. However, if I were to give any explanation I would give the one that appeals to me most and that is, from the Mishnah, 'At five one must begin the study of the Bible, at ten that of the Mishnah, and at thirteen one must assume the Commandments.' "

LAWS CONCERNING MOURNING

"Hadassah, dear, it is sad that your future father-in-law passed away before your wedding. It happens that *simchot* are sometimes marred by death in the family."

"Thank goodness, I have never had a very close association with tragedy until now, Mother. Just what are the customs at this time?"

"During the funeral services the *keriah* is torn. A *keriah* is a deliberate tear made in the garments of the members of the immediate family. This is performed just before the coffin is closed, when one's mourning is still intense. It must be done on the cloth garment near the front of the neck, lengthwise in the cloth, not along the seams. The *keriah* is torn while the mourner stands, to denote that sorrows and troubles must be met bravely by the individual, who must remain strong while bearing sorrow. The *keriah* is torn by an older man, who pronounces the following benediction: 'Blessed are Thou, O Lord our God, King of the Universe, Righteous Judge.'

"The relatives for whom one must mourn are father, mother, son, daughter, wife, husband, brother and sister. One does not mourn a child less than thirty days old.

"The intervention of a festival annuls *Shivah*, the mourning of seven days, or *Shloshim*, the mourning of thirty days; mourning ceases as soon as festivals begin. Although festivals annul *Shivah* mourning, nevertheless the memorial candle is lighted. The festival candles are also lighted.

"The week of mourning is called *Shivah*, when the family sits on low stools or on low chairs. In the olden days it was customary for the mourners to sit on the floor without any leather footwear on their feet. The first meal eaten by the mourners on their return from the cemetery is hard-boiled eggs and bagels. The roundness of the eggs signifies the wheel of fortune, and the changes from happiness to unhappiness and back to happiness, to which man is subject. This meal is generally prepared by friends and neighbors; this is called *seudat havrach*. During the *Shivah* week all services are recited in the home where the relatives sit *Shivah* except on the Sabbath morn when the mourners may go to the synagogue. The *Kaddish* must be recited only in the presence of a group of ten men (*minyan*). The week of *Shivah* gives the mourners a chance to meditate and to adjust themselves to life without the departed, and to start life anew. During this period friends and relatives come to pay their respects. Visitors shake hands with each one in turn saying 'May the Lord comfort you, together with all other mourners for Zion and Jerusalem.' A memorial candle is lit and it is kept burning for a whole week. On the first day of mourning it is not customary to wear the *tallis*.

"The *Kaddish* is recited for a period of eleven months by the sons or nearest male relative of the deceased, three times a day, during each regular service. It is the prayer of sanctification.

"The period after the *Shivah* week is called *Shloshim*, meaning thirty days after the death. During this period the family goes about its affairs, but they do not go to theaters or dances or to any entertainment. The mourning period is carried on for twelve months.

"At the end of a year a tombstone may be unveiled

and friends and relatives gather at the cemetery. The service at the unveiling consists of several psalms and the *El Maley Rachamim*. *Kaddish* is then said by the nearest male relative.

"Every year at the date of death, *yahrzeit* is observed by the lighting of a *yahrzeit* candle. The sons go to the synagogue and recite the *Kaddish* on the eve of the *yahrzeit*, and in the morning and in the evening of the following day.

"Memorial services are recited during the year on such holidays as Yom Kippur, Shemini Atzeret, the last day of Passover, and the second day of Shavuot. Each person reads silently several prayers in which he mentions the names of his parents. The cantor chants the *El Maley Rachamim* on behalf of the departed kin of the entire congregation.

"Unfortunately, Hadassah, it will be necessary for the *El Maley Rachamim* to be recited before your wedding in memory of your departed father-in-law."

BENEDICTIONS AND GRACE

(All prayers and benedictions are said with head covered.)

RITUAL OF WASHING OF THE HANDS

(The benediction before meals is preceded by the washing
of the hands.)

בָּרוּךְ אַתָּה יְיָ אֱלֹהֵינוּ מֶלֶךְ הָעוֹלָם · אֲשֶׁר קִדְּשָׁנוּ
בְּמִצְוֹתָיו וְצִוָּנוּ עַל נְטִילַת יָדָיִם :

*Baruch Atta Adonoy Eloheinu Melech Haolam Asher
Kidshanu B'Mitzvotav V'tzivonu al Netilat Yodayim.*

Blessed art Thou, O Lord our God, King of the Universe, who hast sanctified us by Thy Commandments and
hast commanded us the washing of the hands.
(There should be no interruption between the washing of
the hands and the benediction over bread.)

HAMOTZI:
BENEDICTION ON BREAKING BREAD

בָּרוּךְ אַתָּה יְיָ אֱלֹהֵינוּ מֶלֶךְ הָעוֹלָם · הַמּוֹצִיא לֶחֶם
מִן הָאָרֶץ :

*Baruch Atta Adonoy Eloheinu Melech Haolam Ha-
motzi Lechem Min Haaretz.*

Blessed art Thou, O Lord our God, King of the Universe, who bringeth forth bread from the earth.
(The choicest piece, the crust, is cut for the benediction.)

BENEDICTION OVER WINE

בָּרוּךְ אַתָּה יְיָ אֱלֹהֵינוּ מֶלֶךְ הָעוֹלָם · בּוֹרֵא פְּרִי הַגָּפֶן :

Baruch Atta Adonoy Eloheinu Melech Haolam Boray Pri Hagafen.

Blessed art Thou, O Lord our God, King of the Universe, who createst the fruit of the vine.

BENEDICTION FOR VEGETABLES, HERBS AND FRUIT WHICH GROW ON THE GROUND

בָּרוּךְ אַתָּה יְיָ אֱלֹהֵינוּ מֶלֶךְ הָעוֹלָם · בּוֹרֵא פְּרִי הָאֲדָמָה :

Baruch Atta Adonoy Eloheinu Melech Haolam Boray Pri Haadamah.

Blessed art Thou, O Lord our God, King of the Universe, who createst the fruit of the earth.

BENEDICTION FOR MEAT, FISH, MILK AND BEVERAGES EXCEPT WINE

בָּרוּךְ אַתָּה יְיָ אֱלֹהֵינוּ מֶלֶךְ הָעוֹלָם · שֶׁהַכֹּל נִהְיֶה בִּדְבָרוֹ :

Baruch Atta Adonoy Eloheinu Melech Haolam Shehakol Nihyeh Bidvaro.

Blessed art Thou, O Lord our God, King of the Universe, by whose word all things exist.

BENEDICTION FOR FOOD MADE OF CEREAL FLOUR

בָּרוּךְ אַתָּה יְיָ אֱלֹהֵינוּ מֶלֶךְ הָעוֹלָם · בּוֹרֵא מִינֵי מְזוֹנוֹת :

Baruch Atta Adonoy Eloheinu Melech Haolam Boray Minai Mzonot.

Blessed art Thou, O Lord our God, King of the Universe, who createst the various kinds of food.

BENEDICTION FOR FRUIT

בָּרוּךְ אַתָּה יְיָ אֱלֹהֵינוּ מֶלֶךְ הָעוֹלָם · בּוֹרֵא פְּרִי הָעֵץ:

Baruch Atta Adonoy Eloheinu Melech Haolam Boray Pri Haetz.

Blessed art Thou, O Lord our God, King of the Universe, who createst fruit of the tree.

BENEDICTION OVER THE SABBATH CANDLES

(It is one of the three fundamental duties of a Jewish woman to light candles on the Sabbath. The head is covered, the palms of the hands shield the face during the benediction. After candles have been lit the benediction is pronounced.)

בָּרוּךְ אַתָּה יְיָ אֱלֹהֵינוּ מֶלֶךְ הָעוֹלָם · אֲשֶׁר קִדְּשָׁנוּ
בְּמִצְוֹתָיו וְצִוָּנוּ לְהַדְלִיק נֵר שֶׁל־שַׁבָּת:

Baruch Atta Adonoy Eloheinu Melech Haolam Asher Kidshanu B'mitzvotav V'tzivanu L'Hadlik Nair Shel Shabbat.

Blessed art Thou, O Lord our God, King of the Universe, who hast sanctified us by His Commandments, and commanded us to kindle the Sabbath lights.

BENEDICTION ON A FESTIVAL ON WEEKDAYS

בָּרוּךְ אַתָּה יְיָ אֱלֹהֵינוּ מֶלֶךְ הָעוֹלָם · אֲשֶׁר קִדְּשָׁנוּ
בְּמִצְוֹתָיו וְצִוָּנוּ לְהַדְלִיק נֵר שֶׁל־יוֹם טוֹב:

Baruch Atta Adonoy Eloheinu Melech Haolam Asher Kidshanu B'mitzvotav V'tzivanu L'Hadlik Nair Shel Yomtov.

239

Blessed art Thou, O Lord our God, King of the Universe, who hast sanctified us by His Commandments and commanded us to kindle the festival lights.

ON A FESTIVAL WHICH OCCURS ON A FRIDAY NIGHT

בָּרוּךְ אַתָּה יְיָ אֱלֹהֵינוּ מֶלֶךְ הָעוֹלָם · אֲשֶׁר קִדְּשָׁנוּ
בְּמִצְוֹתָיו וְצִוָּנוּ לְהַדְלִיק נֵר שֶׁל שַׁבָּת וְיוֹם טוֹב :

Baruch Atta Adonoy Eloheinu Melech Haolam Asher Kidshanu B'mitzvotav V'tzivanu L'Hadlik Nair Shel Shabbat Vyomtov.

Blessed art Thou, O Lord our God, King of the Universe, who hast sanctified us by His Commandments, and hast commanded us to kindle the Sabbath and festival lights.

ON THE FIRST NIGHT OF THE FESTIVAL ADD

בָּרוּךְ אַתָּה יְיָ אֱלֹהֵינוּ מֶלֶךְ הָעוֹלָם · שֶׁהֶחֱיָנוּ
וְקִיְּמָנוּ וְהִגִּיעָנוּ לַזְּמַן הַזֶּה :

Baruch Atta Adonoy Eloheinu Melech Haolam Shehecheyanu Vkiyimanu Vhigianu Lazman Hazeh.

Blessed art Thou, O Lord our God, King of the Universe, who has kept us in life, and hast preserved us and enabled us to reach this season.

BLESSING OF CANDLES ON YOM KIPPUR

בָּרוּךְ אַתָּה יְיָ אֱלֹהֵינוּ מֶלֶךְ הָעוֹלָם · אֲשֶׁר קִדְּשָׁנוּ
בְּמִצְוֹתָיו וְצִוָּנוּ לְהַדְלִיק נֵר שֶׁל יוֹם הַכִּפֻּרִים

Baruch Atta Adonoy Eloheinu Melech Haolam Asher

Kidshanu B'mitzvotav V'tzivanu L'Hadlik Neir Shel Yom Hakipurim.

Blessed art Thou, O Lord our God, King of the Universe, who hast sanctified us by His Commandments, and hast commanded us to kindle the Yom Kippur lights.

HAVDALAH BENEDICTION

(After saying the blessing over wine we say the benediction over the candle and the spices.)

בָּרוּךְ אַתָּה יְיָ אֱלֹהֵינוּ מֶלֶךְ הָעוֹלָם • בּוֹרֵא מְאוֹרֵי הָאֵשׁ:

Baruch Atta Adonoy Eloheinu Melech Haolam Boray M'oray Ha'esh.

Blessed art Thou, O Lord our God, King of the Universe, the creator of the lights of fire.

BENEDICTION OVER SPICES

בָּרוּךְ אַתָּה יְיָ אֱלֹהֵינוּ מֶלֶךְ הָעוֹלָם • בּוֹרֵא מִינֵי בְשָׂמִים:

Baruch Atta Adonoy Eloheinu Melech Haolam Borai Minai Bssamim.

Blessed art Thou, O Lord our God, King of the Universe, who created a variety of spices.

CHILDREN'S MORNING PRAYER

מוֹדָה אֲנִי לְפָנֶיךָ מֶלֶךְ חַי וְקַיָם שֶׁהֶחֱזַרְתָּ בִּי נִשְׁמָתִי בְּחֶמְלָה • רַבָּה אֱמוּנָתֶךָ:

Modeh Ani Lfanecha, Melech Chai Vkayam, Shehechezarta Be Nishmati, Bchemlah Rabbah Emunatecha.

I thank Thee before Thee, Living and Everlasting

King, for Thou hast mercifully returned my soul unto me.
Great is Thy faithfulness.

BENEDICTION FOR CHANUKAH

(Before kindling the lights the blessings are said.)

בָּרוּךְ אַתָּה יְיָ אֱלֹהֵינוּ מֶלֶךְ הָעוֹלָם · אֲשֶׁר קִדְּשָׁנוּ
בְּמִצְוֹתָיו וְצִוָּנוּ לְהַדְלִיק נֵר שֶׁל חֲנֻכָּה :

Baruch Atta Adonoy Eloheinu Melech Haolam Asher
Kidshanu B'mitzvotav V'tzivanu L'Hadlick Ner Shel Cha-
nukah.

Blessed art Thou, O Lord our God, King of the Universe, who hast sanctified us by thy Commandments, and
commanded us to kindle the lights of Chanukah.

MAOZ TZUR

מָעוֹז צוּר יְשׁוּעָתִי · לְךָ נָאֶה לְשַׁבֵּחַ · תִּכּוֹן בֵּית
תְּפִלָּתִי · וְשָׁם תּוֹדָה נְזַבֵּחַ · לְעֵת תַּשְׁבִּית מַטְבֵּחַ · וְצָר
הַמְנַבֵּחַ · אָז אֶגְמוֹר · בְּשִׁיר מִזְמוֹר · חֲנֻכַּת הַמִּזְבֵּחַ :

Maoz Tsur Yshuati, Lehah Naeh Lshabeach
Tikon Bet Tfilati Vsham Todah Nzabeyach
Let Tochin Matbeyach Mitsor Hamnabeyach
Oz Egmor Bshir Mizmor Chanukat Hamizbeyach.

Rock of Ages, let our song praise Thy saving power;
Thou, amidst the raging foes, wast our shelt'ring tower.
Furious they assailed us, but Thine arm availed us,
And Thy word broke their sword
When our own strength failed us.
(The first evening we also say the *Shehecheyanu.*)

בָּרוּךְ אַתָּה יְיָ אֱלֹהֵינוּ מֶלֶךְ הָעוֹלָם · שֶׁעָשָׂה נִסִּים
לַאֲבוֹתֵינוּ בַּיָּמִים הָהֵם בַּזְּמַן הַזֶּה :

242

Baruch Atta Adonoy Eloheinu Melech Haolam She-osso Nisism Lavotenu Bayamim Hahem Bazman Hazeh.

Blessed art Thou, O Lord our God, King of the Universe, who hast wrought miracles for our fathers in those days at this season.

BENEDICTION WHEN HANGING THE MEZUZAH

בָּרוּךְ אַתָּה יְיָ אֱלֹהֵינוּ מֶלֶךְ הָעוֹלָם · אֲשֶׁר קִדְּשָׁנוּ בְּמִצְוֹתָיו וְצִוָּנוּ לִקְבּוֹעַ מְזוּזָה :

Baruch Atta Adonoy Eloheinu Melech Haolam Asher Kidshanu B'mitzvotav V'tzivanu Likboah Mezuzah.

Blessed art Thou, O Lord our God, King of the Universe, who hast sanctified us by His Commandments, and enjoined us to put up the Mezuzah.

CHALAH BENEDICTION

בָּרוּךְ אַתָּה יְיָ אֱלֹהֵינוּ מֶלֶךְ הָעוֹלָם אֲשֶׁר קִדְּשָׁנוּ בְּמִצְוֹתָיו וְצִוָּנוּ לְהַפְרִישׁ חַלָּה :

Baruch Atta Adonoy Eloheinu Melech Haolam-Asher Kidshanu B'mitzvotav V'tzivanu Lhafrish Chalah.

Blessed art Thou, O Lord our God, King of the Universe, who hast sanctified us by His Commandments, and commanded us to take the portion of the dough.

LULAV AND ESROG BENEDICTION

בָּרוּךְ אַתָּה יְיָ אֱלֹהֵינוּ מֶלֶךְ הָעוֹלָם · אֲשֶׁר קִדְּשָׁנוּ בְּמִצְוֹתָיו וְצִוָּנוּ עַל־נְטִילַת לוּלָב :

Baruch Atta Adonoy Eloheinu Melech Haolam Asher Kidshanu B'mitzvotav V'tzivanu al Netilat Lulav.

243

Blessed art Thou, O Lord our God, King of the Universe, who hast sanctified us by His Commandments, and commanded us to take the Lulav.

BENEDICTION UPON ENTERING SUCCAH

בָּרוּךְ אַתָּה יְיָ אֱלֹהֵינוּ מֶלֶךְ הָעוֹלָם · אֲשֶׁר קִדְּשָׁנוּ
בְּמִצְוֹתָיו וְצִוָּנוּ לֵישֵׁב בַּסֻּכָּה :

Baruch Atta Adonoy Eloheinu Melech Haolam Asher Kidshanu B'mitzvotav V'tzivanu Leshev Basuccah.

Blessed art Thou, O Lord our God, King of the Universe, who hast sanctified us by His Commandments, and commanded us to sit in the Succah.

BENEDICTION ON KERIAH:
TEARING GARMENTS OF MOURNERS

בָּרוּךְ אַתָּה יְיָ אֱלֹהֵינוּ מֶלֶךְ הָעוֹלָם · דַּיַּן הָאֱמֶת :

Baruch Atta Adonoy Eloheinu Melech Haolam Dayan Haemet.

Blessed art Thou, O Lord our God, King of the Universe, Righteous Judge.

GRACE AFTER MEALS

He who says grace commences thus: "Let us say grace."

The others respond: "Blessed be the name of the Lord from this time forth and forever."

He who says grace proceeds: "With the sanction of these present we will bless Him of Whose bounty we have partaken and through Whose goodness we live.

244

"Blessed art Thou, O Lord our God, King of the Universe, Who feedest the whole world with Thy goodness, with grace, and with loving kindness and tender mercy. Thou givest food to all flesh, for Thy loving kindness endureth forever. Through Thy great goodness, food hath never failed us. May it not fail us forever and ever for Thy great Name's sake, since Thou nourishest and sustainest all beings, and doest good unto all, and providest food for Thy creatures whom Thou hast created. Blessed art Thou, O Lord, who givest food unto all.

"We thank Thee, O Lord our God, because Thou didst give us an inheritance unto our fathers, a desirable, good and ample land, and because Thou didst bring us forth, O Lord our God, from the land of Egypt and didst deliver us from the house of bondage, as well as for Thy covenant, which taught us Thy statutes which Thou hast made known unto us, and for the food wherewith Thou dost constantly feed and sustain us every day, in every season at every hour."

On Chanukah and Purim we add:

"We thank Thee also for the miracles, for the redemption, for the mighty deeds and saving wrought by Thee, as well as for the wars which Thou didst wage for our fathers in the days of old at this season."

On Purim we add:

"In the days of Mordecai and Esther, in Shushan, the capital, when the wicked Haman rose up against them, and sought to destroy, to slay and make to perish all the Jews, both young and old, little children and women, on one day, on the thirteenth day of the twelfth month, which is the month of Adar, and to take the spoil of them for a prey— then Thou didst in Thine abundant mercy bring his counsel

245

to nought, didst frustrate his design, and return his recompense upon his own head; and they hanged him and his sons upon the gallows."

On Chanukah we add:

"In the days of the Hasmonean, Mattathias, son of Johanan the high priest, and his sons, when the iniquitous power of Greece rose up against Thy people Israel to make them forgetful of Thy law, and to force them to transgress the statutes of Thy will, then didst Thou in Thine abundant mercy rise up for them in their time of their trouble; Thou didst plead their cause; Thou didst judge their suit; Thou didst avenge their wrong; Thou deliverest the strong into the hands of the weak, the many into the hands of the few, the impure into the hands of the pure, the wicked into the hands of the righteous, and the arrogant into the hands of them that occupied themselves with Thy law. For Thyself, Thou didst make a great and holy name in Thy world, and for Thy people Israel Thou didst work a great deliverance and redemption on this day. And thereupon, Thy children came into the oracle of Thy house, cleansed Thy temple, purified Thy sanctuary, kindled lights in Thy old courts, and appointed these eight days of Chanukah in order to give thanks and praises unto Thy great Name."

25-YEAR CALENDAR OF JEWISH FESTIVALS

*Festivals begin at sundown the evening before,
almost invariably with the lighting of candles.*

ROSH HASHANAH Commencing Tishrei 1

Jewish year	*Date on common calendar*	
5727	September 15	1966
5728	October 5	1967
5729	September 23	1968
5730	September 13	1969
5731	October 1	1970
5732	September 20	1971
5733	September 9	1972
5734	September 27	1973
5735	September 17	1974
5736	September 6	1975
5737	September 25	1976
5738	September 13	1977
5739	October 2	1978
5740	September 22	1979
5741	September 11	1980
5742	September 29	1981
5743	September 18	1982
5744	September 8	1983
5745	September 27	1984
5746	September 16	1985
5747	September 4	1986
5748	September 24	1987
5749	September 12	1988
5750	September 30	1989
5751	September 20	1990

YOM KIPPUR Commencing Tishrei 10

Jewish year	*Date on common calendar*	
5727	September 24	1966
5728	October 14	1967
5729	October 2	1968
5730	September 22	1969
5731	October 10	1970
5732	September 29	1971
5733	September 18	1972
5734	October 6	1973
5735	September 26	1974
5736	September 15	1975
5737	October 4	1976
5738	September 22	1977
5739	October 11	1978
5740	October 1	1979
5741	September 20	1980
5742	October 8	1981
5743	September 27	1982
5744	September 17	1983
5745	October 6	1984
5746	September 25	1985
5747	October 13	1986
5748	October 3	1987
5749	September 21	1988
5750	October 9	1989
5751	September 29	1990

SUCCOT Commencing Tishrei 15

Jewish year	*Date on common calendar*	
5727	September 29	1966
5728	October 19	1967
5729	October 7	1968
5730	September 27	1969
5731	October 15	1970
5732	October 4	1971
5733	September 23	1972
5734	October 11	1973
5735	October 7	1974
5736	September 20	1975
5737	October 9	1976
5738	September 27	1977
5739	October 16	1978
5740	October 6	1979
5741	September 25	1980
5742	October 13	1981
5743	October 2	1982
5744	September 22	1983
5745	October 11	1984
5746	September 30	1985
5747	October 18	1986
5748	October 8	1987
5749	September 26	1988
5750	October 14	1989
5751	October 4	1990

SHEMINI ATZERET Commencing Tishrei 22

Jewish year	*Date on common calendar*		
5727	October	6	1966
5728	October	26	1967
5729	October	14	1968
5730	October	4	1969
5731	October	22	1970
5732	October	11	1971
5733	September	30	1972
5734	October	18	1973
5735	October	8	1974
5736	September	27	1975
5737	October	16	1976
5738	October	4	1977
5739	October	23	1978
5740	October	13	1979
5741	October	2	1980
5742	October	20	1981
5743	October	9	1982
5744	September	29	1983
5745	October	18	1984
5746	October	7	1985
5747	October	25	1986
5748	October	15	1987
5749	October	3	1988
5750	October	21	1989
5751	October	11	1990

SIMCHAT TORAH Commencing Tishrei 23

Jewish year	*Date on common calendar*	
5727	October 7	1966
5728	October 27	1967
5729	October 15	1968
5730	October 5	1969
5731	October 23	1970
5732	October 12	1971
5733	October 1	1972
5734	October 19	1973
5735	October 9	1974
5736	September 28	1975
5737	October 17	1976
5738	October 5	1977
5739	October 24	1978
5740	October 14	1979
5741	October 3	1980
5742	October 21	1981
5743	October 10	1982
5744	September 30	1983
5745	October 19	1984
5746	October 8	1985
5747	October 26	1986
5748	October 16	1987
5749	October 4	1988
5750	October 22	1989
5751	October 12	1990

CHANUKAH Commencing Kislev 25

Jewish year	*Date on common calendar*	
5727	December 8	1966
5728	December 27	1967
5729	December 16	1968
5730	December 5	1969
5731	December 23	1970
5732	December 13	1971
5733	December 1	1972
5734	December 20	1973
5735	December 9	1974
5736	November 29	1975
5737	December 17	1976
5738	December 5	1977
5739	December 25	1978
5740	December 15	1979
5741	December 3	1980
5742	December 21	1981
5743	December 11	1982
5744	December 1	1983
5745	December 19	1984
5746	December 8	1985
5747	December 27	1986
5748	December 16	1987
5749	December 4	1988
5750	December 23	1989
5751	December 12	1990

CHAMISHAH ASAR BISHVAT Commencing Shvat 15
ARBOR DAY OR FESTIVAL OF THE TREES

Jewish year	Date on common calendar	
5726	February 5	1966
5727	January 26	1967
5728	February 14	1968
5729	February 3	1969
5730	January 22	1970
5731	February 10	1971
5732	January 31	1972
5733	January 18	1973
5734	February 7	1974
5735	January 27	1975
5736	January 17	1976
5737	February 3	1977
5738	January 23	1978
5739	February 12	1979
5740	February 2	1980
5741	January 20	1981
5742	February 8	1982
5743	January 29	1983
5744	January 19	1984
5745	February 6	1985
5746	January 25	1986
5747	February 14	1987
5748	February 3	1988
5749	January 21	1989
5750	February 10	1990

PURIM Commencing Adar 14

Jewish year			*Date on common calendar*	
5726	Adar 14	March	6	1966
5727	V'Adar 14	March	26	1967
5728	Adar 14	March	14	1968
5729	Adar 14	March	4	1969
5730	V'Adar 14	March	22	1970
5731	Adar 14	March	11	1971
5732	Adar 14	February	29	1972
5733	V'Adar 14	March	18	1973
5734	Adar 14	March	8	1974
5735	Adar 14	February	25	1975
5736	V'Adar 14	March	16	1976
5737	Adar 14	March	4	1977
5738	V'Adar 14	March	23	1978
5739	Adar 14	March	13	1979
5740	Adar 14	March	2	1980
5741	V'Adar 14	March	20	1981
5742	Adar 14	March	9	1982
5743	Adar 14	February	27	1983
5744	V'Adar 14	March	18	1984
5745	Adar 14	March	7	1985
5746	V'Adar 14	March	25	1986
5747	Adar 14	March	15	1987
5748	Adar 14	March	3	1988
5749	V'Adar 14	March	21	1989
5750	Adar 14	March	11	1990

PASSOVER Commencing Nissan 15

Jewish year	*Date on common calendar*	
5726	April 5	1966
5727	April 25	1967
5728	April 13	1968
5729	April 3	1969
5730	April 21	1970
5731	April 10	1971
5732	March 30	1972
5733	April 17	1973
5734	April 7	1974
5735	March 27	1975
5736	April 15	1976
5737	April 3	1977
5738	April 22	1978
5739	April 12	1979
5740	April 1	1980
5741	April 19	1981
5742	April 8	1982
5743	March 29	1983
5744	April 17	1984
5745	April 6	1985
5746	April 24	1986
5747	April 14	1987
5748	April 2	1988
5749	April 20	1989
5750	April 10	1990

LAG B'OMER Commencing Iyar 18

Jewish year	*Date on common calendar*	
5726	May 8	1966
5727	May 28	1967
5728	May 16	1968
5729	May 6	1969
5730	May 24	1970
5731	May 13	1971
5732	May 2	1972
5733	May 20	1973
5734	May 10	1974
5735	April 29	1975
5736	May 18	1976
5737	May 6	1977
5738	May 25	1978
5739	May 15	1979
5740	May 4	1980
5741	May 22	1981
5742	May 11	1982
5743	May 1	1983
5744	May 20	1984
5745	May 9	1985
5746	May 27	1986
5747	May 17	1987
5748	May 5	1988
5749	May 23	1989
5750	May 13	1990

SHAVUOT Commencing Sivan 6

Jewish year	Date on common calendar	
5726	May 25	1966
5727	June 14	1967
5728	June 2	1968
5729	May 23	1969
5730	June 10	1970
5731	May 30	1971
5732	May 19	1972
5733	June 6	1973
5734	May 27	1974
5735	May 16	1975
5736	June 4	1976
5737	May 23	1977
5738	June 11	1978
5739	June 1	1979
5740	May 21	1980
5741	June 8	1981
5742	May 28	1982
5743	May 18	1983
5744	June 6	1984
5745	May 26	1985
5746	June 13	1986
5747	June 3	1987
5748	May 22	1988
5749	June 9	1989
5750	May 30	1990

FAST OF TAMUZ Commencing Tamuz 17

Jewish year	*Date on common calendar*	
5726	July 5	1966
5727	July 25	1967
5728	July 13	1968
5729	July 3	1969
5730	July 21	1970
5731	July 10	1971
5732	June 29	1972
5733	July 17	1973
5734	July 7	1974
5735	June 26	1975
5736	July 15	1976
5737	July 3	1977
5738	July 23	1978
5739	July 12	1979
5740	July 1	1980
5741	July 19	1981
5742	July 8	1982
5743	June 28	1983
5744	July 17	1984
5745	July 7	1985
5746	July 24	1986
5747	July 14	1987
5748	July 3	1988
5749	July 20	1989
5750	July 10	1990

TISHA B'AV Commencing Av 9–10

Jewish year	Date on common calendar	
5726	July 26	1966
5727	August 15	1967
5728	August 3	1968
5729	July 24	1969
5730	August 11	1970
5731	July 31	1971
5732	July 20	1972
5733	August 7	1973
5734	July 28	1974
5735	July 17	1975
5736	August 5	1976
5737	July 24	1977
5738	August 13	1978
5739	August 2	1979
5740	July 22	1980
5741	August 9	1981
5742	July 29	1982
5743	July 19	1983
5744	August 7	1984
5745	July 28	1985
5746	August 14	1986
5747	August 4	1987
5748	July 24	1988
5749	August 10	1989
5750	July 31	1990

YAHRZEITEN

Name	Date on Jewish Calendar	Date on Common Calendar

FAMILY ANNIVERSARIES

My parents' wedding
anniversary

Date

_____   _____

My husband's parents'
wedding anniversary

_____   _____

Our wedding anniversary

_____   _____

My birthday

_____   _____

My husband's birthday

_____   _____

The children's birthdays

_____   _____

_____   _____

_____   _____

_____   _____

The children's wedding
anniversaries

_____   _____

_____   _____

Friends' anniversaries   Date

_____   _____

_____   _____

_____   _____

_____   _____

_____   _____

_____   _____

_____   _____

_____   _____

_____   _____

_____   _____

_____   _____

_____   _____

_____   _____

_____   _____

_____   _____

_____   _____

_____   _____

_____   _____

_____   _____

_____   _____

_____   _____

_____   _____

_____   _____

ESSENTIAL BOOKS FOR THE JEWISH HOME

Holy Scriptures, a new translation according to the Massoretic text. Philadelphia: Jewish Publication Society, 1950.

Daily Prayer Book, the Hebrew text with English translation, commentary, notes and introduction by the Chief Rabbi of England, Joseph H. Hertz; first American revised edition, New York City, Bloch Publishing Co., Inc., 1949.

Service of the Synagogue for New Year and the Day of Atonement, latest edition of the festival prayers with an English translation in prose and verse, edited by Rabbi Jacob Davis and Rabbi Naphtali Adler, reprinted from the latest and best London edition. 2 vols. Hebrew Publishing Company, 1962.

Haggadah for Passover, illustrated by Saul Raskin. New York City: Wolozin, 1941.

Jewish Festivals from Their Beginning to Our Own Day, by Hayyim Schauss, translated by Samuel Jaffe. Cincinnati: Union of American Hebrew Congregations, 1938.

The Lifetime of a Jew Throughout the Ages of Jewish History, by Hayyim Schauss, Cincinnati: Union of American Hebrew Congregations, 1950.

Songs of Zion, compiled and edited by Harry Coopersmith. Behrman House, Inc., 1948.

A Book of Jewish Thoughts, edited by Chief Rabbi Joseph H. Hertz. Montreal: Canadian Jewish Congress, 1943.

A Short History of the Jewish People, illustrated edition, revised and enlarged, by Cecil Roth. London: East and West Library, 1948.

The Jews, Their History, Culture and Religion, edited by Louis Finkelstein, Harper, 1950, 2 vols.

The Zionist Movement, by Israel Cohen, edited and revised with supplementary chapter by Bernard G. Richards. New York: Zionist Organization of America, 1946.

Trial and Error, the autobiography of the President of Israel, Dr. Chaim Weizmann. Harper, 1949.

History of the Jews in Canada, from the Earliest Beginnings to the End of the Nineteenth Century, by Benjamin G. Sack. Montreal: Canadian Jewish Congress, 1945.

American Jewish Year Book, a record of events and trends in American and world Jewish life, published annually by the American Jewish Committee and the Jewish Publication Society.

GENERAL INDEX

Anniversaries, 261–62
Arbor Day. *See* Chamishah Asar
    Bishvat

Bar Mitzvah, 232
Benedictions and Grace, 237–46
    after Meals, 245–46
Betrothal and Marriage, 14–18
Books, Essential, 263–64
Bread: Benediction on Breaking of,
    237
    Chalah Benediction, 243
Brith Milah, 229–30

Calendar, 25-Year, 247–59
Calf's Foot Jelly (Petchah), 125
Candles: Benediction on, 239
    Blessing of Yom Kippur, 240–41
Cereal Foods, Benediction on, 238
Chag-Ha'asif, 69
Chalah Benediction, 243
Chamishah Asar Bishvat, 90–94
    Calendar, 253
Chanukah, 78–89
    Benediction, 242
    Calendar, 252
    Grace after Meals, 245–46
Children's Morning Prayer, 241–42
Children's Village, 29
Child Rescue Fund, 28–29
Circumcision, 229–30
Construction Fund, 28

Day of Atonement. *See* Yom
    Kippur
Dietary Laws, 21–24

Feast of Harvest, 69
Feast of Tabernacles. *See* Succot
Feast of Weeks. *See* Shavuot
Festival of Freedom. *See* Passover
Festival of Lights. *See* Chanukah
Festival of the Trees. *See*
    Chamishah Asar Bishvat

Festivals, Benediction for, 239–40
Fruit, Benedictions for, 238, 239

Grace and Benedictions, 237–46
    after Meals, 245–46

Hadassah, 25–31
Hadassim, 29
Hamotzi, 237
Hands, Ritual Washing of, 237
Havdalah Benediction, 241

Jewish National Fund, 27–28

Kashrut, 21–24
Keren Hayesod, 28
Keren Kayemeth, 27–28
Keriah, Benediction on, 244
Kol Nidrei, 61–62

Lag b'Omer, 15, 145–49
    Calendar, 256
Lulav and Esrog, 69
    Benediction, 243–44

Maoz Tzur, 242–43
Marriage, 14–18
Meat, Fish, Milk and Beverages.
    Benediction for, 238
Mezuzah, 19–20
    Benediction when Hanging, 243
Mourning, 234–36
    Benediction on Keriah, 244

Nahalal, 30
New Year. *See* Rosh Hashanah

Passover, 104–44
    Calendar, 255
    Dairy Meals, 131–44
    Menus and Recipes, 114–44,
        220–21ff
Pidyon Ha-Ben, 230–32

Prayers, 237–46
  Grace after Meals, 245–46
Purim, 95–103
  Calendar, 254
  Grace after Meals, 245–46

Redemption of the Son, 230–32
Rosh Chodesh, 15
Rosh Hashanah, 45–59
  Calendar, 246

Sabbath, 32–44
  Candles, Benedictions on, 239, 240
Sephirah, 14
Shavuot, 150–59
  Calendar, 257
Shemini Atzeret, 70
  Calendar, 250
Shivah, 234–35
Shloshim, 234, 235–36
Simchat Torah, 70
  Calendar, 251
Spices, Benediction over, 241
Succah, 68–69
  Benediction upon Entering, 244

Succot, 68–77
  Benediction upon Entering Succah, 244
  Calendar, 249

Tamuz, Fast of, 15
  Calendar, 258
Three Weeks, 160–62
Tisha b'Av, 15, 160–62
  Calendar, 259
Tree Festival. See Chamishah Asar Bishvat
25-Year Calendar, 247–59

Vegetables, Herbs and Fruit, Benediction for, 238

Washing of the Hands, Ritual, 237
Weddings, 14–18
Wine, Benediction over, 238

Yahrzeiten, 61, 260
Yom Haatzmaut, 15
Yom Kippur, 60–67
  Calendar, 248
  Candles, Blessing of, 240–41
Youth Aliyah, 28–29

INDEX TO RECIPES

Almond Cake Filling, 179
Almond Date Squares, 176–77
Almond Fingers, 164–65
Almonds, Mandelbrot, 184
Antipasto, 208
Apple: Crisp, 206–7, 213
  Fritters, 223
  Pie, 214–15
  Pie, Deep-Dish, 121
  Pudding, Farfel, 126
  Roll, 180–81
  Squares, 165
  Strudel, 58–59
  Twists, Fried, 165–66
Apples: Baked, 128
  Charoset, 114
Applesauce, 65
Apricot Whip, 50
Aspic, Cranberry, 86

Bagel, Passover, 220
Bagelech, Cheese, 204
Banana Cake, 166
Banbury Tarts, 167
Barley and Lima Bean Soup, 157
Bean and Barley Soup, Lima, 157
Beans, Mock Liver Appetizer with,
  87
Beef. *See also* Liver; Meat
  Brisket of, Roast, 118
  Kreplach, 64–65
  Pie, 212
  Rib Roast and Browned
    Potatoes, 100
  Steak, Broiled, 125
  Stuffed Peppers, 126–27
  Stuffed Squash, 129
  Tongue, Roast, 115
Beet Borsht, 118
  Cold, 154–55
Beet Mold, 158
Beets: Chremsel, 140
  Harvard, 116
  Pickled, 126
Biscuit Dough for Apple Roll, 181
Biscuits, 163
Black Radish Salad, 128
Blintzes, Cheese, 132
Blintzes, Potato and Liver, 123–24
Blueberry Roll, 86–87
Borsht: Beet, 118
  Beet, Cold, 154–55
  Spinach, 218
Brain Latkes, 56–57
Bran Muffins, 163
Brazil Nut Slices, 202–3

Bread: Chalah, 38–39
  Raisin, 149
  Stuffing, 218
Bread and Butter Pickles, 216–17
Butterscotch Pie, 214
Butterscotch Rolls, 168

Cabbage Salad, 76
  Cole Slaw, 89
Cabbage, Stuffed, 83–84
Cakes: Banana, 166
  Cheese, 169–70
  Cheese, Pineapple, 188
  Cherry Custard, 171
  Chocolate Cream Layer, 172
  Chocolate Fudge, 172–73
  Chocolate Sponge, 132–33
  Coconut, 175
  Date and Nut Loaf, 77
  Date and Orange, 177–78
  Day and Night, 179
  Fruit, Dark, 179–80
  Honey, 51
  Honey Chiffon, 52
  for Jam Squares, 183
  Matzo Spice, 128
  Meringue, 184–85
  Pineapple Cheese, 188
  for Pineapple Squares, 188–89
  Pineapple Upside-Down, 200
  Pineapple Upside-Down, Orange
    and, 73–74
  Sour Cream Coffee, 193–94
  Sour Cream Refrigerator, 220
  Spice Matzo, 128
  Sponge, 116–17
  Sponge, Chocolate, 132–33
  Sponge, Fruit Salad on, 119
  Strawberry Refrigerator, 135–36
  Tropic Aroma, 198
  Wine, 223
Candied Fruit Peel, 203
Candy. *See also* Cherry Balls;
    Chinese Chews; etc.
  Carrot, 223
  Fudge, Chocolate, 203
  Fudge, Maple, 203–4
  Mohn, 103
Cantaloupe Basket, 74
Carrot Candy, 223
Carrot Pudding, 120
Carrot Tsimes with Knadel, 50–51
Carrots: Glazed, 100–1
  for Mock Salmon Patties, 213
Cauliflower au Gratin, 155
Celery Soup, Cream of, 88, 139

Chalah, 38–39
Charoset, 114
Cheese: Bagelech, 204
  Balls, 94
  Balls, Fruit Salad with, 142
  Blintzes, 132
  Cake, 169–70
  Cake, Pineapple, 188
  Knadlech, 204–5
  Knishes, 156
  and Matzo, Baked, 225
  and Noodle Ring, 205
  Pancakes, 206
  Pancakes, Sour Cream and, 89
  Sauce, 209–10
  Soufflé, 205
  Squares, 170
  Straws, 148–49
Cherry Balls, 186
Cherry Custard Cake, 171
Cherry Turnovers, 190–91
Chick Peas, 40
  with Rice, 219
Chicken: Broiled Spring, 157
  Casserole, 67
  with Corn Flakes Stuffing, Roast
    Capon, 84–85
  Giblet Fricassee, 123
  Livers and Mushrooms, 157
  en Papillote, Savory Roast
    Capon, 41–42
  Pie, 211
  with Potato and Liver Stuffing,
    Roast, 49–50
  Soup, 41
  Southern Fried, 75
  Stuffings for Roast. See
    Stuffings
Chili Sauce, 217
Chinese Chews, 170–71
Chocolate: Cream Layer Cake, 172
  Frosting, 173
  Frosting, Soft, 172
  Fudge, 203
  Fudge Cake, 172–73
  Fudge Squares, 173
  Roll, 173–74
  Sponge Cake, 132–33
  Squares, 174
  Torte, 174–75
Chowder, Fish, 139
Chremsel, 140
Coconut: Cake, Delicate, 175
  Fruit Pudding, 122
  Glaze, 197
  Macaroons, 138, 222
  Squares, 175

Coffee Cake, Sour Cream, 193–94
Cole Slaw, 89
Compote of Rhubarb and
  Strawberries, 43
Concord Grape Jelly, 210
Cookies. See also Macaroons; etc.
  Date and Nut Refrigerator, 177
  Farfel, Passover, 221
  Oatmeal, 187
  Oatmeal, Crisp, 187
  Passover, 221, 222
  Pineapple, 188
  Pinwheel, 190
  Poppy Seed, 191
  Refrigerator, 182
  Refrigerator, Date and Nut, 177
  Refrigerator, Passover, 221
  Ski Jumpers, 193
  Spritz, 194
  Thimble, 197–98
Corn Flake Macaroons, 176
Corn Flakes Stuffing, Roast Capon
  with, 84–85
Corn Muffins, 163–64
Cottage Potatoes, 58
Cranberry: Aspic, 86
  Grape Relish, 72
  Sauce, Whole, 210
Cream of Celery Soup, 88, 139
Cream Puffs, 136–37
Custard Cake, Cherry, 171

Dairy Menus, 131–42 passim
Dark Fruit Cake, 179–80
Date Almond Squares, 176–77
Date and Nut Bread, 94
Date and Nut Chews, Chinese,
  170–71
Date and Nut Loaf, 77
Date and Nut Refrigerator
  Cookies, 177
Date and Orange Cake, 177–78
Date Pinwheels, 178
Day and Night Cake, 179
Deep-Dish Apple Pie, 121
Delicate Coconut Cake, 175
Dinner Menus: Chanukah, 83, 87
  Friday Evening, 38
  Passover, 114–42 passim
  Purim, 99
  Rosh Hashanah, 49, 52
  Shavuot, 154, 156
  Succot, 70, 74
  Yom Kippur, 64, 65
Duck with Orange Sauce, Roast,
  53–54

Dumplings, Knadel, 51

Egg and Potato Appetizer, 224
Egg Drops, 71
Eggplant Relish, Chopped, 71
Eggs, Omelet, 135

Farfel Apple Pudding, 126
Farfel Cookies, Passover, 221
Fish. *See also* Salmon; etc.
  Balls (Gefilte Fish), 39–40
  Chowder, 139
  Fried Fillets, 143
  Mold, Gefilte, 133–34
  Patties, 131–32
  Stock, 40
French Fried Potatoes, 75
Fritters, Apple, 223
Frosting, Chocolate, 173
  Soft, 172
Fruit. *See also* Apples; etc.
  Cake, Dark, 179–80
  in Cantaloupe Basket, 74
  Cup, 142–43
  Glaze for Cake, 73
  Mixed Stewed, 67
  Peel, Candied, 203
  Pudding, Coconut, 122
  Salad in Pineapple Basket, 148
  Salad on Sponge Cake, 119
  Salad with Cheese Balls, 142
  Sauce, Hot, 73–74
Fruited Gelatin Mold, 55
Fruited Kugel, 42
Fudge: Chocolate, Quick and
    Easy, 203
  Maple, 203–4
Fudge Bars, 181
Fudge Cake, Chocolate, 172–73
Fudge Squares, Chocolate, 173

Gefilte Fish, 39–40
  Mold, Baked, 133–34
Gelatin. *See also* Aspic; Jelly
  Beet Mold, 158
  Fruited Mold, 55
Giblet Fricassee, 123
Ginger Squares, 119
Ginger Sticks, 221–22
Gingerbread, 182
Glaze, 216
  Coconut, 197
  Fruit, 73
Glazed Carrots, 100–1
Grape Cranberry Relish, 72
Grape Jelly, Concord, 210

Grapefruit Halves, Grilled, 154
Greek Salad, 209
Green Peppers, Stuffed, 126–27

Haddock: Fried Fillets, 143
  Patties, 131–32
Halibut Chowder, 139
Halishkes: Meat, 83–84
  Vegetable, 219–20
Hamantashen, 101–2
Harlequin Pears, 93
Harvard Beets, 116
Herring: Chopped, 66
  Pickled Fillets, 65–66
Hominy, Pea Soup with, 84
Honey Cake, 51
  Chiffon, 52
Honey Teiglach, 55–56
Horse-Radish, Prepared, 40

Ice Cream, Maple, 207
Ingberlach, 119, 221

Jam, Quick Strawberry, 211
Jam Squares, 183
Jelly. *See also* Aspic; Gelatin
  Calf's Foot (Petchah), 125
  Grape, Concord, 210
  Roll, 134
  and Sour Cream Dessert, 208

Kasha: Stuffing, Fillets of Sole
    with, 88
  Varnishkes, 158
Kezel, Orange and Lemon, 226
Kichel, 43–44, 183
Kishke, 42–43
Kisses, Meringue, 177
Knadel, Carrot Tsimes with, 50–51
Knadlech, 114–15
  Cheese, 204–5
Knishes, Cheese, 156
Kreplach, 64–65
Kugel: Noodle, 42
  Potato, 119

Latkes. *See also* Pancakes
  Brain, 56–57
Lemon: and Orange Kezel, 226
  Pie, 215–16
  Sauce, 58–59
Lima Bean and Barley Soup, 157
Liver: Broiled, Smothered in
    Onions, 127
  Chopped, 117

Mock, Appetizer, 87
and Mushrooms, 157
Pie, 225–26
and Potato Blintzes, 123–24
and Potato Stuffing, 50
Shepherd's Pie, 212–13
Varenikes, 227
Livers and Mushrooms, Chicken,
157

Macaroons: Coconut, 138, 222
Corn Flake, 176
Mandelbrot, 184
Mandlach, 49
Maple Ice Cream, 207
Marmalade: Peach, 210
Pineapple, 225
Matzo: Balls, 114–15
and Cheese, Baked, 225
Meal Pancakes, 143
Spice Cake, 128
Mayina for Passover, 225–26
Meat. *See also* Beef; Veal
Balls, 123
Balls in Tomato Sauce, 53
Halishkes, 83–84
Loaf, 120
Prune Tsimes, 226
Sauce, Spaghetti with, 212
Shepherd's Pie, 212–13
Menus: Chamishah Asar Bishvat,
93
Chanukah, 83, 87
Friday Evening, 38
Lag b'Omer, 149
Passover, 114–42 *passim*
Purim, 99
Rosh Hashanah, 49, 52, 57
Shavuot, 154, 156
Succot, 70, 74
Yom Kippur, 64, 65
Mixed Stewed Fruit, 67
Meringue, 169, 174, 185
Cake, 184–85
Kisses, 177
Mocha Cake Filling, 198
Mock Liver Appetizer, 87
Mock Salmon Patties, 213
Mohnelach, 103
Mother's Sweibec, 184
Mousse, Strawberry, 101
Muffins, Bran, 163
Muffins, Corn, 163–64
Mushrooms and Chicken Livers,
157
Mushrooms and Sweetbreads, 99
Mustard Pickles, 217–18

Nahit, 40
with Rice, 219
Noodle: and Cheese Ring, 205
Kugel, 42
Stuffing, Turkey with, 71–72
Noodles: Passover, 127
for Soup, 66
Noon Menu, 56
Nut: Butter Balls, 185–86
and Date Bread, 94
and Date Chews, Chinese, 170–
71
and Date Loaf, 77
and Date Refrigerator Cookies,
177
Nuts, Soup, 49

Oatmeal Cookies, 187
Crisp, 187
Old-Fashioned Rice Pudding, 207
Omelet, 135
Orange: and Date Cake, 177–78
Halves, Sweet Potatoes in, 72
and Lemon Kezel, 226
and Pineapple Upside-Down
Cake, 73–74
Sauce, 59
Duck with, 53–54
Oranges, Baked, 131

Pancakes. *See also* Blintzes; Latkes
Cheese, 206
Cheese and Sour Cream, 89
Matzo Meal, 143
Potato, 85
Pastry. *See also* Pies; Strudel;
Tarts; etc.
Swiss, 186–87
Peach Marmalade, 210
Peach Tarts, 76–77
Pears, Harlequin, 93
Pea Soup: with Hominy, 84
Yellow Split, 74–75
Peppers, Stuffed, 126–27
Perch, Baked Stuffed, 141
Petchah, 125
Pickled Beets, 126
Pickled Herring Fillets, 65–66
Pickles: Bread and Butter, 216–17
Mustard, 217–18
Pies. *See also* Tarts
Apple, 214–15
Apple, Deep-Dish, 121
Beef, 212
Butterscotch, 214

Chicken, 211
Lemon, 215–16
Liver, 225–26
Liver, Shepherd's 212–13
Rhubarb and Strawberry, 159
Shepherd's, 212–13
Pike, Baked Stuffed, 141
Pilaf, Turkish, 206
Pineapple: Basket Salad, 148
and Beet Mold, 158
Cheese Cake, 188
Cookies, 188
Marmalade, 225
Pudding, 130–31
Squares, 188–89
Upside-Down Cake, 200
Upside-Down Cake, Orange and, 73–74
Pinwheel Cookies, 190
Pirishkes, 190–91
Poppy Seed Candy, 103
Poppy Seed Cookies, 191
Potato: and Egg Appetizer, 224
Kugel, 119
and Liver Blintzes, 123–24
and Liver Stuffing, 50
Pancakes, 85
Pudding, Sweet, 227
Puffs, 121–22
Soup, 133
Stuffing, 115, 137–38
Stuffing, with Liver, 50
Varenikes, 54–55
Potatoes: Browned, Roast with, 100
Cottage, 58
Creamed Mashed, 143
French Fried, 75
Roasted, 130
Scalloped, 142
Sweet, in Orange Halves, 72
Prune Torte, 191–92
Prune Tsimes, 226
Prune Whip, 138
Puddings. See also Kugel
Carrot, 120
Coconut Fruit, 122
Farfel Apple, 126
Pineapple, 130–31
Rice, 207
Sweet Potato, 227

Quick and Easy Fudge, 203
Quick Strawberry Jam, 211

Radish, Horse-, Prepared, 40
Radish Salad, Black, 128
Raisin Bread, 149

Raisin-Filled Crescents, 202
Raspberry Jam Torte, 124
Refrigerator Cake: Sour Cream, 220
Strawberry, 135–36
Refrigerator Cookies, 182
Date and Nut, 177
Passover, 221
Relish, Cranberry Grape, 72
Relish, Eggplant, Chopped, 71
Rhubarb and Strawberry Compote, 43
Rhubarb and Strawberry Pie, 159
Rice: Browned, 218–19
and Nahit, 219
Pudding, 207
and Tomato Soup, 100
Turkish Pilaf, 206
Rum Balls, 186

Salads: Beet Mold, 158
Black Radish, 128
Cabbage, 76
Cabbage, Cole Slaw, 89
Fruit, with Cheese Balls, 142
Fruit, in Pineapple Basket, 148
Fruit, on Sponge Cake, 119
Greek, 209
Spring, 138
Salmon: Broiled, 136
Chowder, 139
Patties, Mock, 213
Rolls, 209–10
Sauces: Cheese, 209–10
Chili, 217
Cranberry, Whole, 210
Fruit, Hot, 73–74
Lemon, 58–59
Meat, for Spaghetti, 212
Orange, 59
Orange, Duck with, 53–54
Tomato, 53
Savory Roast Capon en Papillote, 41–42
Schav, 218
Scones, Southern, 164
Scotch Curls, 192
Sea Bass, Baked Stuffed, 141
Shepherd's Pie, 212–13
Shortbread with Chocolate Bits, 193
Shortcake, Strawberry, 144
Ski Jumpers, 193
Smetene Torte, 192–93
Sole: Fried Fillets, 143
with Kasha Stuffing, Fillets of, 88

Patties, 131–32
with Potato Stuffing, Fillets of,
137–38
Soufflé, Cheese, 205
Soup: Beet Borsht, 118, 154–55
Celery, Cream of, 88, 139
Chicken, 41
Egg Drops for, 71
Fish Chowder, 139
Lima Bean and Barley, 157
Noodles for, 66
"Nuts," 49
Pea, with Hominy, Split, 84
Pea, Yellow Split, 74–75
Potato, 133
Schav, 218
Spinach Borsht, 218
Tomato and Rice, 100
Vegetable, 135
Sour Cream: and Cheese Pancakes,
89
Coffee Cake, 193–94
and Jelly Dessert, 208
Refrigerator Cake, 220
Torte, 192–93
Southern Fried Chicken, 75
Southern Scones, 164
Spaghetti and Meat Sauce, 212
Spice Cake, Matzo, 128
Spinach Borsht, 218
Sponge Cake, 116–17
Chocolate, 132–33
Fruit Salad on, 119
Spring Salad, 138
Spritz Cookies, 194
Squash, Stuffed, 129
Strawberry: Dessert for Passover,
224
Jam, Quick, 211
Mousse, 101
Refrigerator Cake, 135–36
and Rhubarb Compote, 43
and Rhubarb Pie, 159
Shortcake, 144
Tarts, 216
Whip, 208
Strudel, 194–97
Apple, 58–59
Stuffings: Bread, 218
Corn Flakes, 85
Kasha, 88
Matzo, 130
Noodle, 71–72
Passover, 221
Potato, 115, 137–38
Potato and Liver, 50
Sweetbreads and Mushrooms, 99

Sweet Potatoes in Orange Halves,
72
Sweet Potato Pudding for Passover,
227
Sweibec, Mother's, 184
Swiss Pastry, 186–87
Syrup, Peach, 77

Tarts: Banbury, 167
Peach, 76–77
Strawberry, 216
Tutti-Frutti, 167–68
Tea Menus, 93, 149
Teiglach: Filled, 197
Honey, 55–56
Thimble Cookies, 197–98
Tomato and Rice Soup, 100
Tomato Sauce, Meat Balls in, 53
Tomatoes, Broiled, 127
Tongue, Roast, 115
Tortes: Chocolate, 174–75
Prune, 191–92
Raspberry Jam, 124
Smetene (Sour Cream), 192–93
Tropic Aroma Cake, 198
Tsimes: Carrot, with Knadel, 50–51
Prune, 226
Turkey with Noodle Stuffing,
Roast, 71–72
Turkish Delight: Rolls, 198
Squares, 199–200
Turkish Pilaf, 206
Turnovers, Cherry, 190–91
Tutti-Frutti Tarts, 167–68

Upside-Down Cake, Pineapple, 200
Orange and, 73–74

Varenikes: Liver, 227
Potato, 54–55
Varnishkes, 158
Veal: Brisket, Stuffed, 129–30
Chops, Breaded, 121
Petchah, 125
Steaks, Breaded, 57
Vegetable Halishkes, 219–20
Vegetable Soup, 135

Walnut Cake Filling, 179
Walnut Squares, 200
Whitefish, Baked Stuffed, 155
Wine Cake, 223

Yeast Delights, 201
Yellow Split Pea Soup, 74–75